DEMON KISSED
CURSED ANGEL WATCHTOWERS

MICHELLE MADOW

DREAMSCAPE PUBLISHING

PROLOGUE

I hover among the clouds, gazing down upon the city that I'm being sent to on assignment.

Callejon del Beso—the Alley of Kiss. I watch as the first rays of sunlight appear over the city, remembering how this area used to be before the collision—vibrant and bursting with energy. Most of that's gone now. Now only a small portion of the previously sprawling metropolis lights up with life. The rest of it—along with the rest of the continent that used to be called Mexico—is dark and full of despair.

Most of the *planet* is now dark and full of despair.

In my hundreds of years of existence, I've seen plenty of darkness and war. But nothing so devastating as what happened half a century ago, when a witch cast a spell that opened the gates to all thirteen Hell dimensions. These dimensions were full of demons, and the spell released their spirits upon the Earth.

I don't understand why the witch did it. I don't think I'll ever know. Witches are an unpredictable, ungodly race...

which is why I wasn't surprised when I found out that angels are being called upon to go down to Earth to fix their mess.

What *did* surprise me was that I was one of the angels chosen. The task ahead requires an angel with more strength and experience than I've acquired during my few hundred years of existence. Why choose me when so many others are better suited for the job?

Because the opening of dimensions wasn't the worst consequence of the witch's spell. The spell also created rifts in the Earth, dividing it into thirteen continents and causing endless death and destruction.

I hate war. I remember how much my heart hurt when cities such as Warsaw and Aleppo were bombed to ruins in the twentieth and twenty-first centuries.

That's what most of the world looks like today.

After five years of chaos, the Demon King Ezekiel took control of Callejon del Beso by unleashing a curse upon the continent. The curse is that of *greed*. Everyone who lives in the continent is affected by the curse, and they're slaves to the demon.

Since assuming control, Ezekiel has built up the continent. A small portion of the city resembles the world before the collision—it's booming and lively. At the center is the Watchtower—the gleaming, luxurious skyscraper where Ezekiel lives and reigns.

But the humans who live in such luxury are few and far between. Most are slaves in the work camps outside the city, bound to a lifetime of hard labor to ensure that the demon and his followers are left wanting nothing.

It's my job as a messenger angel of God to go down to Earth and kill the demon Ezekiel, freeing the continent and the humans who live there from his curse forever.

I'm going down to Earth immediately after sunrise. I should feel ready. After all, out of all the angels in Heaven, I was the one chosen for this task. There *must* be a reason for that.

But I feel as far from ready as ever.

CHAPTER ONE

To break the curse, I'll possess a human that God assigned to me. The human's name is Adriana Medina—an eighteen-year-old socialite and the daughter of one of the most prominent men on the continent. Her father lords over a labor camp in the countryside, but Adriana recently moved in with her sister Teresa and Teresa's husband Marco in the city so she can find herself a suitable husband.

For the past few days, I've been learning everything possible about Adriana's life so when I'm in her body, no one will suspect that anything has changed.

I should feel prepared. But I don't. Because once I enter Adriana's body, I'll also be a slave to the curse of greed that Ezekiel placed upon the continent.

I'll fight the curse with every fiber of my being… but will that be enough?

A breeze stirs next to me, and Uriel appears by my side in a glowing orb of light. The seraph angel is much larger than I am

—double my size, at least. Flames dance around his wings, and he glows with the brightness of Heaven itself.

"Rebekah." He says my name with disdain, his nose turned down at me. "I trust you're prepared for the task ahead?"

"As prepared as I possibly can be," I say, although my voice wavers slightly.

Uriel's lips straighten into a firm line. "I do not know why God has chosen you when there are more experienced messenger angels in Heaven who would excel at the task ahead," he says. "But he *has* chosen you, and it's not my place to question the will of God—only to deliver it."

"So why are you here?" I ask. "Surely you have better places to be?"

"I'm here to give you the final piece of information you need to ensure your mission is a success."

"The final piece?" I perk up at his words. "What more am I allowed to know?"

"You didn't think you were going to be sent into the city without instructions about *how* to kill Ezekiel, did you?" he asks.

"I don't know." I shrug, since yes, that was exactly what I'd thought. "I assumed that part of my task was to figure out how to kill him on my own."

"If you *want* to figure out how to kill him on your own, be my guest…" Uriel holds his hands up and backs away, his wings rising behind him.

"No!" I call out, stopping him. "Of course I want to know how to kill him."

"That's what I thought." Uriel smirks and floats back to me, although his wings remain raised. I suspect to remind me of his glory—as if I need reminding. "To kill Ezekiel, you must impale him through the heart with my Flaming Sword."

I suck in a sharp breath. "But your Flaming Sword…"

"Was stolen by Ezekiel when I journeyed to Earth to battle the demons in the chaos times following the collision of dimensions," Uriel finishes. "No need to remind me—I know. I'm pretty sure all of *Heaven* knows. Which is extremely embarrassing—especially since Ezekiel evoked the power of the sword to cast the curse of greed upon the continent and enslave the humans who live there."

"So I need to steal the Flaming Sword back from Ezekiel himself?" I huff. "Fantastic."

"Yes," he says simply. "Which means you must first *locate* the sword."

"I thought you could always sense where the sword was, since you forged it yourself?" I ask. "Isn't the essence of the sword tied to your soul?"

"It is." His face hardens, and the flames on his wings grow taller, licking the clouds above us. "Except that after cursing the continent, Ezekiel hid the sword and had a witch cast a boundary spell around it. Until the boundary spell is removed, I can't sense the sword."

I press my lips together, soaking in the meaning behind his words. "So even if I'm able to find the sword, how am I supposed to remove the boundary spell?" I ask. "You know as well as I do that angels can't reverse spells. Especially because I'll be possessing a *human*. I'll be powerless."

"This is the part you're not going to like…" Uriel starts.

"What is it?" I hold my gaze with his, waiting for the next piece of bad news.

"A witch will need to remove the boundary spell."

I back up, repulsed. "You want me to work with a *witch*?" I ask, needing to make sure I understand this correctly.

"Yes." Amusement dances across his face. "Precisely."

"But there are barely any witches left on the continent!" I sputter. "Ezekiel killed them after taking control."

"The key word is *barely*," Uriel says. "As you know, Ezekiel didn't kill *all* the witches on the continent. Some went into hiding, and they now practice in secret."

"So how on Earth am I supposed to find one?" I ask. "And even if I *do* find a witch, how am I supposed to work with one? In case you've forgotten, a witch started this entire mess in the first place! Why would any of them want to help me? And even if by some miracle I find one who will, witches are erratic and volatile. I absolutely *cannot* work with one. There must be another way to reverse the boundary spell. A way that *doesn't* involve teaming up with a witch."

"Are you questioning the orders of God?" Uriel puffs out his chest, towering over me.

"No." I glance down, shrinking under his gaze. "Of course not. It's just…" I pause, taking a second to organize my thoughts. "God really wants me to work with a witch?"

"Do you think I'm making this up for my own amusement?"

I say nothing, since yes, the thought *had* crossed my mind.

"Look." Uriel takes a deep breath, and for the first time since gracing me with his presence, the snark is gone from his tone. "I wouldn't make something up for my own entertainment when the fate of an entire continent is at stake." He pauses, allowing his words to sink in. "But if it helps, God wouldn't have chosen you for this task if it was impossible for you to complete. God is all knowing and all seeing. If you make the correct choices, you *can* succeed on this mission and free the humans who live on this continent from being bound to Ezekiel and the curse he thrust upon them."

"Thank you." I glance down at the city below, getting ahold of myself as I watch the first rays of sunlight inch above the horizon. "You're right—I shouldn't have doubted God's decision to appoint me to this task. I'll do better once I'm down there. I promise."

If I'm able to resist the curse, I think, although I don't say it out loud.

"Good." Uriel relaxes, the flames on his wings simmering down. "Now, the sun is starting to rise. Do you have any final questions before you descend to Earth?"

More than I have time to ask before the sun completes its ascent. Instead, I simply ask, "What if I get stuck on something while I'm down there? Will I be able to call on you for advice?"

"No," he says sharply. "The curse is strong, and I cannot put myself in the position to be affected by it."

"But I can?" I nearly roll my eyes, but stop myself.

"You will be possessing a human," he reminds me. "God instructed you to do this for a reason—because if you lose yourself to the curse, there's not much harm you can cause in human form. And I have it on good authority that you'll be locked in that form until you complete your task. But if an angel—specifically a *seraph* angel like myself—were to be affected by the curse, the results could be disastrous. It's a risk I cannot take. So once you're down there, you're on your own. But the sun has nearly risen, so God bless and good luck."

He raises his wings, the flames consuming him, and he's gone.

CHAPTER TWO

I teleport down to Earth, appearing in the bedroom of Adriana Medina. But I remain invisible, because while I'm not in a corporeal form, I can't affect or be affected by the world around me. Which means that until entering Adriana's body, I won't be affected by the curse.

Adriana is fast asleep, and I look around, studying the place I'll live until I complete my mission. A sparkly dress lies haphazardly across a chair—she must have thrown it there after getting home last night. There's a trash can next to her bed. The television is on but muted, playing the only channel available—the Watchtower broadcast that plays infomercials around the clock, along with the occasional bits of breaking news from the city.

Adriana groans in her sleep and adjusts herself in her bed. Her makeup is smudged and running down her cheeks, one arm draped over the edge of the mattress. Her dark hair forms a halo on her pillow. She looks so calm and peaceful.

But I feel awful for her. Because her free will is about to be yanked away, and *I'm* the one who's going to do it.

In the few times I've been sent down to Earth to convey a message, it's been in my natural form—although I, of course, hid my wings and angelic glow. I've never possessed a human. It's not something angels are typically ordered to do, since God values the free will of all creatures on the Earth. *Demons* are the ones who possess humans, and they take advantage of them in horrible ways. I've heard terrible stories from angels who have been sent down to assist with exorcising them from their hosts.

The thought of possessing a human feels wrong on many levels. Mainly because I dislike the idea of taking away Adriana's free will, but also because while I'm in her body, I won't be able to use my angelic powers.

But it's not my place to question God's plan. He wouldn't send me on this mission if it were impossible for me to succeed. I *must* trust in Him.

So I float above Adriana, sink my body into hers, and allow my soul to fill the shape of its new human form.

CHAPTER THREE

I awake to a wrenching pain in the pit of my stomach.

It feels like there's poison swirling in my gut, and I swallow down the urge to be sick. My mouth tastes dry and vile, and I groan and curl up into myself, although the movement only makes me feel worse.

What's happening? Did something go wrong when I possessed Adriana's body? Because surely humans don't feel like this all the time. They wouldn't be able to function if they did.

My eyes feel glued together with crust, but I manage to pry them open. The sunlight streaming through the window pounds into my head. I clutch my stomach again, trying to swallow down the nausea creeping up my throat, but it's forcing itself up, and this time, there's no keeping it down.

I lean over the bed and retch into the trash can, emptying my stomach until the pit of poison is gone. The experience is disgusting, but at least I feel slightly better.

Despite how miserable I feel, I should get out of bed since I have a mission to accomplish—but I feel too awful to move. Instead, I lay there, clutching my stomach and wishing I could magically make a glass of water appear on the nightstand next to me.

I'm just about to fall back asleep—maybe once I wake up again, I won't feel so miserable—when someone knocks on the door.

"Adriana?" a female voice asks softly. "Are you awake?"

She doesn't give me time to answer, instead opening the door and peeking inside. I know who she is immediately—Adriana's older sister Teresa. Like Adriana, she has dark hair, brown eyes, and tan skin, although she's slightly taller. Her eyes are kind and concerned, making her look older than her twenty-three years.

She glances down at the trash can, her nose scrunching in disgust. "Rough night last night?" She doesn't wait for me to answer, instead striding inside and placing a glass of ice water on the nightstand.

I reach for it, chugging the water in a few gulps. In that moment, it's the most divine substance I've ever tasted.

"Thanks," I say once I'm finished, placing the glass back on the nightstand. "How did you know I needed that?"

"I heard you throwing up from my room," she says. "And I thought you should know that Sofia called—she'll be here in an hour to pick you up for brunch."

The mention of food makes my stomach churn. "I don't think I can go," I say, wrapping my arms around myself again. "I think I'm sick."

"Seriously?" Teresa laughs, which surprises me, since she was being so kind until now. "You've championed through hangovers since moving here. Unless all that partying is starting to catch up with you?"

"*This* is a hangover?" I grimace and slowly force myself to sit up in bed. My head pounds, but my stomach is feeling slightly better since getting sick. "Why would someone do this to themselves?"

"You got carried away last night," she says. "It happens. It's hard to blame anyone for it, given the situation we're in..." She glances at the window, her eyes far off. I have a feeling she's referring to the curse, and I want to ask her about it, but she blinks the sadness away and returns her attention to me. "Do you want me to call Sofia and tell her you can't make it?" she asks. "She sounded really excited, since it'll be your first time having brunch at the Watchtower, but—"

"The Watchtower?" Fear races through my veins at the mention of the place where Ezekiel lives. "We're going there?"

"*You're* going there," Teresa clarifies. "I'm having brunch with Marco at home. Unless you want to stay here and eat with us? I'm making pancakes—your favorite."

The offer is tempting. After all, I don't *want* to step inside that Watchtower and meet one of the demons who's caused so much misery to the planet. But the sooner I locate a witch, reverse the barrier spell around the sword, and use it to kill Ezekiel, the sooner I can return home.

Perhaps Teresa has an idea about where I can find a witch? But Teresa seems too kind to associate with witches, and she might become suspicious if I ask about them. I'm better off asking Sofia—from what I know of Adriana's cousin, she's even more of a party girl than Adriana. Surely, she must know something.

"Thanks for the offer," I tell Teresa. "But if I promised Sofia that I'd go to brunch with her, then I'm going."

"Okay…" Teresa studies me, her forehead creasing. "Are you sure everything's all right?" she asks. "I know you're not feeling a hundred percent, but yesterday you couldn't wait for brunch in the Watchtower. Now you look terrified."

"Like you said, it's my first time having brunch in the Watchtower," I say, wracking my mind for a feasible reason—other than the real reason—for why I look worried. I glance around Adriana's room, and it hits me the moment I see the sparkly dress discarded on the chair. "And I have no idea what to wear!"

That's something a socialite party girl would worry about, right?

"Are you asking for my help?" Teresa looks confused, but grateful.

"Yes," I say, realizing I really *do* need her help. After all, I have no idea where to start with dressing myself for this occasion. I've never paid much attention to fashion, and the last thing I want is to look horribly out of place.

"Go shower," Teresa says with a sigh. "It'll help you feel better. I'll lay out some outfit options for you to choose from once you're ready."

"Are you sure?" I ask.

"Yes!" she says. "Go. I've got this."

She shoos me toward the bathroom, and I shoot her a grateful smile, sending up a quick thank you to God that, throughout this mission, I'll have Teresa nearby to help guide my way.

CHAPTER FOUR

The shower does miracles for my hangover. And with the warm water rushing over me and clearing my senses, I'm grateful for being assigned to possess a human who can afford such luxuries as heated running water.

I'm also grateful that I don't feel affected by the curse.

But curses are tricky and unpredictable. Hopefully if I *do* become affected, I'll know and be able to resist it.

Once out of the shower, I dry off and examine the human in the mirror. With her tan skin, slim figure, dark hair that flows over her shoulders, and huge brown eyes, Adriana is a beautiful human. This is an advantage for me, because I know from my hundreds of years of existence that life is easier for the ones considered more beautiful than most. I don't think it's right or fair, but humans are generally kinder and more giving to those they consider attractive.

I pray that during my time here, I'll be able to use that advantage to help me succeed with completing my task.

But it's not Adriana's perfect features that my eyes are

drawn to. It's the tattoos around her wrists. The thick stripes of gold showing that Adriana, like every other human on this continent, is a slave to the demon Ezekiel, bound to him by the traces of his blood within the ink.

Luckily, Adriana's tattoo is gold, marking her as a member of the highest—and smallest—caste of humans. Most Golds have enough money that they don't need to work, although the men must also serve as guards or tax collectors to the demon. The most respected Golds, such as Adriana's father, lord over the labor camps throughout the continent.

Underneath the Golds are the Silvers—the educated, upper-class citizens who work jobs that the old world would have called "white collar." They generally have most everything they want, although unlike the Golds, they have to work for their money.

Below them are the Greens—the entertainers, artists, craftspeople, merchants, and welders. The Greens don't live cushy lives by any means, but they're comfortable. Comfort is hardly appreciated in a continent cursed with greed, but they have more than most.

In the shantytowns outside of the city live the Reds—those who serve the citizens of the city. The shantytowns lack electricity and plumbing, and the Reds are barely paid enough money to get by.

But at least they're paid. That's more than can be said for the Blues.

Most humans on the continent bear blue tattoos around their wrists. They're slaves in the labor camps in the countryside, working day and night to provide the natural resources that those in the city need to live. Their lives are miserable—hopeless. They cannot escape from their bonds of slavery, and many of them die young, from exhaustion and overexertion. The labor camps literally work them to death.

Out of all the citizens in the continent, they need my help the most.

Here, in Adriana's glistening bathroom, it's easy to forget about the Blues toiling away in desolate conditions to provide for this luxurious life in the city. The Golds turn a blind eye to it.

But I won't forget. I'll do everything in my power to save them. Not just them—I'm going to save *everyone* on this cursed continent.

I'll start with going to the Watchtower, and then I'll find a witch to help me.

CHAPTER FIVE

The Watchtower isn't far from Teresa's house—only a few blocks—but Sofia picks me up in her car anyway. Only the Golds have cars, and the ones who do only have one per family. This is because cars are no longer produced, and the only ones that function now are electric. Gasoline cars are worthless, and most have been deserted or destroyed for parts.

Sofia rolls down the windows and blasts a CD—I recognize the British, all-female pop group as one that was popular in the nineties. She cranks the volume, obviously wanting to be noticed, and it works. People turn their heads to stare at us as we roll by, craning their necks to get a glimpse inside the car. It's like we're celebrities.

As Golds, I suppose we *are* celebrities to most people.

With the music blasting, I can't have a conversation with Sofia, but I don't mind. It gives me time to think.

We approach the Watchtower, and I gaze up at the giant building. Its shimmery, bright blue exterior is blinding, making the other buildings seem dull in comparison. On the crowded sidewalks outside, people have set up shop, selling sparkly trinkets and other accessories. The merchants all have green tattoos around their wrists, and their customers are Golds and Silvers.

We pull up to the front of the Watchtower, and a valet opens the door for me. His tattoo is red.

"Good morning." He smiles pleasantly and closes the door behind me. "Have a wonderful day at the Watchtower."

"Thank you." I smile back, wondering if I should tip him. But I'm only carrying limited coins. What if I want those extra coins later to buy something for myself?

I blink the thought away, surprised at having it cross my mind. I shouldn't care about buying anything for myself. Once I complete my mission, nothing Adriana owns will be mine. So I reach into my purse and remove a small copper coin—which, like all coins in the city, bears the insignia of the Flaming Sword upon it—and hand it to the valet.

His eyes widen, and he glances skittishly around before shoving the coin into his pocket. "Thanks, miss." He nods and runs around to the other side of the car, getting in and driving away to park it.

"Why did you do that?" Sofia asks from next to me.

"Do what?" I ask.

"Tip the valet." From the way she says it, I assume tipping isn't customary around here.

Fantastic—I haven't even been here for twenty-four hours, and I'm already making mistakes.

"To thank him for his service," I answer simply.

"That's what our *taxes* are for." She says the word in disgust, and gives me a once over. "You look... different," she observes, and I have a feeling she doesn't mean it as a compliment. "Did you let your sister dress you or something?"

I glance down at my jeans, realizing they *do* look different from Sofia's miniskirt and crop top. Does Adriana usually dress like Sofia? I hope not. I can't imagine feeling comfortable in something that leaves no part of my body to the imagination. But looking around, I see a variety of styles—the clothes look like they've been plucked from various time periods—and I don't feel as out of place anymore.

"Never mind." Sofia rolls her eyes and heads toward the entrance. "Let's get some Bloody Marias into our systems—it certainly seems like you need a few."

I take a deep breath and follow her inside the lair of the demon.

CHAPTER SIX

The inside of the Watchtower is a bustling city unto itself. It reminds me of the glamorous hotels that existed in Las Vegas before the dimensions collided—full of shops, restaurants, bars, entertainment, and yes, even a casino.

We walk through the casino to go to the restaurant. Despite it being before noon, the tables and slots are full of people trying to get lucky. People of all different castes are playing—Golds, Silvers, Greens, and even the occasional Red. The only caste missing is Blue—which makes sense, since the Blues are imprisoned in their labor camps in the country.

Bartenders—all of them Reds—continuously bring drinks to the gamblers. Some of the people they're serving look so bleary-eyed that I wonder if they've been in the casino all night. A gut instinct tells me they have.

We pass by a gleaming white car on a podium with a big red bow tied around the hood, and Sofia stops in place, her eyes wide. "We should try our hand at winning *that* after brunch," she says, pointing at the car. "Maybe we'll get lucky."

"But you already have a car," I say, confused about why she wants *another* one. Especially when there are so many other, not as fortunate, people in the city who don't have a car at all.

"Exactly." She laughs. "If I win, I'll have *two* cars! Or I can sell it. I wonder how many coins it's worth? Probably a small fortune." Her lips curve into a small smile, as if she's already planning what she'll buy with the money. Then she looks at me and frowns. "You're no fun today." She pouts.

"Sorry," I apologize, recalling what Teresa said when she came in my room this morning. "I had a rough night last night."

"You bet you did!" Her eyes brighten, and I have no idea why she's excited, but I'm glad I said *something* right. "That guy you were dancing with was all over you—practically in love with you! And I remember him saying he'll be at brunch this morning. Did you ever get his name?"

"I don't think so." I glance around, hoping she doesn't realize I have no idea what I'm talking about.

"Makes sense," she says. "After how much we drank, I'm glad we remember him at all!" She laughs again, and I have the impression that Sofia's one of those people who amuses herself more than she amuses others around her.

She leads the way around the casino until we're in front of a restaurant called SALT. The place is packed, and I watch as a server carries a clear cauldron of blue liquid to a table. Everyone there grabs one of the thick colorful straws coming out of the cauldron and drinks from it.

"That's the Heaven & Hell," the hostess says, apparently having noticed me looking at the ginormous drink. Her skintight outfit is more revealing than Sofia's, and she has glitter all over her skin. Her tattoos, of course, are red. "You *must* try it. It's divine."

I nod, since I *am* curious to find out what it tastes like, and follow her to an elevated circular booth in the middle of the restaurant. It seems large for two people, but apparently Sofia reserved it specifically.

"Enjoy," the hostess says, placing menus in front of us.

"Tell our waitress to bring us some Bloody Marias as soon as possible," Sofia says, looking around the room in anticipation. "We're ready to get this party started!"

"Will do." The hostess nods. "Did you also want a Heaven & Hell?"

"Later," Sofia says with a wave of her hand. "We'll have one right before the music starts."

The hostess nods again and hurries away, presumably to deliver our requests to the powers that be in the kitchen.

I examine the menu, listening to Sofia prattle on about some guy she met last night. As long as I nod and acknowledge what Sofia's saying, she continues to talk—which is fine by me, because the less I talk, the less chance of Sofia realizing I'm not Adriana.

Everything on the menu is pricey, which explains why most of the people dining here are Golds, with the occasional Silver splashed into the mix. We'll likely spend on one meal what an entire family of Reds makes in one month.

The waitress brings over two glasses of tequila, along with tomato juice and a bunch of sauces and spices so we can mix our drinks precisely how we like them. She takes our orders, and I ask for the pancakes, remembering Teresa mentioned them being Adriana's favorite.

Sofia mixes her drink, and I follow her lead, since I've never made a Bloody Maria before.

"Cheers!" she says once she's finished brewing her masterpiece, raising her glass in the air.

"Cheers." I click my glass with hers and take a sip of the drink. It's thick and spicy, and I'm surprised to find I like it.

The drink helps calm my nerves, making me think straight again. I'm here to gather information about witches, and I can't continue putting off the conversation I need to have with Sofia. Especially because from what I've seen of her so far, Sofia is flighty and impulsive—exactly the sort of behavior I would expect from a witch. Or at least from someone who associates with them.

God wouldn't instruct me to possess someone who has no possible connection to witches. I have to assume Sofia is the first step in figuring out exactly what that connection is.

All I need to do is ask her.

CHAPTER SEVEN

Sofia loves talking about the various guys on her "current dating rotation," so I use that to breach the conversation.

"So," I begin, figuring I might as well be out with it. "Do you have some kind of trick for making all these guys go crazy for you? A love spell, perhaps?" I waggle my eyebrows, mirroring the body language I've observed in Sofia so far this morning.

"No." She brings a hand to her chest and laughs, sounding nervous. "Why would you think that?"

"I don't know." I shrug and smile mischievously. "But if you *did* know anything about that sort of stuff, I hope you wouldn't keep it all to yourself."

"Well, I don't." She sits back and crinkles her nose. "Why would you think I know anything about *witches*?" She says the word like it's dirty—the same way I said it while speaking with Uriel earlier.

"You really know nothing about them?" I ask.

"No!" she exclaims. "Why are you even asking me such

a thing?"

"I'm sorry, it's just…" I press my lips together, searching for some sort of explanation.

"You don't think a witch cast a spell on you—do you?" She scoots closer to me, her eyes flashing with concern—and with a hunger for gossip. "Because my mom always says that if you suspect you're the victim of a witch's spell, you need to wear red socks and underwear inside out to prevent the spell from reaching you. You have those things, right? If you don't, we can go shopping after brunch."

That advice is an old wives' tale passed down from generation to generation on this continent—and while I don't know a ton about witches, I *do* know that won't work. Which means Sofia is very good at hiding her knowledge of witches, or she truly knows nothing about them.

Unfortunately, Sofia doesn't strike me as particularly intelligent—*and* she sounds truly scared by the thought of witches—so my instinct tells me it's the latter.

"I don't think anyone's cast a spell on me." I laugh, as if the notion is ridiculous. "It was just a joke. Sorry."

Sofia studies me for a few seconds, looking suspicious. "Well, it wasn't very funny," she finally says, sticking her nose in the air. "I don't know what it's like in your home sector, but a mention of witchcraft is taken seriously here in the city. Luckily you only said something to me, and since we're cousins, I won't think too much of it. But don't joke around like that with anyone else. They won't take it as lightly as I did."

She chugs the rest of her drink, and I get the impression that this conversation is over.

Which leaves me wondering—in a city that's fearful of even *mentioning* witches, how am I supposed to figure out where to find one?

CHAPTER EIGHT

The waitress brings out the Heaven & Hell drink, and everything after that is a blur. The restaurant blacks out the windows, the DJ mixes music in his booth, and the staff passes out glow sticks and plastic light-up jewelry. People dance on tables, scantily clad women blast smoke machines into the crowd, and musicians in flashing costumes play instruments in time with the songs. My favorite is the electric violinist—he's absolutely mesmerizing.

Violin is my favorite instrument—I play myself—and while I watch him, I itch to play so badly. Hopefully Teresa has a violin at her house. If not, I'll have to figure out how to acquire one. After all, I need to do *something* to relax my mind and help me think on this mission. Playing music is the perfect solution. Especially since Adriana used to play herself. She isn't as talented at it as I am, but that's certainly something I can hide.

Now I'm waiting in line for the bathroom, and my head is starting to clear. I look in the mirror and see my reflection—a plastic halo glows around my head, and my cheeks are flushed from dancing. Sofia's friends showed up soon after the waitress dropped off our humungous drink... how long had we been dancing and watching the show?

I glance down at my watch, and my eyes widen at the time. I've wasted *hours* at this party—hours that could have been spent moving forward with my mission. This is unacceptable. I can't think of an explanation for how this happened other than that I allowed the curse to take over. I was having fun, and at the taste of it, I wanted *more*.

But I have to fight it. I have to get home.

I finish in the bathroom and push through the crowd to get to our table. Sofia's dancing on top of it with one of the guys we apparently met last night. Their bodies are so entangled that it's difficult to see where she stops and he begins.

"Adriana!" She waves from over his shoulder. "There you are! Come dance with us."

Her friends reach forward to help me up, but I don't take their hands.

"It's late," I yell up to Sofia, pointing at my watch. "I have to get home!"

"But the party's not over!" She kneels so she can talk without screaming. "And I'm not even close to being sober enough to drive."

She has a good point, and I don't want her driving drunk. But the longer I stay here, the more I fear being affected by the curse. I need to leave. I don't want to abandon Sofia, but her friends are here—they'll make sure she gets home safely.

"I'm going to walk home—it's only a few blocks," I tell her. "You'll be okay without me, right?"

"You're leaving?" Sofia asks, shocked. "Are you sure?"

I feel someone's hand on my butt, and I glance over my shoulder, meeting eyes with some guy I've never seen before. I slap his hand away, and he calls me a bitch before hurrying toward another group of unsuspecting girls.

"Yes, I'm sure." I look around, feeling suddenly confined by the flashing lights and thumping music. It's too busy, and too loud. "Have fun, and I'll see you later!"

I give her a quick hug and hurry through the restaurant, finally able to breathe again once I'm out of there.

As I walk through the casino, I contemplate my predicament. Sofia has no idea where to find a witch. So who should I ask? I look around, knowing I should figure this out now, but I'm exhausted. Adriana must not have slept well the night before. I hadn't been able to fully shake off the hangover I'd woken up with, *and* I'd just spent all day drinking and partying.

All I want is to go back to Teresa's house and get a good night's sleep.

Then I'll wake up refreshed and ready to figure out how to find a witch in the morning.

CHAPTER NINE

The walk home is only a few blocks, but the sun is starting to set. I can't get rid of the feeling that someone's following me. But every time I turn around, no one's there. I must be paranoid.

Still, I walk faster, eager to get back to the house.

As I get closer, there are less and less people on the streets, until I'm the only one walking. I'm a block away when someone turns the corner ahead, nearly crashing into me. We stop walking, and I stare up at him, hardly able to breathe. He's incredibly attractive—tall, with dark shaggy hair and ice-blue eyes—but his looks aren't what's taking my breath away. It's the way he's looking at me.

As if he's been searching for me his entire life, and has just now finally found me.

"Julia?" he asks, sounding completely spellbound.

My gaze is trapped in his, and I don't know what to say. Clearly, he's mistaking me for someone else. And for reasons I don't understand—since obviously I've never met this man before—I can't help but feel disappointed.

Whoever Julia is, she's lucky to have someone who cares for her so much.

"No," I tell him, despite *wishing* I were this person he's searching for. "I'm Re—" I pause, realizing I almost introduced myself with my own name. I almost said Rebekah. "I'm Adriana."

"Oh," he says. "You just look so much like…" He studies me, as if he's waiting for me to recognize him—or like he's waiting for me to say that yes, I *am* this Julia he's asking about.

Perhaps Adriana's met him before? But no… that can't be possible. If she had, he would know her name.

"Never mind," he says, the dazed look leaving his eyes. "You just remind me of someone… but that's impossible. She couldn't be here. I must have mistaken you for someone else."

"Sorry," I say, even though I have nothing to apologize for.

He continues staring at me, and I glance around to see if anyone else is nearby. They're not. It's only the two of us, and the sun's nearly set.

I should make an excuse and be on my way. But something about him… I can't put my finger on it, but something about him is *different*.

"You shouldn't be on the streets by yourself after dark," he says casually. "Where are you heading?"

"If I shouldn't be on the streets after dark, why should I tell you where I'm going?" I ask with a small smile. "Isn't that even *more* dangerous?"

"Touché." He smirks. "But you shouldn't be afraid of me."

"Who says I'm afraid of you?" I tilt my head, pushing away a strand of hair that falls in front of my eye. "Although since we've never met, I shouldn't exactly trust you, either."

"You should," he says quickly. "Trust me, I mean."

"And why's that?"

"Because I would never hurt you." He says it so seriously that I automatically believe him.

Now I'm the one who watches him, my breath taken away again. Why is this stranger having such a big effect on me?

"I'm on my way home." I motion around the corner. "It's close."

"I'll walk you," he says. "Make sure you get there safe."

"Okay." I swallow and follow his lead. I could be making a mistake by trusting him, but I'm more comfortable walking with him than walking alone. I no longer feel like someone's watching me. I feel *safe*.

"You live with your family?" he asks, his hands shoved into the pockets of his leather jacket.

"With my sister and her husband," I answer. "I moved in with her two weeks ago."

"Makes sense," he says. "If you'd been here longer, I would have noticed. I would never forget a face like yours."

I don't know what to say to that. Again, I feel bad that I'm not the person he hoped I was—Julia.

We walk for a few seconds without speaking.

"Why did you move here?" he asks, breaking the silence. "Did something happen to your parents?"

"No," I tell him. "Nothing like that. My parents live in Sector Six, and now that I'm old enough, I wanted a change of scenery. So I moved in with my sister in the city." I stop walking, resting my hand on the gate that leads to Teresa's house. "This is me," I say, although I don't move to enter. Instead, I look up at him, waiting for I don't know what.

All I know is that I'm not ready to leave.

"Well, *Adriana*," he says, emphasizing my name. "Meeting you has been… a pleasure. I'm glad you decided to move here."

"Thanks," I say, and then I chuckle, realizing how awkward that reply was. "I mean, I'm glad I met you, too."

That wasn't much better. But he's apparently amused, because he smiles. Not just a small smile, but the kind that reaches his eyes.

"Be safe." He reaches forward, tucking a loose strand of hair behind my ear.

I stand frozen. As his skin brushes mine, heat travels all the way down to my toes. I must look as spellbound as he was earlier. But before I can figure out how to respond, he turns around, and as quickly as he appeared, he's gone.

It's only once I'm inside that I realize—I never saw the color of his tattoos.

CHAPTER TEN

I spend the next day walking through the city, trying to pick up *any* signs about where I might find a witch. After Sofia's warning yesterday, I don't ask anyone about witches, but I try my best to observe everything I can.

I find nothing that helps me.

There are either no witches left in the city, or they've done a fantastic job of going into hiding. I assume it's the latter. Because if there are no witches in the city, why would I have been sent here at all?

There must be something I'm missing.

I head home before sunset, remembering the mysterious stranger's advice that I shouldn't walk the streets alone after dark. I also feel like an idiot for not asking for his name.

But I'm trying not to think too much about him. After all, as an angel, I'm supposed to be above basic human impulses like being affected by a handsome stranger. Whatever I felt for him couldn't have been real.

Those feelings must have been caused by that potent

Heaven & Hell drink I had at brunch. Because while angels love humans, and sometimes even fool around with them while on missions, we don't fall *in* love with them. Those who do are severely punished. They're cast out of Heaven and become fallen angels—demons.

I shiver at the thought. But I push away the worry, because I'm getting ahead of myself. All I did was acknowledge beauty, which is far from forbidden. Appreciating the beauty in God's creations is equivalent to praising Him, and certainly nothing to be ashamed about.

How ridiculous of me to jump from admiring a beautiful man to worrying about falling in love with him.

But if I see that man again, I *will* find out his name. Especially because—for some reason I can't pinpoint—I have a feeling that he's important to my mission.

I arrive home and have dinner with Teresa and Marco, allowing them to lead the conversation. The less I say, the less likely it is that they'll realize I'm not Adriana. Teresa looks at me a few times in concern, and I worry that she's onto me, but she seems to believe my excuse that I'm tired from a day of shopping. It isn't completely a lie, since I *did* buy a few things so I could speak with the shopkeepers.

I'm glad when I'm finally upstairs and alone in my room, because after a day of wandering around and discovering nothing, it's harder and harder to push away the tendrils of defeat creeping into my soul.

And so, I drop to my knees beside my bed and pray for an answer from God. Well, not an answer, since God doesn't come down from Heaven and answer prayers directly. He doesn't communicate with messenger angels at all—he communicates with seraph angels like Uriel, who then deliver messages to us. But I *do* pray for a sign, or a push in the right direction.

I'm nearly finished with my prayers when there's a knock on the door.

I jolt up, panicked, because all forms of religion are banished here. Demon worship is all that's acceptable—specifically the worship of Ezekiel. I *cannot* be caught praying.

So I jump into bed and pick up the closest book on my nightstand—a self-help book about dating from the early twenty-first century.

"Come in," I say, opening the book to a random page and trying to relax.

Teresa comes in, looking worried. "Hey." She wraps her arms around herself and glances around the room. "Do you have a few minutes to talk?"

"Yeah, sure." I shut the book and put it back on the nightstand. "What's up?"

She closes the door and situates herself on the foot of my bed. "I got a concerning call from Aunt Carmen today," she says, and I'm grateful that Uriel briefed me enough that I know Aunt Carmen is Sofia's mother—Adriana's mom's sister.

"About what?" I sit up in panic. Did I make a mistake by not staying at the restaurant yesterday and waiting to leave with Sofia? Did she drive drunk—despite saying she wouldn't—and get in an accident? "Is Sofia okay?"

"Sofia's fine," Teresa says, and I immediately relax. She presses her lips together and continues, "I hope you know that Sofia cares about you, and that you won't take what I'm about to tell you out on her."

"What happened?" I ask, getting nervous again.

"Sofia told Aunt Carmen that you asked her about witches

yesterday at brunch," Teresa says. "It scared her, and she's worried about you."

I sit there, shocked. Sofia *tattled* on me? Why would she do that? And how am I supposed to explain this to Teresa?

"I assured Aunt Carmen that it's nothing to worry about," she continues before I can work out a response. "But Adriana... you've never shown any interest in witches before. *Why are you asking about them now?*"

"Dating," I spurt out, glancing at the book on my nightstand and remembering the lie I told Sofia yesterday. "Sofia has such good luck with dating—I joked about her maybe having help from a witch. Like love spells, or potions or something. But that's all it was—a joke. I promise."

The lie sits heavy on my tongue. I hate lying to Teresa, since she seems to truly want the best for Adriana. But she also seems like a good person, and the last thing I want is to bring her into this and potentially put her in danger.

Her brows knit together—she doesn't look convinced. "If there's another reason... I hope you know you can talk to me," she says. "I understand if you're curious about these things. And I promise I won't judge you for it."

She seems to truly mean it. Which makes me wonder—is *Teresa* the sign I prayed for? Does she have information about how I can find a witch?

I find that hard to believe. She's so calm and levelheaded—she's not the type of person who would be involved with such things.

But she *did* enter my room right when I was finishing praying.

That could be a sign from God that I'm meant to ask Teresa for guidance. It *would* make sense for Him to instruct me to possess someone who's living with a person who can help me.

I need to have faith in Him and see what information—if any—Teresa might have.

"How can you say that?" I ask her. "What do you know about witches?"

"I know more than you think." She sighs, as if the confession pains her. "And I *can* answer your questions. But I have a feeling you weren't asking Sofia about witches because you're curious about a silly love spell. And if I'm going to answer your questions, I need you to be honest with me about why you were asking her about witches at all."

CHAPTER ELEVEN

This is my chance to find a witch. It *must* be.

I have to trust Teresa—and I have to trust God.

So I quickly send Him a prayer, letting Him know that I trust Him. I hope I'm doing the right thing.

"You're right," I admit. "I didn't ask Sofia about witches because I was interested in a love spell."

"Thank you for being honest with me." Teresa nods, her eyes warm and caring, and she waits for me to continue.

I fidget, not knowing where to start. "You said you can answer my questions," I say, since I need to get more information before telling her anything that resembles the truth. "But *how* can you be so sure about that? Do you know any witches?"

"I do," she says, her expression serious. "In fact, I'm very close with one. Closer than you might imagine. But, Adriana—I'm putting a lot on the line by trusting you with this. You have to promise not to mention this to anyone—not even Mom and Dad. Okay?"

"I promise," I say, and it's an easy promise to make, since I intend to complete my mission and vacate Adriana's body as soon as possible. "How do you know this witch?" I ask. "Is there a way you can arrange for me to meet her?"

"Perhaps." Teresa glances away from me, and then returns her gaze to mine. "But first I need to know why you want to speak to a witch to begin with."

"I just… need their help with something," I say, playing with the edge of my comforter. "I need to reverse a spell."

She presses her lips together, studying me. "That's vague," she says. "I was hoping you would tell me more than that."

"I'm sorry," I say. "But—you said you know a witch. Wouldn't it be more helpful if I'm able to talk to her?"

"It would be." Teresa stares at a painting on my wall—one of palm trees swaying on a beach. Her eyes are far off, and I can tell she's deep in thought. "Adriana," she finally says. "You're my sister, and you know the only reason I would ever keep something from you is for your own safety, right?"

"Right," I say, even though I don't know enough about their relationship to tell if that's the truth or not.

"Good." She nods and wrings her hands together. "Well… there's no easy way to say this, so I'm just going to spit it out."

I watch her, waiting for her to continue.

"I don't just *know* a witch," she says, holding her gaze with mine. "It's more than that. You see… I *am* a witch."

CHAPTER TWELVE

"*You what?*" I lean back in shock. Teresa is the last person who could ever be a witch. She's the opposite of everything witches represent.

How can this be true?

"I'm a witch," she repeats, and then she lowers her eyes, picking at her fingernails. When she refocuses on me, her gaze is full of resolve. "This might be easier to explain if I start from the beginning."

"Okay." I nod, making every effort to remain calm. "I'm listening."

She takes a deep breath, and begins. "I started showing signs of my powers around the age of fourteen," she says. "I was terrified, and I told no one, because I would be killed if I was discovered. I also knew no one would ever suspect me of being a witch, because it's very rare that a witch is born from two non-magical parents."

"It is," I say, since I do know that much.

"Keeping my true self from you and the rest of the family

was the hardest thing I've ever had to do," she continues. "I wanted to trust you all—you're my *family*—but Dad's the Lord of Sector Six. His obligation is to Ezekiel and the continent. I feared he would turn me in if I told him. And even if I told you all and you kept my secret, if I was ever discovered and it was found out that my family was keeping the secret for me, you would all be killed as well. I couldn't put you at risk like that. I wouldn't be able to live with myself if I did."

"So why tell me now?" I ask. "What changed?"

"You did," she says. "By asking about witches at all. I know you—you're stubborn. If you're determined to find a witch, you won't stop until you do. Better that you talk to me than continue to search around the city and risk getting into trouble if the wrong people find out what you're asking about."

I nod, since I *do* agree with her there.

"You're taking this much better than I thought you would," she says. "I thought you would be mad."

"What would you have done if I was mad?" I ask. "Put a spell on me so I forget this conversation?"

"It's an option," she says. "I won't lie and say it isn't. Although a memory spell requires a potion, not a chant."

I take a few seconds to digest her words. "How am I supposed to trust anything you say?" I fling my arms down next to me in frustration. "How do I know you won't use your magic—or a *potion*—to make me believe whatever you want me to believe?"

"Because you're my *sister*," she says, blinking away tears. "I love you. I would never do anything that isn't in your best interest. If you want me to never use magic on you, tell me, and I won't. Or if you want me to give you a potion so you forget this entire conversation and you're free of the burden of knowing what I truly am, I can do that for you, too. Just tell me, and I'll do it. I promise."

"Don't perform any magic on me," I say sharply. "Don't take away my free will."

"Okay," she says. "Understood."

We sit there like that for a few seconds, both of us unsure how to continue.

But I know what I must do now. Teresa was honest with me about who she is, so I need to do the same and trust her with the truth of who *I* am.

But first, I have a few more questions.

"Does Marco know?" I ask. "Or did you keep this from him, too?"

"He knows," she says. "You see… when I first realized what I am, I started sending anonymous notes to find out what others knew about witches. Of course, I was limited to the Golds who lived at the sector, but I was desperate to find someone I could talk to—someone who would understand what I was going through. Everyone ignored the notes—most destroyed them entirely, not wanting to be associated with anything regarding witchcraft. Then, when I was sixteen, Marco was stationed as a new guard. By that point, I expected that no one would acknowledge my notes, but I had to try. And you have no idea how happy I was when I found out that Marco was a witch, too. He promised to help me. At first, we pretended to date as a cover for when he would teach me how to use my powers. But soon, we fell in love for real. You know what happened from there—he proposed to me the day I turned eighteen. Unlike me, he was born into a family of witches, and I moved with him to the city so I could be part of their underground coven."

"Wow," I say, truly in awe of her bravery, even though I don't particularly care for her kind. "But don't you worry about getting caught? Wouldn't it be easier if you stopped using your magic altogether?"

"It would," she says. "But the more we practice, the stronger we are. And we can't risk letting our kind die out. Because as witches, we're not as affected by the curse as humans are. We don't know why that is, but we suspect that the magic in our blood helps us resist."

"I wish I could resist it." I pull my legs to my chest and wrap my arms around them. "It would make everything easier."

"It's not your fault that you can't," she tells me. "There's no spell or potion that can reverse the curse—trust me, we've tried. Someday, we hope to free everyone from Ezekiel's control, but we're so outnumbered, and we don't know where to begin. The people in the labor camps are too weak to fight, and everyone else is so greedy that they turn a blind eye to the fact that most people here are kept in deplorable conditions, working to death to provide the resources that keep the minority living in luxury. But I don't know why I'm telling you this." She sighs and pushes her hair behind her ears. "You only wanted help with reversing a spell. I shouldn't be burdening you with the talk of such treason, especially since there's nothing you can do to help."

"That's where you're wrong." I reach for her hand to stop her fidgeting, hoping to prepare her for the bomb I'm about to drop. "Because I can end this curse. But I need your help to do it."

CHAPTER THIRTEEN

"What?" Teresa laughs. "How can you do anything to end this curse?"

"I have a lot to tell you," I say. "It's going to be a lot to take in at once, and I'm sorry for that. But you trusted me with your secret, and now it's time for me to trust you with mine."

"What secret?" she asks, more serious now. "What are you talking about?"

"I'm not Adriana," I begin. "My name's Rebekah, and I'm an angel sent down by God to find Uriel's Flaming Sword and use it to kill the demon Ezekiel, which will end the curse forever."

"You *what*?" Teresa blinks, and her eyes flash with a myriad of emotions, eventually settling on anger. "Are you playing some kind of joke on me?"

"No," I continue. "I'm completely serious. And I'm so relieved to find out that you're a witch, because I *need* the help of a witch to help me succeed on this mission. You see, after Ezekiel stole the Flaming Sword from Uriel and used it to curse the continent, he hid the sword and had a witch create a boundary spell around it. The spell makes it impossible for angels to locate the sword. Only a powerful witch can locate it, and once it's found, the boundary spell needs to be removed so I can steal the sword back and use it to kill Ezekiel. Now that I know you're a witch, you *must* be the witch meant to help me do this."

Teresa shakes her head, pressing her fingers to her temples. "Hold up," she says, lowering her hands and looking straight at me. "If you're here, where's my sister? Is she still back at our parents' house in Sector Six? It's actually been *you* this entire time I thought she's been living with me?"

"Not exactly." I bite my lip, knowing how important it is to phrase this as delicately as possible. "I only arrived yesterday morning."

"Arrived," Teresa repeats, deadpan. "And how did you 'arrive,' exactly?"

"I was commanded by God to possess Adriana's body."

Teresa pulls her hand out of mine and leaps off the bed. She holds her palms out and chants in Latin, the words making my head pound like the worst migraine ever. The pain is blinding, and my ears ring at a deafeningly high pitch. I press my fingers to my temples, desperate to make it stop.

"What are you doing?" I ask, although since my hearing's dimmed, it comes out as a scream. "You're hurting me!"

"Damn right I'm hurting you." Teresa stops chanting for a second to speak. "I'm forcing you out of my sister's body."

"You're *exorcising* me?" I lower my arms in shock, but then she starts chanting again, and I keel over from the pain. It's like she's ripping my soul from my body. I scream again, closing my eyes and doing everything in my power to cling to Adriana's body. Angels have better holds on humans than demons do—which is why it's far more dangerous to exorcise us—but I won't be able to resist the spell forever.

"Stop!" I say, screaming again from the pain. I feel myself slipping away—I can't hold on for much longer. "I was instructed to enter Adriana's body by *God himself*! He wants to save this city. I don't know the details of His plan—no one does—but He has reasons for everything. He wouldn't have told me to enter Adriana's body unless it was the best chance for success!"

Her only response is to chant louder and step closer to me, her palms inches away from my chest, sucking my soul right out of this body.

I scream again and keel over further, now curled in a ball on the floor next to the bed. "Don't do this—to me *or* your sister," I beg, tears flowing from my eyes. "It's dangerous to force an angel from a human body. It harms the human."

She continues to chant, and I scream again, the outer parts of my soul peeling away from Adriana's body. I can't hold on for much longer.

Then the door swings open, banging against the wall. Marco stands in the opening.

"What the hell is going on in here?" he yells.

Teresa pauses her chanting, lowering her hands as she looks at him. "Adriana's possessed," she says. "Help me force this demon from her body."

"No!" I plead to Marco. I try to stand, but the pain cripples me, and I fall back to the floor. "I'm not a demon—I'm an angel, sent here by God to break the curse Ezekiel placed upon the continent. I'm telling the truth, I swear it."

Marco studies me for a few seconds. Then he walks over to Teresa and wraps his hands around her wrists, gently lowering her arms.

I suck in a deep breath, the pain alleviating as my soul settles back into Adriana's body.

"What are you doing?" Teresa asks him. "I need you to help me get rid of the demon."

"If she's who she says she is—an angel—we can't do this," he says, and I relax, grateful he's on my side. "Not without possibly permanently harming Adriana."

"And if she's lying?" Teresa glares at me, and returns her gaze to Marco's. "If she's a demon?"

"There's only one way to find out," Marco says, staring at me in challenge. "She needs to stand inside a demon trap."

CHAPTER FOURTEEN

Teresa clenches her fists, and I have a feeling that it's taking all of her willpower to stop herself from continuing to exorcise me. "Fine," she eventually agrees. "You stay here and guard her. Make sure she doesn't escape. I'll find the materials we need."

"She'll be fine," Marco says, and then he looks down at me, an eyebrow raised. "Won't you?"

"Yes." I can barely speak, and I don't make a move to stand up—I'm still in too much pain to do so. "I am who I say I am. But I don't blame you for wanting proof."

Teresa glares at me, distrust splayed across her face. "We'll see about that," she says. "But Marco's more skilled at exorcising than I am. So if you try anything funny on him, he'll force you out in a second." With that, she turns around, leaving the room.

Now that she's gone, the silence between Marco and me hangs awkwardly in the air.

"Thanks," I say to him, my voice shaking after what I just

went through. The pain is ebbing away, and I feel like I can get up, but I worry that any sudden movement might make Marco attack. "Is it okay if I move to sit on the bed?" I ask. Better safe than sorry.

"Yeah," he says. "But if you try to jump out the window or something, you'll regret it." He sounds tough, but he smiles, and I think he knows I have no intentions of trying to escape.

I move up to the bed, stretching out my limbs to make sure everything's all in one piece. It is. "Thanks for coming in when you did," I tell him. "I wouldn't have been able to hold onto this body much longer."

A shadow passes over his eyes. "The body you're talking about is Adriana's—Teresa's sister," he reminds me—as if I need reminding. "Did Adriana give you permission to possess her?"

"No." I shake my head, taken aback by the question. "God ordered me to do it."

"Directly?" Marco asks.

"No," I tell him. "God doesn't speak to messenger angels. He told Uriel—the seraph angel—and Uriel relayed the message to me."

"And you don't think Adriana had a right to be asked?"

"God didn't tell me to ask her." I clench my fists, irritation building at the audacity of his questions. "He told me to possess her. So that's what I did."

"*Uriel* told you to possess her," he says.

"Same thing."

"Not exactly." He stands still, studying me. "Did you question what you're doing at all?" he asks. "Or are you just following orders?"

"You speak about following orders as if it's a bad thing," I say. "And maybe following orders from some people is. But not from God. God wouldn't order me to do something if it wasn't the best way to go about the mission."

"So you don't think Adriana deserved a say in this?"

"It wasn't my place to ask." I hold his gaze, although guilt pangs in my chest, because I don't entirely disagree with his statement.

Before we can continue the conversation, Teresa bursts back inside, carrying a large piece of poster board.

"What's that?" I ask.

She says nothing, instead flipping over the poster so I can see.

I'm staring at a drawing of a demon trap. I'd recognize that circled pentagram with symbols inside the edges anywhere. She must have drawn it downstairs while Marco and I were up here talking.

She lays it on the ground near my feet. "Now's the time of truth." She looks at me in challenge and points to the trap. "Get up and stand in it."

CHAPTER FIFTEEN

I want to point out that if I were a demon, I would have used my demonic powers to incinerate them or kill them in some other horrible way, but I doubt that would go over well. At this point, they *must* know I'm not a demon. But I understand needing definite proof, so I step inside the trap.

"Good." Teresa nods. "Now step out of it."

I hold her eyes and do as she says. I can't stop myself from smiling once I'm out of the trap. Because if an actual demon—either possessing a human or in his natural form—were to step inside a trap, he wouldn't be able to step out. He would be stuck there until whoever trapped him either vanquished him or broke one of the lines of the circle, setting him free.

"Do you believe me now?" I ask.

"I believe you're not a demon," she says. "I don't have much of a choice. But am I happy that God asked you to possess my sister? No—not at all."

"I understand," I say. "But I promise that I'll keep Adriana safe."

"How do I know that?" she asks. "You're just a spirit possessing her."

"I'm more than just a spirit," I tell her. "My name is Rebekah, and I have my own form. I'm an *angel*. God ordered me not to go about this mission in my form, but I still have one."

"Okay," Teresa says. "But if anything happens to Adriana—if, God forbids, she gets killed because of what you're doing—you can just leave her body and float back up to Heaven in your true form. But my sister will be gone. Forever. Or at least, she'll be gone until I see her again after death."

"You make it sound so easy for me, but it's not," I say softly. "You see, I'm bound to remain in Adriana's body until I complete my mission. If I fail, I won't be allowed back into Heaven. I'll be cast out."

"You'll become a fallen angel," Marco realizes. "A demon."

"Yes," I say. "And I'll remain one unless I'm given a chance to redeem myself. Not all fallen angels are given such a chance—and sometimes when they are, they don't know they're being tested unless they pass." I shiver at the possibility of suffering such a fate. "So you see, I *must* succeed. My life is tied to Adriana's. If she dies, I'll fail the mission, and I'll be cursed to an eternity as a demon."

Teresa still watches me with suspicion, although she seems less tense than earlier. "I just want you out of my sister's body as quickly as possible," she says.

"I want the same," I agree. "Because leaving Adriana's body means I've completed my task and ended the curse. The faster I can do that, the faster everyone living on this continent will be freed. And I don't want anyone here to suffer for a second longer than they have to."

"I want the same thing," Teresa says. "But I don't like my sister being involved. She's an innocent in this war—a *human*."

"I understand," I say, because I do. "But God chose her. I don't know His reasons, but I promise you that He has them. It's all tied to a bigger plan. We have to have faith in Him and trust Him."

"I know, I know—I heard you the first time." Teresa glances down at the demon trap and huffs. She's obviously frustrated, but at least she isn't still trying to exorcise me, so I give her time to take this all in.

Finally, after a few moments of silence, she refocuses on me. "As much as I don't like these circumstances, it sounds like we're on the same side," she admits. "We both want to end this curse and keep Adriana safe."

"Yes." I nod. "We do."

"Okay." She takes a deep breath, her eyes full of determination. "So… where should we start?"

CHAPTER SIXTEEN

"Uriel can normally sense where his Flaming Sword is, because he forged it with fire from his own soul," I explain again, since I now have her full attention. "But the boundary spell the witch cast around it is strong. Uriel can no longer sense his sword."

"And with a locater spell, another witch can still find it?" Teresa asks.

"Yes," I say. "If they're strong enough."

"Then I suppose we're about to do a locater spell."

"Right now?" I ask. "I mean, you don't need time to prepare?"

"Yes, right now," she says. "There's no reason to wait."

"I'll get the crystals from the safe," Marco volunteers.

"And I'll get the table set up," she says. "Rebekah—you'll come with me."

I can tell she doesn't want me to know where this safe is that Marco will be grabbing the crystals from, and I don't blame her for being wary about trusting me. After all, I'm a stranger in her home. I'm just grateful that she's stopped trying to exorcise me and is now working with me. So I follow her downstairs and set up the table as she asks, doing as she says and not asking any questions.

Once finished, the table is covered with a black cloth, and there are three candles in the center. Teresa lights them. Once finished, she reaches for Marco's hand.

Watching them, and looking at the setup in front of us, it hits me that I'm about to witness witches doing magic. I've never been in the presence of witches conducting a spell. Like all angels, I keep my distance from witches and their ungodly magic.

"I'm assuming you've seen the Flaming Sword before, correct?" Teresa asks me. "The *real* Flaming Sword, and not the replica used for the continent's insignia?"

"Of course." I straighten, slightly offended that she felt a need to ask. "All angels have seen Uriel's Flaming Sword."

"Good," she says. "Your help—as someone who's seen the sword with your own eyes—will be beneficial in the accuracy of the spell."

"My help?" I sputter. "You want me… to do *magic*?"

"Not most of it, but your help will make the spell more effective," Teresa says, and she turns off the lights, the only glow in the room now coming from the candles. "Is that a problem?"

The dim lights make me feel trapped and closed in, and I rest my hands on the table for something to help steady myself. "I've just never done magic before," I explain. "I wouldn't know where to start."

"I thought you were an angel?" Marco asks. "Don't angels have magical abilities?"

"Yes," I say. "But that's different."

Teresa raises an eyebrow. "How so?"

"Our magic is part of who we are—who we were created to be," I explain. "I can't use my magic while in this form, but when I use it to do something—for example, to heal a human—I don't have to use any spells or potions. I just think of what I want to do, and it happens." I want to add that my magic is *natural*, but I don't want to offend them by accusing their magic of being unnatural—even though it *is* unnatural—so I leave it at that. "I wouldn't know the first thing about assisting with a spell."

"Luckily for you, Marco and I will be doing the hard part," Teresa says. "Your part is easy. Just hold our hands, close your eyes, and picture the Flaming Sword."

"Okay," I say, since that doesn't sound *too* bad. "That's it?"

"Yep," she says. "By holding our hands and thinking of the sword while we do the spell, you'll be sending the energy of the object in question—the sword—to us. It'll help our location spell be more accurate. I won't be able to sense exact coordinates, but I'll be able to get a general vicinity. Now—are you ready to begin?" She holds out her hand and watches me, daring me to take it.

I step forward, first taking Teresa's hand, and then Marco's. Together, we form a circle around the table. Their faces glow with the light of the flames, as I'm sure mine does, too.

This feels so... dangerous. As if I'm doing something wrong. Rationally, I know I'm not—since this is what I've been sent here to do—but witch magic has been something I've thought of as forbidden for so long. I never thought there would be a day when I would willingly participate in a spell. But here I am, doing just that. It's crazy and scary and invigorating all at the same time.

"I'm ready," I say, surprised by how much I mean it.

"Once I start chanting, I want you to close your eyes and picture the Flaming Sword," Teresa instructs me. "Don't stop picturing it until I break the circle. Okay?"

"Yes." I nod. "Okay."

She starts chanting—the spell is in Latin—and I close my eyes, picturing the sword. I recall Uriel holding it half a century ago before marching into battle—how he lifted it above his head, the gold gleaming in the sunlight, and ignited the sword with his flames. I remember how optimistic I and the other messenger angels were as we watched him—how we believed that with the sword, he would defeat the demons on Earth, win the war, and force the demons back into the Hell dimensions where they belong.

We didn't expect him to be defeated—to have the sword stolen from him, forcing him back up to Heaven. And we certainly hadn't expected the sword to go missing. Throughout history—for thousands of years—that sword had been by Uriel's side. It represents *strength* and *hope*. We must get it back.

Teresa gasps and pulls her hand away from mine.

"What?" I flex my hand and look at her. "Did I do something wrong?"

"No," she says, breathless. "Not at all. You did great."

"Then what happened?"

Fear flickers over her eyes. "I saw where the sword is being hidden," she says.

"And?" I ask. "Where is it?"

"One of the places I was hoping it *wouldn't* be," she says grimly. "The Watchtower."

CHAPTER SEVENTEEN

A few days later, we're no further along with figuring out how to get the sword from the Watchtower than we were after finishing the spell.

We're all eating lunch in the kitchen when the television screen suddenly lights up. An image of the Watchtower with "special announcement" written in front of it appears on the screen, and alert music blasts from the speakers.

"What's happening?" I ask.

"Whenever there's an announcement that everyone needs to see, Ezekiel broadcasts it to all the televisions in the continent," Teresa explains, putting down her sandwich and facing the screen. "It doesn't happen often. Something big must have happened."

I stop talking and stare at the TV. The shot shifts from the overview of the Watchtower to a large man in a fancy suit holding a microphone. I nearly ask if he's Ezekiel, but then I see the green tattoos on his wrist. He must be an entertainer —an actor.

He holds the microphone closer and begins. "Good morning, citizens!" he says with a grin. "I'm interrupting your day with some exciting news. I know it's only been a few weeks since the last selection, but I just received word that, as of this morning, none of King Ezekiel's concubines remain alive. He must have picked a bad bunch last time, because they usually last for a *little* longer than that!" He laughs, his smile huge, as if he's truly amused that these concubines had been murdered so quickly. "I'm sure all you lovely ladies will be thrilled to know that he's looking for ten new concubines to come live in the Watchtower, and he'll be hosting the selection next week. So mark your calendars for next Saturday night at eight sharp. As always, the ball is open to anyone who can afford a ticket and an outfit fit for the occasion. And remember—if you're a woman who wants to be considered as a concubine, wear a red dress to the ball so Ezekiel knows you're interested! I'll be there all night covering the event for those who won't be lucky enough to attend. I can't wait to see you there!"

He smiles again, and then the broadcast cuts out, switching to an infomercial advertising beautiful ball gowns.

"What was *that* about?" I ask, forcing my eyes away from the gorgeous dresses to focus on Teresa and Marco.

"How much do you know about Ezekiel's concubines?" Marco asks me.

"Not much," I admit. "Just that he selects ten girls each year to live with him in the Watchtower, and he usually ends up killing them all."

"That pretty much summarizes it," Teresa says. "When he held his first selection, he claimed to be searching for a queen. He was supposed to choose one of the ten of them to marry."

"But that's not how it happened?" I guess.

"Nope," she says. "He killed them all before the year was up

—apparently none of them were good enough for him. And so, year after year, he holds more selections, but he never finds a queen. Even if some of the girls survived the year, he asked them to leave after the year was up so he could make room for ten new girls. Now, everyone knows he's not looking for a queen. He simply keeps the girls around for entertainment. If they step out of line and anger him, he kills them. Usually all ten of them don't make it, but some years at least one or two survive and are kicked out. Killing them all after a few months is extreme, even for him."

I raise my hand to my mouth, horrified. "If he kills them… why would anyone want to be selected as a concubine?" I ask.

"Because if they survive, they're elevated to a Gold," she explains. "They're given an apartment and a generous amount of money every year for the rest of their lives. For so many women in the city, becoming a concubine is a ticket to a life of luxury and wealth that they couldn't otherwise dream of."

"So their own greed causes them to risk their lives," I realize.

"I suppose it does," she says, her eyes sad. "The only other way to switch castes is through marriage—but then, both people become the lower caste, so it's not something people seek to do."

"So if a Gold man wants to marry a Green woman, he would have to become a Green for her," I say.

"Yep," Marco says. "As you can imagine, this happens *very* rarely in a city cursed with greed. No one's willing to give up their status for anything—not even for love."

"The only way to move *up* in caste is to survive a year as one of Ezekiel's concubines and become a Gold," Teresa says. "The chance gives the women of lower castes hope."

"They want to become a Gold so badly that they'll die for

it." I look down at the tattoos wrapped around my wrists—around *Adriana's* wrists—and shudder. The people here are truly bound in chains to Ezekiel.

And I'm the only one who can free them.

Another infomercial comes on—this one advertising shoes that go with ball gowns and yet are still comfortable to wear while dancing the night away. The actress glides across the floor, lifting her dress up to show off her high-heeled shoes, a huge smile on her face. I can't imagine *any* pair of heels being that comfortable, but the actress is convincing enough that I want to try them on for myself and see.

Suddenly, the phone rings, yanking me out of my thoughts. How did I allow myself to be swayed by a stupid infomercial after learning such horrible things about the selection and Ezekiel's concubines? I know it's the fault of the curse, but it's still my responsibility to do everything I can to resist it.

Teresa walks over to the phone and answers it. "Hi, Sofia," she says, looking at me while she speaks. "Yes—Adriana's right here. I'll hand you over to her." She drops the phone from her ear, and I walk over to take it from her.

"Hey," I say, trying to force some enthusiasm into my tone.

"Adriana!" Sofia squeals. "Did you see the announcement from the Watchtower?"

"Of course," I say, and I glance over at the television. The lady is still dancing in the heels, but now with a handsome man guiding her. They gaze at each other in adoration, and I almost believe they're truly in love.

"We *need* to go shopping," she says.

"We do?" I ask.

"Of course!" she says. "It's your first selection ball! Anyone who's anyone will be there—including the hottest *single* Gold men on the continent. We *must* go."

I take a deep breath and lean against the wall. The last thing I want is to go to this ball where Ezekiel is searching for women that he'll end up killing. I don't want to be anywhere *near* Ezekiel. He's a horrible, disgusting monster.

But I was sent here to kill him. *And* I now know he's hiding the Flaming Sword in the Watchtower. Attending the ball could prove beneficial to my mission.

I won't let my own worries and fears keep me from succeeding in what I was sent here to do.

"You're right," I say, suppressing a sigh. "Of course we need to go."

"Great!" Sofia chirps. "And we need to go shopping *now*, before all the best dresses get snatched up. I'll be over to pick you up in ten minutes—be ready to head out!"

She hangs up before I can answer, and I stare at the phone in my hand, amazed with how much just changed in the span of a few minutes.

It looks like I'm going to this ball after all.

CHAPTER EIGHTEEN

Sofia's car is packed—three of the girls I recognize from brunch are in there. Apparently she forgot to tell me that this is going to be a *group* shopping trip, but I slide into the car anyway.

We arrive at the street that Sofia says has the *best* shopping in the entire city, and after we park, I follow her and the girls out of the car. As Sofia guessed, the street is packed. Mostly Golds, but I notice some Silvers as well.

"We *have* to go to Maria's," Sofia says, hurrying down the street. "Before all the best gowns are taken!"

I recognize the store name as the first one advertised on the infomercials. The girls all squeal in excitement and rush down the street. I follow them, looking around at everything we pass.

I see a music store, and I stop walking at the sight of a beautiful violin displayed in the window. Sucking in a sharp breath, I can nearly *feel* what it would be like to rest that violin upon my shoulder and play.

"Come on," Sofia nags, pulling at my arm. "Why'd

you stop?"

"Can we stop inside that music store so I can check out that violin?" I ask. "I'll be fast."

Her eyebrows furrow. "You play violin?" she asks.

"I did when I was younger." I shrug. "I want to pick it up again."

"Hmm," Sofia says. "I guess we can stop by on our way back. *After* we find our dresses."

She pulls me away from the store, and I go along with it, placated by the fact that we'll return to the music store later. As long as I come home at the end of the day with that violin by my side, I'll be happy.

Except *hours* into dress shopping, Sofia still hasn't found a dress she likes. I found one soon after starting, and the other girls found theirs after a bit more searching. But apparently nothing is good enough for Sofia. I huff from my spot on the couch, waiting for her to model the next one she's trying on.

She comes out of the dressing room and twirls in a shimmery green ball gown.

"It's beautiful!" I say, even though she's tried on others that were much better.

"No, it's not." She pouts. "I look like a plant."

The shopkeeper comes back over to us, holding a few more dresses. "I brought over some more for you to try," she says to Sofia. "These are the *best* in the store—I promise."

"We'll see about that." Sofia takes them and marches back into the dressing room.

I look out the window—it's already getting dark—and sigh. "What time do most of the stores close around here?" I ask one of Sofia's friends—a girl named Ana.

She glances at her watch. "We have another hour, at least."

My heart drops, since I have a feeling that Sofia will be here until the store closes. Which means I'll lose my chance of stopping by that music store on the way back.

I *really* want that violin. Playing violin not only relaxes me, but it also helps me think. I flex my fingers, wanting nothing more than to wrap my hands around that bow and create music. Once I have the violin, perhaps I'll be better able to sort through my thoughts and figure out a plan to steal the Flaming Sword from the Watchtower. Maybe seeing that store today was a sign from God that I *need* to buy that violin.

All I know is that I refuse to return home without it.

"I'm going to stop by that music store really fast," I tell the girls. "You'll still be here in half an hour, right?"

"You're going alone?" Ana asks.

"Yeah," I say. "This is a busy street, right? It's safe?"

"It is," one of the other girls says. "Just stay on the main street, and you'll be fine."

"Will do," I say. As I head out, I hear one of them mutter something about "stupid country girls" and another say something about how I was being a downer, anyway.

I feel like I can breathe again the moment I step onto the street, and I head back to the music store. It's still open, and I smile at the sight of the violin in the window.

The instrument is *perfect*, and I use nearly the rest of my coins to buy it. I'm grinning as I step back out on the street, the bag with my new dress on one side and the violin in its case by my other, excited to get home and play. I'm feeling happier than I have all day.

I'm halfway back to the dress store, stopping to wait for a car to cross the street, when someone tugs at the bottom of my shirt. A young child around the age of six. His hair's unwashed, there's dirt smudged on his face, and his eyes are sad. The tattoos around his wrists are red. I look around for someone nearby who might be his parent, but everyone I see is a Gold or a Silver.

"Hey there," I say with a smile. "Are you lost?"

He nods, still looking up at me with those soulful, wide eyes, and my heart goes out to him. I have to do *something* to help.

I kneel so I'm closer to his level. "We need to find your parents," I say. "Do you know where you saw them last?"

"That way." He points down a dark, narrow street nearby. I don't see anyone in it, but it curves around, so it's possible for people to be on the other side. Perhaps that's where the more affordable shopping is—it would explain why his parents are there instead of here. He must have wandered over here accidentally and gotten scared in the crowd.

"Okay." I move my violin to my other hand, somehow managing to hold it and the shopping bag together, and reach for the boy's hand with my now-free one. "Let's go find your parents."

He nods and walks with me down the road—it's narrower than I thought at first, more of an alley than a street. It's colder in here, and darker, and I shiver as a strong wind blows by.

I hesitate and glance over my shoulder. Sofia's friends told me to stay on the main street. But this boy needs help. Everyone else is too busy trying to get in their last bit of shopping before the stores close, so if I don't help him, no one will. I stand straighter and continue forward, following him around the corner.

The moment I turn the corner, someone runs at me from behind and wraps their arms around me, holding a knife to my neck. His tattoos are red.

His rancid breath is hot against my face as he says, "Scream and I'll slit your throat."

CHAPTER NINETEEN

Someone else—a woman who's also a Red—runs forward and scoops the boy up in her arms. She has the same small build and soulful eyes as he does. She must be his mother. She also holds a knife, and she watches me closely, as if she's preparing to attack if I make one small move.

"I don't mean him any harm," I say, hoping to reason with them. "I was just helping him find his parents. That's all. I was trying to *help* him. Let me go. *Please.*" My eyes fill with tears, my voice shaking as I speak.

"Stupid, stupid girl," the man mutters in my ear. "Drop your bags and empty your pockets. Now."

I drop the shopping bag and my violin to the ground. My heart breaks as the case hits the pavement.

"Your purse, too," the man says. "And any other coins you have hidden in your pockets. Don't try to hide anything from me—because I'm going to check, and if you hold anything back, I promise that pretty little Gold face of yours that you'll be sorry."

I move to drop my purse to the ground, but before I can, someone else rushes into the alley—he moves so quickly that I can barely make out his features. All I know is that in seconds, the knife is no longer pressed against my skin, and the man and woman are splayed on the pavement, blood gushing from their necks and forming puddles around their twitching bodies. Seconds later, they're still.

A rivulet of blood creeps closer to my violin, and I pick up both it and the shopping bag with my gown. The boy is huddled over his mom's body, crying and begging her to wake up.

I look over at the man who did this—he's standing against the wall of the alley, his arms crossed and a satisfied smirk on his lips. I recognize him instantly—the mysterious stranger who walked me home from brunch the first day I was here.

"You killed them." I clench the bags to my sides, unable to keep the anger from my tone. "You *murdered* that boy's parents right in front of him."

He flips the knife in his hand and slips it into his belt. "All that trouble and I don't even get a thank you?" he asks.

"You *killed* them," I repeat. "They just needed money, and you took their lives."

"Apparently, you need some education about how things work in the city," he says. "Because you don't think they were going to let you go after you handed over your precious coins, do you?"

I press my lips together, because yes, that's exactly what I thought.

"You *did* think they were going to let you go." His eyes twinkle with amusement. "Didn't you?"

"Of course," I say. "They just wanted money. Why wouldn't they let me go after getting it?"

He peels himself away from the wall and walks toward me, his ice-blue eyes capturing me in his gaze. "Because, Adriana," he starts, and I can't stop the warm feeling that shoots up my chest at the realization that he remembers my name. "You've seen their faces. You know who they are. If you report them... they'd be killed for stealing from a Gold. Once they had everything they needed from you, they would have slit your throat and left you in this alley to rot—at least until the stench got so strong that someone discovered what remained of your corpse. Now *they're* the ones who will rot in this alley—not you. So, you see, you should be thanking me."

He's standing so close that I can barely think. I can barely breathe. All I can feel is my heart pounding in my chest, beating so hard that I fear it might burst if it speeds up anymore.

He glances away from me to look at the child, who's still crying over the body of his mother. "Go," he tells him. "And make sure to remind your people what happens when a Red tries to steal from a Gold."

The boy nods and runs away, gone in an instant.

I hold my hand to my neck, hit with the realization that I nearly died. I tried to help someone and almost died for it. If I *had* died, I would have failed my mission. I would have been cast from Heaven.

This man—whose name I still don't know—he saved my life.

"What's your name?" I ask. "This is the second time we've met... and I never got your name."

His eyes flash with surprise, and he takes a step back, as if I said something wrong. "You don't know?" he finally asks.

"No." I laugh, although I feel guilty about it a second later, since the bodies of my attackers are still sprawled around us.

This isn't a time for merriment. "You never told me your name. How would I know?"

"No," he muses. "I suppose I didn't."

"Well…" I prod, but then I wonder—is there a reason why he's keeping his name secret? His jacket covers his tattoos, and he has incredible fighting skills. He must have gone through intensive training to learn how to fight like that.

Is he some kind of vigilante? Perhaps even a witch, able to resist the curse, who rescues people in need?

"You don't have to tell me if you don't want to," I say. "Although, you *did* save my life. I would at least like to know your name."

"Matthew," he says suddenly. "My name is Matthew."

"Well, thank you, Matthew," I say. "For saving my life."

I adjust my bags, and Matthew's eyes flicker to the one with the dress.

"Is that for the ball?" he asks.

"It is," I say. "Are you going as well?"

He raises an eyebrow. "Are you asking me to the ball?"

"No!" I say, and I widen my eyes, realizing how horrible that sounded. Especially because I *like* the idea of possibly going with him. We may have only met twice—and both times in strange situations—but around Matthew, I feel… safe. "I mean, do you want me to ask you?" I continue. "Because if you do, then I suppose we could go together, although I think my cousin might be upset because she thinks I'm going in a group with her…" I trail off, realizing I'm babbling. How embarrassing.

"I'm sorry," he says with a smirk. "I didn't mean to get you excited. I already have a date."

"Oh," I say, my heart dropping. "Sorry. Of course you do."

"No need to apologize," he says. "If I didn't have a date

already, then you better believe I would go with you. I'm sure you'll look beautiful in that dress."

"Thank you," I say, and my cheeks flush again. He must think I'm ridiculous. "And thank you again—for saving me. I don't know how you knew I was here, but I'm in your debt."

"It's wasn't difficult to spot you being led into that alley," he says. "Most Golds don't fall for tricks like that from Reds anymore. But when I saw it was *you*, I knew I had to do something."

"Well, that was very generous of you," I say. "To risk your life like that. I doubt many others would do the same."

"I also doubt many others are as talented with a knife as I am." He reaches for his knife, throwing it high in the air and catching it by the handle.

"True," I say, and then I look around, realizing we've been casually standing here, chatting in this alley. Where two people lay dead. "What's going to happen to them?" I ask, motioning to the corpses.

"Someone will eventually find them," he says. "Just like they would have found you, if those thieves had gotten their way."

I shiver at the reminder that I could be dead in this alley instead of them—my soul possibly already condemned to fall from Heaven.

"Well… thank you again," I say, although I'm not sure I'll ever be able to thank him enough. "Like I said, I'm in your debt."

"There's no need for that." He waves away my words. "Saving you was… my pleasure."

He watches me intensely, his eyes studying my face—as if he's searching for something in my features. My blood stills under his gaze, and I feel lightheaded and dizzy. I move closer to him, and he does the same, until we're standing only inches apart. His eyes travel down to my lips, and my heart races with the sudden realization that he's going to kiss me.

What surprises me more is that I *want* him to kiss me.

Somehow, we move closer together. Before I know what's happening, his lips are on mine. I fall into him, my heart racing, wanting more. His lips are warm, and this feels so *right*.

But the kiss is short—sweet—and his fingers trail against my cheek, as if he's memorizing every inch of my face.

I open my eyes, surprised by the sadness in his gaze. He's looking at me as if this is the last time he'll ever see me. But why? I don't know what this is between us, but it feels like it's only the beginning.

There's so much I want to ask him. But then my foot bumps into something—the corpse of the man who tried to rob me—and I'm yanked back to reality. Where we're standing in an alley where two people just died.

"My cousin's probably getting worried about me," I realize. "I've been gone for so long…"

"Of course," he says. "I'll walk you back to the street, where you'll be safe."

"Thank you," I say for what feels like the millionth time today, and I allow him to lead me toward the street that's bright with lights and bustling with determined shoppers. "We *will* see each other again," I ask once we're back to the street. "Won't we?"

He doesn't answer.

When I glance over at him to see why, he's not there. I whip my head around, searching for him, but I can't find him anywhere. He's gone.

Why did he disappear? How did he even get away that quickly? And more importantly… what's he hiding from me?

I might have thought he was just a figment of my imagination. But imaginary people can't save others from murdering thieves. He's real. And after that kiss—after seeing the way he looked at me—forgetting him will be impossible.

At least I know he'll be at that ball.

And when we're both there, I'll finally discover who the mysterious Matthew is once and for all.

CHAPTER TWENTY

Teresa and Marco are sitting in the living room when I get back. In the time that I've lived here, I've never once seen them hang out in this room. Which I suspect means one thing—they're waiting for me.

They're sitting on opposite sides of the couch, not looking at each other. Teresa has her arms crossed in front of her chest, her eyes angry. Marco seems calmer, and he sits up straighter when I come in. Something's *definitely* up.

"Hi." I look back and forth between them as I close the front door. "What's going on?"

"Marco has a plan about how you can get access to the Watchtower," Teresa says, her voice soft and eerily calm. "Sit down."

I place the violin and bag with my dress on the ground and do as she asked.

"What's your plan?" I direct the question toward Marco.

"After the announcement this morning about the upcoming ball, I had an idea," he starts.

"A *ridiculous* idea." Teresa scoffs. "There's no way it'll work."

"Even if it's ridiculous, I still want to hear it," I say, and then return my focus to Marco.

"As I was saying," he continues. "Next week, Ezekiel is holding the ball where he'll choose ten new concubines to live with him in the Watchtower for a year. Obviously, this ball is a good chance for you to meet him. As Golds who live in the city, it's customary for us to go, so we'll all be attending regardless. But the ball is only for one night. We need you to have access to the Watchtower *every* night. So I started thinking— what if you didn't attend as a guest? What if you auditioned to be a concubine?"

"What?" I gasp, unsure I understood correctly. "You want me to be one of Ezekiel's *concubines*?" I say the word in disgust, a shiver running down my spine at the prospect.

"See?" Teresa glares at Marco. "She thinks it's as ridiculous as I do."

"No." I shake my head. "I mean... on one level, it makes sense. I'll have access to Ezekiel that I wouldn't have otherwise. But isn't he known for *killing* his concubines? Won't I just be putting myself in danger?"

"He doesn't kill every concubine," Marco says. "The ones he likes survive."

"He's not going to like me," I say. "I'm here to kill him."

"Which is why you'll have to hide that from him until you figure out exactly where the Flaming Sword is and devise a plan to end him."

I press my lips together, saying nothing. The thought of putting myself in such proximity to Ezekiel terrifies me. If he finds out who I am before I'm able to kill him, I'll fail my mission for sure.

But I also see Marco's point. That sword is hidden in the

Watchtower. I'll have a much better chance of locating it if I live in the Watchtower myself.

Marco must be able to tell that I'm considering his idea, because he continues. "You'll need to get Ezekiel to trust you," he says. "It's been done before, by previous concubines who survived. Sometimes, it seemed like Ezekiel even cared for them."

"Demons aren't capable of love," I tell him. "Lust, yes. Obsession, perhaps. But not love. A creature that evil can't truly experience love."

"Perhaps not," he says. "It would explain why Ezekiel has never found a queen. But you don't need him to love you. You just need him to trust you. If he trusts you, he'll be more likely to reveal where he keeps the sword. Once you figure that out, come to Teresa and me. We'll figure out what to do next from there."

"It's not a bad first step," I say. "Assuming, of course, that Ezekiel doesn't kill me first."

"You're here to kill him," Marco says. "There's no getting around the danger that accompanies such a mission."

"True," I say.

"You're not actually considering this?" Teresa stares at me, her eyes wide.

"Of course I'm considering it," I tell her. "It's the most solid plan any of us have had so far. Unless you've thought of something better?"

"I don't think you understand," Teresa says. "When Ezekiel kills his concubines… it's brutal. Sometimes it's for the simplest things. If he doesn't like something one of them does, he snaps his fingers and incinerates them on the spot. You'll be putting yourself in harm's way every single day. Not just yourself—you'll be putting *Adriana* in harm's way. I will not let my sister be murdered because her body was the one chosen for you to possess. No way. Not happening."

"I'm sorry," I tell her, because I truly am. I don't want her to lose her sister either. Just like I don't want to fall from Heaven if I fail. "But what if I wasn't in Adriana's body? Then would you think the plan was a good one?"

"I don't know." Teresa shrugs. "But it's irrelevant, because you *are* in her body. Unless something happened and you've been given permission to be released?"

"No," I say. "And you know that it's in my best interest to protect her. But this plan is the best we have right now."

"Perhaps," Teresa says. "But no one will believe that you're serious about auditioning."

"Why's that?" I ask.

"Because no Gold has auditioned to be a concubine since Ezekiel's original selection."

CHAPTER TWENTY-ONE

"How's that possible?" I look to Marco for confirmation, because he seems to be the one who's able to think more logically.

"It's true," he says. "Like we told you earlier, the main reason that women audition is because it's the only way for them to rise in status. If they're already a Gold, why would they bother?"

"Because they want to be chosen as queen?" I ask.

"People accepted long ago that Ezekiel wasn't going to choose a queen," Teresa says. "Golds auditioned in the original selection because they wanted to be royalty—being the queen was the only rank higher than being a Gold. But he killed every single one of them. After seeing the bloodbath of the concubines, no other Golds have taken the risk. Why would they, when we already live a life of luxury and comfort?"

"So if I audition, it will cause quite the stir," I say.

"That's an understatement," Teresa says. "You'll be singled out from the start. If you're chosen, you'll stand out even more

—which I worry will make it even more likely that you'll be killed."

"Or it could work to her advantage," Marco points out. "Ezekiel loves a good show. It would hardly be interesting if he killed the only Gold to audition in half a century."

"*If* she gets chosen," Teresa shoots back. "Over a hundred girls auditioned last time, and only *ten* of them are selected. The odds are not in our favor."

"She'll get chosen." Marco snorts. "Adriana's beautiful—more beautiful than many of the girls Ezekiel's chosen in the past. But most importantly, she's a Gold. I can't imagine him not being intrigued by a Gold auditioning to be a concubine."

"He'll surely wonder *why* she's auditioning," Teresa says. "I can't imagine anything she could say that would sound remotely believable. He'll suspect her from the beginning—and he'll be even more likely to kill her."

"I could say that I want to become his queen," I say softly. "Adriana moved here to find a suitable husband. Who could be more suitable—and of higher rank—than Ezekiel himself?"

"He's narcissistic enough that he would probably believe it," Marco says.

"Except he's no longer looking for a queen," Teresa reminds us. "Everyone knows that. He doesn't think any of us are good enough to be his queen."

"Unless I believed I could change his mind," I say. "Like you said, Adriana's beautiful. She's a Gold. And not just *any* Gold—her father is the lord of one of the sectors. Why wouldn't she think that she's qualified to be queen?"

"She's *eighteen*," Teresa says. "She can barely take care of herself—let alone an entire continent."

"She would hardly be the first teenage queen," I say. "I've seen many queens crowned at her age—some even younger."

"None of them married a *demon king!*" Teresa clenches her fists to her sides, her eyes wide in terror.

"True," I admit. "But Henry the Eighth was horrible enough to his wives that he might as well have been a demon."

She cracks a smile, but it's gone quickly.

"I'm as scared as you are, but I think this plan can work," I say, serious again. "I think you know that, too. But to make it work, I'll need help and support—from *both* of you."

"I don't like it." Teresa huffs and sits back in the couch.

"I know you don't," I say. "But do you think it gives me a chance to complete my mission?"

She sighs and runs her hands through her hair, staring out the window, her forehead creased in thought.

I say nothing, giving her time to process. Marco does the same.

"It does give you a chance," she finally admits. "As much as I hate it, I can't think of any other way that would give you more access to the Watchtower."

"Then it's settled." I swallow and clasp my hands in my lap, the terrifying reality of the situation hitting me all at once.

But I have to remain calm—for all our sakes.

And so, I raise my head and say, "Next week at the ball, I'm going to audition—and be chosen—to be one of Ezekiel's concubines."

CHAPTER TWENTY-TWO

The week before the ball was full of shopping and prepping. I needed a red dress, since everyone auditioning to be a concubine had to wear one. But Teresa didn't want anyone to see me buying one, since a Gold purchasing a red ball gown this week would surely get the entire city talking. She wants everyone to be shocked when I show up to audition—including Ezekiel. So she hired a top-notch fashion designer—a Green named Flory—to create a gown for me. Flory jumped at the job, especially because Teresa paid her a hefty bonus of gold coins to ensure she kept our plan a secret.

It takes nearly an hour to get me in the dress and able to properly maneuver myself while wearing it. It fits snugly around my waist—so snugly I worry I might get short of breath while dancing—but it *has* to be tight since it's strapless and needs some way to stay up. The corset is so intricately beaded that it sparkles in the light, and the skirt's so full and fluffy that three people could easily fit inside. It reminds me of a wedding dress, but bright red instead of white. I have to hold my arms out to make sure not to smoosh it, and I fear it'll be a miracle if I don't trip over it at some point during the night.

Now, I sit at my dressing table while Flory does the finishing touches on my hair. She has me wearing it down—she claims it looks more youthful that way, and Ezekiel loves youthfulness. She's curled it and is adding various sparkly gems to it. Meanwhile, I stare into the mirror at my face, which has been made up expertly, down to the fake eyelashes encrusted with gems. There's no denying that Adriana is breathtakingly beautiful.

I feel like Cinderella about to attend the royal ball.

Except that instead of dancing with a prince, I'll be dancing with a demon.

My heart flutters in anticipation. So much of this comes down to getting Ezekiel to like me. If it wasn't for all the makeup covering my face, I'm sure I would have looked pale with terror.

"Make sure not to pull the tab too early," Flory says. She's been repeating it to me all night. "You don't want to ruin the surprise."

"I know," I tell her. "I'll wait until they announce my name and I'm at the top of the steps. I promise."

"He'll be smitten the moment he lays eyes on you." She arranges my hair over my shoulders and smiles. "You're going to be the most glamorous woman auditioning. Not just auditioning—you're going to be the most glamorous woman at the entire ball!"

∽

Once I'm finished getting ready, Flory helps me into the back of the car. I have to sit in the center seat. The dress takes up so much space that it presses against both doors. Marco's driving, and Teresa's in the passenger seat. They both look incredible—him in a white-tie suit, and her in the purple gown I'd initially bought on my shopping trip with Sofia.

Flory waves as we pull out of the driveway. She's wearing a beautiful dress herself—full and yellow. But there's no room for her in the car—my dress takes up too much space—and according to Teresa, it wouldn't be proper for Flory to arrive in a car with Golds anyway. She'll walk from our house, and then take the trolley home at the end of the night with the other Greens.

We soon pull up at the valet in front of the Watchtower. The moment I step out of the car, two Gold guards rush to my side and stop me in my path. They're both young, probably in their mid-to-late twenties. The first one—the taller one—eyes me, and his brow furrows in confusion.

"Only those auditioning to be one of Ezekiel's concubines can wear red tonight," he informs me. "You'll need to go home and change. But you must hurry, because the doors close in an hour, and once they closed, no one's allowed in."

"There's no need for that." I hold my head high and arrange the skirt around myself. "Because I *am* auditioning to be one of his concubines."

"You are?" The other guard balks. "But... you're a Gold."

"And your point is?" I try my best to sound irritated so he won't pick up on how terrified I truly feel. Plus, this is practice. If I can't convince Gold guards that I'm auditioning because I *want* to be chosen as a concubine, then there's no chance that Ezekiel will believe me.

"I'm sorry, miss," the first guard says, bowing his head. "It's just that, as I'm sure you know, this is quite unprecedented. No Golds have auditioned since the very first selection."

"I know," I tell him. "And it's no wonder Ezekiel has been unable to find a proper queen amongst all the Silvers, Greens, and Reds he has to choose from." I scrunch my nose, as if the thought of him only having to choose from such "lowly" castes disgusts me. "It's about time that someone who's *worthy* of him steps up for the role. And who's worthier than a Gold? And not just *any* Gold, but the daughter of the Lord of Sector Six?"

I look back and forth between them, daring them to contradict me.

"Apologies," the first man says. "I was simply surprised, that's all. I meant no disrespect."

"But you do know that Ezekiel is no longer searching for a queen?" the second guard asks. "His concubines are for... entertainment. Nothing more."

"That's because he has yet to meet me." I fluff the gown around myself, keeping the haughtiness in my tone. "Now, please step out of my way. I have a ball to attend."

I glance at Teresa, and she nods at me. I must be doing a decently convincing job.

"We actually didn't originally approach you to stop you from coming to the ball," the first guard says. "We approach everyone who arrives in a red dress, since all the ladies auditioning must come with us through the side entrance to the waiting room. Once there, you'll be assessed, and if deemed acceptable, you'll remain there until it's time to announce you at the party."

"Although you have nothing to worry about," the second guard says. "You'll surely pass the assessment with flying colors."

I nearly chuckle at how flabbergasted he still is. Instead, I clear my throat to compose myself. "Obviously I'll pass," I tell them, as if I'm so confident that the thought of failing has never crossed my mind. "Now, please, lead the way."

I take one last glance behind me at Teresa and Marco, and then follow the guards around the towering Watchtower, each step one closer to coming face to face with Ezekiel.

CHAPTER TWENTY-THREE

The side entrance is just a plain, unmarked door guarded by an older man. He's wearing the black uniform of the guards, and I don't even need to look at his wrists to know he's a Gold.

He gives me a once over, his eyes widening when he sees my tattoos.

"Is this a joke?" he inquires. "We haven't had a Gold audition—"

"Since the first year of the ball," I interrupt, heaving a sigh. Am I going to have to go through this with every person I encounter? "And not having any Golds audition is clearly the reason why Ezekiel hasn't been able to find a queen. Now, will you let me inside? It's hot out here, and I don't want to perspire in my dress." I fan myself to further my point.

Playing the part of a spoiled Gold socialite is turning out to be far easier than I'd anticipated.

The man raises an eyebrow and glances at the guards on

my sides. The taller one nods, as if confirming that I'm serious. I hold the man's eyes and wait for whatever he's going to say next.

"Very well," he says, eyeing my gown once more. "You certainly meet the necessary requirements. Go ahead."

He opens the door, and the two guards escort me inside a large waiting room. The door is barely wide enough for my dress, and the guards have to help me squish it down on the sides so I'm able to fit through. Once I make it, I re-fluff the gown and pull up the bodice, looking around.

The room is plain, and it's full of about sixty other women in red dresses. Some of them are sitting, while others stand and examine themselves in the mirrors along the walls, doing final touch-ups to their hair and makeup. Most of them are chatting with each other, but a few sit alone in the corners, looking utterly terrified.

As I enter, a few of the girls turn to look at me. They whisper to the girls next to them, and soon enough, silence descends upon the room. They just stare at me, gaping as if I walked in naked.

My cheeks flush, and every bone in my body aches to turn around and run back to Teresa's house. But I suspected something like this would happen, so I hold my head high and continue inside.

Looking around at their tattoos, I see a few Silvers and Reds, but most of them are Greens. They all wear beautiful red dresses, but nothing as extravagant as mine. I feel suddenly self-conscious, and I reach to tuck my hair behind my ears, but I stop myself. Because not only will Flory kill me if I mess up the curls, but I also don't want any of these girls to see how nervous I am. I can't risk ruining my cover.

Suddenly, a petite, round-faced girl stands up—a Silver—and walks toward me. Her form-fitting dress is mermaid styled at the bottom, showing off her curves. "Adriana Medina?" she asks, her arms outstretched and a smile on her face.

"Yes." I take her hands, since she hasn't given me any other option. "Have we met?"

"No, we haven't," she says, and her smile is so contagious that despite how self-conscious I feel, I can't stop myself from returning it. "I'm Elizabeth Chavez—I teach arts and culture at the school for Golds. Your cousin Sofia is one of my students. I've seen you pick her up from school a few times."

"Of course." I nod, even though I've never picked Sofia up from school since entering Adriana's body. Now that Elizabeth is closer, I can see a few lines around her eyes. Her height makes her look young for her age, but since she's a teacher at the high school, I assume she must be somewhere in her late twenties. "It's nice to officially meet you."

"Come, sit with me," she says. "We have so much dancing to look forward to tonight—we must rest our feet while we still can!" Linking her arm around mine, she leads me to a couch on the side of the room. She looks around at a few of the other girls—who are still staring—and smiles at them as we pass. "Your dress is so beautiful," she continues. "Where did you find it? I searched nearly every store in the city and didn't see anything close to this lovely."

"My stylist picked it out," I answer. "She has wonderful taste... although it's so huge. I must admit I'm worried that it'll be impossible to get through the night without crashing into someone."

"I'm sure everyone will move out of your way to ensure that won't happen." She arrives at the couch and sits down, patting the cushion next to her for me to join. I do so. Once I'm situated, I realize the other girls have stopped staring and have resumed chatting amongst themselves.

For the first time since entering the room, I feel like I can breathe again.

"Thank you for saving me," I say to Elizabeth, keeping my voice low so the other girls can't hear.

"Anytime," she says. "There aren't many Silvers here—maybe five of us so far in all—and while our receptions haven't been quite as icy as yours, they've been pretty close."

"Why?" I ask. "Don't Silvers audition every year?"

"Yes, but not many," she says. "And the Greens and Reds think they deserve this chance more than Silvers. Which is unfair if you ask me, since they don't know our personal stories…" She brings her hands together, sadness passing over her eyes. "But there's no need to get into that." She smiles again, her cheeks rosy, and continues before I can ask what she means. "I must say that I'm as curious about you as the rest of them," she admits. "What made you decide to audition?"

"I moved to the city to find a husband," I start, although I don't want to give her the same reason I gave to the Gold guards, since she's being so kind to me and I don't want to insult her caste. So I decide to wing it, and hope what I'm about to say is believable. "When I heard the announcement that Ezekiel's looking for new concubines, I got this *feeling*. It's hard to explain, but something in my gut told me I needed to be here to meet him and have the chance to get to know him. I couldn't ignore it. And so… here I am."

"Ezekiel *is* handsome, isn't he?" she says with a small smile. "The most handsome man on the continent, without a doubt."

"I've never seen him," I admit. "I only moved here recently."

Before she can reply, I hear arguing at the doorway.

I turn to see what the commotion is about, catching sight of a young Red woman in a plain dress seconds before she clutches her hands to her chest and lets out a heart-wrenching wail.

CHAPTER TWENTY-FOUR

"What's going on?" I ask Elizabeth, my voice rising in panic. "What are they doing to her?"

"They're not hurting her," Elizabeth assures me. "Well, not physically, at least."

"Then why is she crying?"

"She's been turned down from the ball," she explains. "From the looks of her dress, I assume that Ezekiel's advisor—the man at the door who let you inside—didn't deem her worthy of attending."

Guards take each of her arms and pull her away from the door. As she's dragged away, I notice that her dress *is* plain and homely, reminding me of something a poor girl from the prairies might wear to church than something fit for a ball.

"That's hardly fair," I say. "It's probably the best she can afford."

"The selection process has never been fair," Elizabeth says. "Many girls tonight had gorgeous dresses, but were turned down because they weren't considered beautiful enough for

Ezekiel. So you see, having an acceptable dress is only part of it."

"But there are a few Reds here," I observe. Although when I look around again, it's impossible not to notice that every woman is extraordinarily gorgeous. "How do they afford their tickets and dresses?"

"The Reds choose a few of their own each year who they want to enter—usually the most beautiful women who want a chance of a better life—and pool together their coins and resources to buy them tickets and dresses," she explains. "It's not uncommon to see them wearing the same dresses that girls have worn in prior years. That girl must not have had the community behind her, but decided to try anyway."

"It was very brave of her," I say.

"I suppose." Elizabeth shrugs. "Although I think you're the bravest one of us all, coming here to remind Ezekiel why he started these selections in the first place—to find a queen."

"I don't see why it's such a far-fetched possibility that he'll ever find a queen," I say.

"Half a century of his not finding one would say otherwise," she says kindly. "Although... I've always believed in fate. Perhaps that *feeling* you had truly means something."

"Perhaps," I say, despite knowing she's wrong, since that *feeling* I claimed to have had never existed at all. "But enough about why I'm here." I rearrange my dress, angling myself back in her direction. "Why did *you* choose to audition?"

"My husband passed away a few months ago," she says sadly. "Like many in the city, he had a bit too much fun at the casinos... although I didn't realize *how* much until after his death. The debt he left me was exorbitant. More than I can ever pay off with a teacher's salary, especially with two kids of my own to take care of."

"I'm so sorry," I tell her, my heart hurting for both her loss and her predicament. "What about your family? Have they offered to help?"

"My father is my only living family member," she says. "He's also a teacher, and while he isn't in debt, he spends all that he makes. He did what he could to help, but it barely made a dent. No Silver man will marry me, because no one wants to take such a large debt on themselves, and obviously no Gold will marry me because they don't want to lose their rank and become a Silver. So... here I am." She motions around us and smiles. "If I'm selected to be a concubine and I survive the year, I'll become a Gold and will be given enough money that I'll easily be able to pay off my late-husband's debt. My children and I will be provided for forever."

"And... if you *don't* survive the year?" I hate that I have to say it, because Elizabeth is being so kind to me and I don't want to upset her, but the possibility needs to be addressed. "Your children just lost their father. They can't lose you as well."

"I *will* survive the year." Her eyes burn with determination—a fierceness I haven't seen in her until now. "I have no other option."

"Yes, you do," I say suddenly. "My family is well off—we have more money than we could ever need. I can take care of the debt for you. You can leave this place now and go back with your children. You don't have to go through with this."

"No." She shakes her head, her expression overcome with emotion. "That's kind of you, truly. But I could never take your money. Then I would be forever in your debt."

"No, you wouldn't be," I tell her. "I *want* to do this for you. Let me, please." I place my hands over hers, hoping she'll take the gesture as permission to accept my offer.

She glances down at her lap and pulls her hands away. "You're just trying to eliminate your competition, aren't you?" she asks, smiling to let me know she's joking.

"I suppose that would be a plus to my offer." I try to return her lighthearted humor, despite the seriousness of the conversation. "Does that mean you'll take it?"

"No," she says, and my heart drops, since I don't know what else I can say to convince her. "I appreciate the offer, truly. But I want more than just money—I want to become a Gold. I want my *children* to become Golds. I can only do that by being a concubine for a year. I can do this. I *will* do this. After all, Silvers have historically always been the most likely to survive."

"Really?" I ask. "Why's that?"

"You barely know anything about all of this, do you?" She laughs. "It's like you've been living on another continent entirely."

I still, panic flooding my veins. Did I say too much? Did I blow my cover?

"I didn't grow up in the city," I remind her, trying to remain calm. "I grew up in Sector Six. We're so far away from the city, I suppose it *does* feel like a different world at times."

"I've never been to the sectors," she says. "But I've met other Golds who moved from them to the city. They obviously didn't know everything about how things work around here, but they knew enough."

"My parents kept me very sheltered." I make up the excuse on the spot. "It's why I left the sector for the city right after turning eighteen. So, anyway," I say, desperate to resume the previous conversation. "Why are Silvers more likely to survive?"

"Because we're far more prepared for a life of luxury than

the Greens and Reds." She's about to say more, but a Gold guard—the tall man who escorted me inside the waiting room—opens the door on the other side of the room and calls for our attention.

"It's about to start!" She squeals softly. "I'm so glad we got to chat. I hope we're both chosen—it'll be wonderful to have a friend living in the Watchtower."

"Yes, it would be." I smile, realizing that even though we'd only talked briefly, I already consider her a friend. Surely life in the Watchtower will be far more bearable with a friend by my side.

But at the same time, I hope she isn't chosen. Her children need her, and the risk of them losing another parent is far too dangerous.

The only reason I can think that she's risking her life for the chance to become a Gold is because of the curse. She seems to have a kind heart—but her decisions, like everyone else's in this city, are tainted by the greed forced upon them.

"You'll line up in order of caste, and in alphabetical order within each caste," the guard instructs, his voice booming through the room. "Lowest caste to highest. Your assigned guard will escort you to the top of the staircase of the ballroom, where you'll be officially introduced. Once you're all introduced, the first dance will begin, and Ezekiel will choose his first dance partner. As a reminder—you are not to ask Ezekiel to dance. If he wants to dance with you, he will ask you. If he doesn't ask you to dance by the end of the night, you're automatically eliminated from the audition. Now, take your spots. Ezekiel's anxious to make your acquaintances."

It's easy to find my spot, since I'm the only Gold—which means I'm last. There's another Silver between Elizabeth and me, but I'm glad to see that we're close to each other. And while I know that convincing her to not audition will be impossible, I promise myself that no matter what happens, I won't let her children be responsible for their father's debt.

Then, as I wait for the other girls to arrange themselves in line, I realize that if I do what I'm here to do—kill Ezekiel—the debt won't matter at all.

Because he'll be dead, and everyone living here will be released from his curse forever.

CHAPTER TWENTY-FIVE

There are about seventy girls auditioning. We're each assigned a Gold guard, and mine is the short one who met me at the valet. His name is Carlos, and he makes sure that he knows how to correctly pronounce my name for my entrance.

"And your profession?" he asks me.

I pause, unsure what to say. Like most Gold women, Adriana doesn't work. She completed her final year of school in the spring and came to the city soon after. She would probably be offended if anyone thought she needed a job.

If Adriana would be offended, then that's exactly how I need to act.

"Profession?" I balk, as if insulted by the question. "Does shopping count?"

I want to cringe at how ditzy it sounds. But my job is to play this part, so I laugh, as if entertained by my own comment. It was very much something Sofia would do.

"Right." Carlos stumbles over the word. "I'm sorry. Of

course you don't have a profession. However, all the other girls do, which is why we're told to ask."

"I'm not like the other girls," I say, straightening my shoulders for extra emphasis. But I also hope I'm not laying it on *too* thick. After all, I don't want everyone in the Watchtower to hate me. Making enemies won't help me find the Flaming Sword. "Perhaps, instead of a profession, you can announce me as the daughter of Manuel and Silvia Medina?" I suggest.

"Yes, I can do that." He smiles, and I'm glad to have put him slightly at ease. "Better yet, I'll include their status as the lord and lady of Sector Six. That way there'll be no mistaking who you are."

"Thank you," I say, relieved that he approves of my idea. "Is there anything else you need to know?"

"That's all," he says, and then he continues to explain how the introduction will progress—where I need to walk, where I need to stand, and any other small details.

Once he's finished explaining the process, we wait in silence for my turn. The line is getting shorter—they're nearly through the Greens. Eventually, it's time for the Silvers. At Elizabeth's turn, she glances behind herself and gives me a thumbs-up. I smile and return the gesture.

"Good luck!" I call to her.

"You too," she says, and then she's out the door. She's followed by the Silver who stood between us. Once she leaves, Carlos and I are the only ones left in the room.

"Are you ready?" he asks, extending his arm for me to take.

"Yes." I place my arm in his, hoping that by *saying* I'm ready, I'll feel it.

"Are you sure about that?" he asks. "You're shaking."

"I am?" I squeak, doing my best to steady myself. "That's strange. It must just be from how excited I am."

He nods, seeming to believe me, and leads me out of the waiting room. But inside, I'm terrified. I'm minutes away from meeting Ezekiel. What if he sees through my cover? What if he senses what I am? I have so many questions, and no answers.

Why can't I be fearless, like Uriel and the other archangels? This would be so much easier if I wasn't so worried about everything that might go wrong.

Although, someone once said that being fearless doesn't mean one has no fears. Being fearless means having fears, but facing them anyway. And so, as we reach the elaborate double doors and Carlos leaves my side, I prepare myself to do just that.

"Adriana Medina, a Gold, the daughter of Lord Manuel and Lady Silvia Medina of Sector Six." Carlos's voice echoes into the hall.

As I step through the doors to the top of the staircase, I pull the tab on the side of the dress just like Flory instructed. The feathery bright red wings sprout from my back, and the crowd gasps, clapping in appreciation.

Now that it's done, I focus on the crowd. The moment I do, I see him. Matthew. He's staring at me, and when his eyes meet mine, he flashes me the same smirk he did the night he saved me in the alley.

My heart races at the memory of the short kiss we shared. My cheeks must be as red as my dress. I'm so happy to see a familiar face—and not just *any* familiar face, but one that instantly makes me feel safe.

But he's standing at the bottom of the staircase, in front of the packed crowd.

That's the place where Ezekiel's supposed to be waiting. Carlos told me that Ezekiel would be at the bottom of the stairs, and that we are supposed to take his hand when we reach him so he can walk us to the line of girls.

I look around the bottom of the staircase, but no one else is there. Only Matthew. His eyes are locked on mine, and he tilts his head slightly, as if waiting for me to join him.

Horror washes over me as realization dawns. Because try as I might to come up for a reason for what I'm seeing, there's no explanation other than Matthew not being who he said he was. He lied to me. In fact, *Matthew* was never his name at all.

His name is Ezekiel.

CHAPTER TWENTY-SIX

"Adriana?" Carlos says, softly enough so only I can hear. "You need to walk down to Ezekiel now."

There's no more denying who he truly is. And so, I take one step, and then the next, lifting my skirt so I don't trip. My feet feel like lead weights. It's like I'm in a haze, and my thoughts swirl like an angry storm as I walk closer to him. Because the man who walked me back home after brunch and saved me from those Reds in the alley is Ezekiel. The *demon* I came here to kill.

I felt safe with a demon. I trusted a demon. I *kissed* a demon.

Disgust rises in my throat. But what makes it even worse is that when I look at Matthew—*Ezekiel*—I'm not disgusted. My heart races at the sight of him, as if it's operating separately from my brain.

How am I supposed to face him—what am I supposed to *say* to him?

My judgment must be deranged. How could I not have

known it was him the moment I saw him? Ezekiel's the only one in this continent who isn't enslaved. He's the only one without—

He's the only one without tattoos around his wrists.

Both times we met, I never saw his tattoos. I assumed his jacket was covering them. But the reason I hadn't seen his tattoos wasn't because they were hidden.

It's because he doesn't have them at all.

Suddenly, I'm in front of him, and he reaches out his hand. "Adriana," he says, his silky voice so familiar as he speaks my name.

I want to call him out for lying to me—for *tricking* me. For kissing me when he knew I didn't know who he was.

Why did he give me a fake name? What purpose did it serve?

"You had no idea it would be me, did you?" he asks softly.

Blinking away my fear, I snap into focus. I shouldn't be surprised that Ezekiel lied and tricked me. That's what demons do. They lie, they hurt, and they kill.

Matthew never existed. He's *always* been Ezekiel. Yes, it's shocking, but the reason I'm here hasn't changed. I need to gain his trust so I can kill him.

So instead of lashing out at him with my anger and confusion, I use it as fuel.

Because if he's going to play me, then I can do the same back to him.

"I didn't know when I met you." I smile and place my hand in his, calling upon everything within me not to shudder when our skin touches. "I only realized a few days ago."

"And now you're here," he murmurs, pulling me closer—so close that our faces are only inches apart.

"I hope you're not disappointed?" I tilt my head and raise an eyebrow playfully.

"To see you?" He smirks. "Never."

We arrive where the others are standing, and I take my place in line, looking up at Ezekiel under my lashes. He's still watching me, his gaze intense and conflicted as he steps back to examine the group.

"All the hopefuls are here," the announcer says from the top of the steps. "It's time for Ezekiel to decide which of these lovely ladies will share the first dance with him."

Ezekiel makes a play of looking at each one of us. He winks at one of the girls—a Green in a clingy dress with a neckline so low that it drops nearly to her navel—and my stomach falls.

Will he choose her? I hope not. I *want* him to choose me.

Because if he chooses me, it means I'm one step closer to succeeding in my mission.

Finally, his gaze lands on mine. I allow my lips to curve up into a small smile, and I tilt my head again, allowing my hair to fall softly over my cheek.

Pick me, I think. *I want you to pick me.*

"Adriana Medina," he says, and it's like there's a line of magnetic energy between us as he speaks my name, connecting us together. "Would you like to join me for the first dance?"

"I would love to," I say with a smile.

The crowd claps as I drop into a curtsy. Suddenly, Ezekiel is beside me, taking my hand and leading me to the center of the ballroom.

CHAPTER TWENTY-SEVEN

"You're trembling," he observes, wrapping one arm around my waist and taking my hand with his other one.

"From happiness." I gaze up into his eyes, which are so familiar to me from the other two times we've met. Just like then, my instinct tells me to trust him.

It *must* be because of the curse. I want him to be the person I thought he was—Matthew.

But that person doesn't exist, and I can't let myself forget it.

"And excitement, anticipation, and a million other amazing things," I add.

The music starts, and he leads me across the floor in a waltz. Adriana's body knows how to dance, and I'm also prepared for this, since Teresa and Marco went over the steps with me this week. We glide around the floor in a way that I hope looks effortless.

"You said you learned who I am a few days ago," he says, his eyes glued on mine. "Were you not upset that I was dishonest with you? Were you not angry with me?"

"At first, yes," I admit. "But then I realized—a name doesn't make someone who they are. Despite what you call yourself—Matthew, or Ezekiel—you're the same person who walked me home that first night and saved my life the second. Those moments were real. *They're* what matter. Not anything else."

"You don't have to call me Ezekiel," he says. "It sounds so formal."

"What should I call you, then?"

"I prefer for those close to me to call me Zeke."

I nearly stumble with surprise, but catch myself just in time. "Would you consider me to be close to you?" I ask.

"Did I not ask you to dance with me first?"

"You did," I reply.

"Then yes, Adriana," he says. "Right now, you're the closest person to me in this entire room."

I'm unsure if he means that metaphorically or physically, but I smile just the same. "We've only met three times," I remind him. "I mean, I'm honored to hear it, but surely there are others you're closer to than me?"

"It's hard to explain." His eyes drift, and for the first time since we started dancing, I feel a distance between us. "But I've felt like I've known you from the moment I saw you."

As I remember it, he thought I was someone else—someone named Julia—but I know better than to bring that up. "I felt the same way, too," I say instead. "After you said you would be at the ball tonight, and after..." I lower my eyes, my cheeks heating at the memory of our kiss.

"After..." He watches me closer, clearly hungry for me to continue.

I lean closer to him, lowering my voice. "After our kiss," I say, the words for his ears only. I feel his breath slow, and I lean back, gazing into his eyes as we glide across the dance floor. "I couldn't stop thinking about you. You told me you already had a date, but it didn't change my feelings. It didn't change how much I wanted to see you again. Which is why, after I learned who you are, I exchanged my other dress for this red one. I couldn't have watched you from afar all night as you danced with the other girls. I wanted you to give me a chance. No—I *needed* you to give me a chance." The words come out stronger than anticipated—as if they're not a complete lie.

Because deep down, I know they're not. The feelings I'm sharing with him—as twisted and convoluted as they are—are real.

"I couldn't believe my eyes when I saw you at the top of those steps," he says. "I heard talk that a Gold was auditioning, and while I *wanted* it to be you, I didn't dare hope. If I did, none of the other girls would have lived up to my expectations, and next week, we would be right back where we are now."

I shiver at his implications. "What do you mean by that?" I ask, doing my best to sound intrigued and not frightened.

"It's not important, because you *are* here," he says, his eyes dark. "That's all that matters. But you looked so shocked when you first saw me. In that moment, I could have sworn that you didn't know it would be me."

"It was just stage fright," I say. "Remember—I grew up in one of the sectors. Being here, in front of so many people... it was overwhelming. But then you took my hand and all that fear washed away. I felt safe. Like I always do around you."

He tightens his grip around my hand, as if he never wants to let it go.

"How do you feel now?" he asks.

"Like I'm living in a dream," I answer honestly. "This is all so incredible. It hardly feels real."

"It is real," he says, and we spin around, his gaze locked on mine. "So you better get used to it."

CHAPTER TWENTY-EIGHT

Once the dance ends, Zeke does as he must and chooses another woman in red to dance with. Much to my dismay, he chooses the one he winked at—the one with the neckline that dips down to her navel. Her name is Maria. When they start dancing, I notice her dress has a slit that goes up to her thigh.

It strikes me as strange that he went from me to her so quickly, but despite how charmed I feel in Zeke's presence, it's the nature of a demon. Completely unpredictable.

We're allowed to mingle with the crowd now, and it doesn't take me long to find Teresa and Marco seated at one of the tables. I join them, glad to give my feet a break after dancing in heels.

"That went well." Teresa's voice is cool and unemotional, but her eyes are swirling with questions. I'm sure she'll give me quite the inquisition once we get home tonight.

"Yes," I say with a smile, aware that partygoers are listening to our conversation and watching us from the corners of their eyes. "Do the women chosen for the first dance always get selected?"

"They most always do," she says.

"You have nothing to worry about," Marco adds. "Ezekiel seems smitten with you."

Teresa tenses at his comment. I can tell she's still not comfortable with putting her sister in such danger, but I'm glad she's helping us. Because now that I've danced with Ezekiel—*Zeke*—I feel more confident than ever that this plan will work.

And while I feel foolish for thinking it, after the dance we shared, it feels like he trusts me already.

"Did I hear him say something about the two of you meeting before?" Teresa leans forward, watching me with suspicion. "Because if you *did* meet him sometime before moving in with me, you would have told me, wouldn't you?"

"It's nothing like that," I say quickly, realizing she thinks I knew him in my true form—as *Rebekah*. Which would have been impossible, since Ezekiel fell from Heaven before I was created. But I can't say that now, with people listening, so instead I say, "We met briefly twice, *after* I moved here." I annunciate the word *after*, hoping it's clear that I mean after I possessed Adriana's body. "I'll tell you the details later."

"You sure will," she says, and I know I'm in for a long night after the party ends.

"So," I say, wanting to change the subject. "At these balls, does Ezekiel ever dance with the same woman more than once?"

"It's been known to happen," Marco says, and he turns to look at Teresa. "It did for Gloria, right?"

"Yes." She nods. "As I remember, he danced with Gloria *three* times at her audition ball."

"Who's Gloria?" I ask, looking back and forth between the two of them.

"She's a friend of Marco's mom," Teresa says simply. "She was Ezekiel's favorite concubine back in her day."

"She made it through the year?" I ask.

"She did," Teresa confirms. "People thought she might have had a chance of being queen. But she was sent out of the Watchtower after her year, just like the other women who've survived. That was the year people gave up hope that a queen would someday be chosen."

"Where is she now?" I look around, wondering if I've seen her yet.

"She's not here," Teresa says. "She keeps to herself."

"Oh." I deflate, disappointed.

"Did you want to meet her?" she asks.

"Well… I think it would be smart to connect with her," I say. "If I'm going to survive in the Watchtower, I should learn as much as I can from someone who's already done so. Don't you think?"

"I think that's a brilliant idea," Marco says. "You'll like her. She's… more like us than you might think."

From the meaningful way he says it, I assume he means she's also a witch. Which is good, since the more witches I can meet around here, the better.

I bring my hand to my lips, nearly laughing at the thought. Whoever would have believed that I'd be looking *forward* to meeting a witch?

It's crazy how much has changed in such a short amount of time.

Before we can continue the conversation, a friend of Teresa's approaches, and Teresa introduces us. The night progresses in that vein for a while—light conversation and meeting acquaintances of Teresa and Marco.

Ezekiel continues to select different girls to dance with. I know he sees where I am—our eyes have locked numerous times—and I expect he'll invite me to dance again. But he doesn't.

Instead, about halfway through the party, he asks *Maria* to dance again.

My heart drops as I watch them on the dance floor. But there *must* be a reason why he chose her instead of me. Perhaps he's undecided on if he wants to eliminate Maria from the competition, and he's dancing with her again because he needs more time to make up his mind.

That must be it. After the connection I felt between us, and the way he told me to get used to being here with him, it's silly to think he might not choose me as one of the ten selected women.

Next, Zeke asks a Red who he hasn't had a turn with yet to dance. She's tall and gangly, and her heels make it so they're nearly the same height. She's beautiful in a fierce, runway model sort of way, but her head hangs as she walks, giving me the impression that she's shy.

He whispers something in her ear, wraps his arm around her back, and takes her hand in his. Jealousy pulses through me at the sight of them together, just as it has been all night as I watched him dance with the other girls, the heat of it burning like a pit in my stomach. I try to rationalize with myself that he has to dance with the others—and that I shouldn't be jealous, since he's a demon and I'm eventually going to kill him—but the feeling won't go away, as hard as I try.

The moment the music starts, it's clear the Red lacks the

grace of the other girls. Her legs are so long that she's stumbling more than dancing. It's like her limbs refuse to work together, and her cheeks are bright red—probably from embarrassment.

Zeke's lips are pressed in a straight line as they dance—he looks even more tortured than she does. He leads in her a twirl, and she somehow manages to trip over his foot. Her legs get tangled together, her ankle rolls to the side, and before anyone can rush forward to help, she's on the floor, her head dropped in shame.

Zeke stares down at her, and his eyes turn black—all over, even where they used to be white. He towers over her, his hands clenched tightly to his sides, and the next thing I know, she's engulfed in flames.

The flames vanish, as if they were never there at all, and the only thing left is a pile of ash where the girl used to be.

CHAPTER TWENTY-NINE

Zeke *incinerated* her.

I stare at the pile of ash, frozen in horror.

Suddenly, the partygoers erupt into applause. At first I'm confused, but it doesn't take long to realize that they *have* to act entertained. It's like when medieval kings beheaded people in the town square and everyone came to watch and cheer. Zeke is their *king*. If they don't act like they support him, they could be killed next.

I look away from the ash, returning my focus to Zeke. He stares straight at me—his eyes back to their normal brown. But there was no mistaking what I saw seconds ago. The inky blackness that had filled them entirely.

Zeke is a monster.

I don't know why I'm surprised. After all, I *knew* he was a demon. But I suppose I still didn't think him capable of such evil. The way he danced with me—his touch so soft, his words so sweet—it was like he was the same person I met on the street.

But after seeing the full evil he's capable of, I will *not* be tricked again.

Ezekiel is evil. He deserves to die.

And *I'm* going to be the one to kill him.

In the meantime, I join the clapping, forcing myself to smile. Perhaps he'll ask me to dance next. I *want* him to ask me to dance with him next—at least it will mean there's one less girl who will be at his mercy.

But he turns away from me, walks over to Elizabeth, and asks her to dance. I hold my breath the entire time they're on the floor, but Elizabeth is a wonderful dancer—perhaps the best of all the girls tonight. Her eyes shine, her smile is full of life, and while I can't hear what they're saying, she and Zeke appear to be having a lively conversation.

Eventually, their dance ends. As the night goes on without him choosing me again, my confidence wanes.

"Perhaps we should go out there and dance?" I suggest to Marco. "To remind Ezekiel that I'm here?"

"Are you crazy?" Teresa leans back in horror.

"Not that I'm aware of," I say. "I'm just trying to think of a way to get his attention."

"Well, that's a terrible idea," Teresa says. "Have you seen any of the other girls in red dance with someone other than Ezekiel?"

"No," I say, realization dawning. "I thought that was because they're keeping themselves free so he can ask them to dance next."

"That's part of the reason," she says. "But Zeke doesn't like other people touching what's his. And tonight, all the women in red dresses are his. The last time a woman in red danced with another man at the ball, Ezekiel incinerated them both on the spot."

I shiver, able to picture it now that I saw him do the same thing to someone else.

"It wasn't a bad idea," Marco assures me. "It would work on most men."

"But Ezekiel isn't most men," I say.

"Exactly. Plus, he keeps looking over at you," Marco adds. "Even though he's a demon, Ezekiel is still a man, and his signals are clear. He hasn't forgotten you're here. In fact, he hasn't stopped thinking about you all night."

"He has a funny way of showing it," I mutter.

"Relax," Teresa says. "He's probably already decided that you'll be selected, so he's giving some of the other girls a chance."

"I hope so." I look at her with raw determination, more eager than ever to finish this job. "He *has* to pick me."

"I know." Teresa nods, her fierce expression mirroring my own. "And he will. Just wait. The ball is nearly over, so it won't be much longer until he announces his choices."

"Good." I look over at Zeke, who's dancing with Maria again. He has that infuriating smirk on his lips, and he's looking down at her as if he wants to eat her alive. "I can't wait."

∽

It's not long until the music stops and Ezekiel vanishes, appearing instantly at the top of the grand stairway.

"Will all the women in red line up at the bottom of the steps?" He glances at what's left of the pile of ash—it's smaller now, since people have been dancing through it all night—and smirks. "Well, those who are still alive and able to walk."

My stomach twists at the reminder of that poor girl, and

fire shoots through my veins as I walk past her ashes, finding a spot among the other women at the bottom of the steps. I hold my head high, looking straight at Ezekiel. I can't *wait* for the chance to kill him.

But I can't risk him catching on to my thoughts, so I soften my gaze and stare up at him hopefully.

His eyes meet mine, and they turn cold before passing me by. Worry fills my chest once more. I want to be confident, but it's like he's done a one-eighty since we shared that first dance. I don't understand it. What could I have done to offend him between then and now?

I have no idea, but all I can do now is pray for the best.

"If I didn't dance with you tonight, go to the back of the room," Ezekiel instructs. "You're automatically eliminated."

More than half the girls turn around and scurry away. I glance at those remaining—there are about thirty of us, of whom only ten will be chosen. I remind myself about what Marco told me—about his being sure that Ezekiel will pick me—and I rearrange my skirts, standing straighter.

"I've selected my ten," Ezekiel says, and everyone in the room goes silent. "If I call your name, walk up the steps and stand behind me. I want everyone to get a good look at the beautiful women who will be living in the Watchtower for the next year."

He begins listing off names, starting with Maria. Of course. He danced with her the most out of everyone. She struts up the steps, standing behind Ezekiel and popping out her hip so her entire leg shows through the slit in her dress.

He says four more names. When he says Elizabeth's sixth, my heart drops. So much for her being safe. She joins him and the others at the top of the steps, smiling radiantly at the crowd.

He says two more names, and my blood turns to ice as my odds continue to decrease.

When he calls the ninth, I hold my breath, waiting. There's one more left. Maybe he's saving his favorite for last? But he's refusing to meet my eyes, and I know before he calls the final name that it isn't going to be mine.

"Yolanda Hernandez," he concludes.

A Red girl who appears to be barely fifteen holds her hands to her chest, as if in shock that she was chosen, before making her way up the steps.

My heart drops at the realization that my instincts were right. He didn't choose me.

Did he figure out who I am? Did I do something to give away that I'm Rebekah, and not Adriana? I doubt it, because if he figured it out, he surely would have lashed out at me like he did to that poor girl he reduced to ashes.

So what could it be?

I have no idea, but right now, the possibility of finding the Flaming Sword and killing Ezekiel feels farther away than ever.

"The ten standing behind me are the best of the best." He looks over the top of the crowd, still refusing to meet my eyes. "In four days, they'll be welcomed to the Watchtower, and a feast will be held in their honor. As always, the feast will be broadcast live. Until then, goodnight."

He raises his arms, flames erupt around him, and he disappears.

CHAPTER THIRTY

"I don't get it." Marco paces around the kitchen island, running his hands through his hair. He tossed his shoes and jacket off the moment we got inside, his sleeves are pushed up, and his tie is undone, draped around his neck. "I saw the way he was looking at you. It's the way a man looks at a woman when he's already half in love with her."

"Maybe this is a good thing," Teresa says from her seat across from me. "Adriana was going to be in too much danger at the Watchtower. Ezekiel passing her over must be a sign that we need to come up with another plan."

I sigh and cover up a yawn. Since getting back to the house, I told them the details about both of my meetings with Ezekiel. They reprimanded me for going with that Red boy in the alley, but other than that, they're as confused as I am.

Now it's far past midnight, and we've been talking in circles for what feels like hours.

"This makes no sense." I kick one of my discarded shoes,

and it hits the leg of Teresa's chair. "There *has* to be an explanation."

"Like what?" Marco asks. "Ezekiel is our king. He gets what he wants. If he wanted you, he would have chosen you."

"I don't know," I say. "But there's only one way to find out."

"And what 'way' is that?" Teresa asks slowly, yawning as well.

"I'm going to ask him to reconsider."

"Hell no you're not." Teresa jolts forward, her eyes awake again. "Do you have a death wish? Have you forgotten what he did to that Red girl—when he *incinerated* her?"

"Playing it safe stopped being an option the moment I entered the Watchtower to audition to be a concubine," I say calmly. "I can't sit around here and do nothing. First thing tomorrow, I'll go to the Watchtower and ask to speak with him. If there's even a chance he'll reconsider, I have to try."

Teresa turns to Marco, who's stopped pacing. "Well?" she asks him. "Aren't you going to convince her to stop this madness?"

"It might not be madness." He leans against the wall, his forehead crinkled in thought. "I mean, it *could* end badly. But it could also get his attention."

"Have you forgotten that my *sister* is in there?" Teresa points at me and stands up, her angry gaze on Marco. "I will *not* let anything happen to Adriana. I won't let Rebekah put my sister in more danger than she's already in."

I want to tell her that Adriana was in danger that moment I was assigned to possess her for this mission, but I don't. Because she already knows that. Instead, I watch as she stomps out of the room, leaving Marco and me sitting in silence.

"Give her some time to cool down." He picks up his jacket,

this conversation apparently over. "Right now, I think we all need some sleep. We'll talk about this again in the morning."

He heads upstairs, and I don't care what either of them said.

Tomorrow morning, I'm going to that Watchtower—and I'm going to convince Ezekiel to change his mind and make me one of his concubines.

CHAPTER THIRTY-ONE

I barely sleep. My mind whirs with memories of the ball, replaying the night as I try to figure out what went wrong. But I come up with nothing. One moment, I was confident that Ezekiel favored me. The next, he acted as if I didn't exist.

I suppose that trying to rationalize the situation is silly. After all, he's a *demon*. Demons are even more erratic than witches.

Well, than *most* witches. I must admit that Teresa and Marco have begun to change my mind about their species.

I wake with the sun the next morning and get dressed, styling my hair and makeup in a way that I know brings out Adriana's beauty. Once finished, I stare at my reflection and take a deep breath.

The plan is crazy. Nothing will stop him from incinerating me on the spot.

But it's the only plan I have. And at this point, I have nothing to lose. After all, I remember the way he looked at me both times we met on the street, and when he danced with me at the ball. I remember the way he kissed me in the alley. I know that demons can't truly care for people, but if he wanted me dead, he could have let those Red thieves kill me. Instead, he saved my life.

There must be a part of him that wants me to remain alive.

I remind myself of that as I leave my room, walk down the steps, and head for the front door.

But when I go to *open* the door, it's stuck. I pull at it harder, but it's no use. No matter how hard I try, the door refuses to budge. I try the back door as well, but it's the same thing. Even the *windows* are impossible to pry open.

"Teresa!" I march up to the master bedroom and fling the doors open. She and Marco are fast asleep, but she stirs, moving slowly to see what's going on. "Did you cast some kind of spell to keep me locked in the house?"

She sits up and stretches, a satisfied smile on her face. Marco stays where he is and pulls the blanket over his head.

"It's a boundary spell, and until I lift it, no one's getting in or out of this house," she says, still smiling smugly. "I can't allow you to follow through with your crazy plan to confront Ezekiel."

"Why not?" I cross my arms and glare at her. "Do you have any better ideas about how to proceed with the mission?"

"No," she admits. "But we'll figure one out. There has to be another way we can approach this—a way that *won't* get my sister killed."

"Ezekiel's not going to kill me," I say. "If he wanted me dead, he would have let those Reds kill me in that alley. He wouldn't have gone out of his way to *save my life*."

"You're giving him too much credit," she says. "You forget that I've seen him with his concubines before. Certain ones always capture his attention, infatuating him for a brief period. Most of them end up dead. Because he *kills* them. He's a monster. You—an *angel*—should know that better than anyone else."

"I do," I say. "But I honestly don't think he wants me dead. At least not right now."

"Why not?" She sneers. "What makes you so special?"

I search for an answer, but nothing comes to me. Luckily, I don't have to respond, because someone rings the doorbell, interrupting the conversation.

I hurry to the window, anxious to see who it is. "It's one of the guards," I say, pressing a hand against the glass. "Carlos—the one who escorted me to the ball last night. He's holding…" I squint, making sure I'm seeing this right. "A large envelope. Some kind of letter?"

Marco throws the comforter off himself and gets out of bed, walking over to the window. Teresa huffs and comes over to join us.

"Remove the spell," Marco says to Teresa. "We should hear what he has to say."

"I'll remove the spell, but *she's* not getting anywhere near the doors," she says, glancing at me. "You two stay up here. I'll go down and see what he wants." She throws a shawl over her shoulders and heads out, leaving Marco and me alone.

I move to follow her, but he hurries in front of the door, barring my exit.

"You're really going to go along with whatever she says?" I ask him. "You haven't even said what *your* opinion is about my plan."

"Your plan is impulsive and it puts Adriana at risk," he says bluntly.

"Auditioning to be a concubine also put Adriana at risk," I point out. "But the two of you supported me in that."

"That's different," he says. "If you were chosen, you would do everything possible to placate Ezekiel, to keep him from lashing out at you. This plan to confront him will only anger him. It will surely get you—and Adriana—killed."

"I won't 'confront' him, per se," I tell him. "I'll just… nicely ask him if he might consider changing his mind."

"Questioning Ezekiel's decision *will* anger him," he says, his eyes strong and determined. "There's no predicting what he'll do when he's angry. And I love Teresa, and I will *not* let her lose her sister."

I want to tell him he's wrong, but I can't fault him for doing what's right by the woman he loves. So I walk back over to the window, catching sight of Carlos letting himself out through the gate. He's no longer holding the letter.

I try to open the window, but find the boundary spell back in place.

Now that I'm trapped in the house again, I hurry downstairs, eager to find out why Carlos had stopped by.

It *had* to have something to do with me. What else could it be?

When I get downstairs, I find Teresa standing in the living room, the letter in her hand.

"Well?" I ask. "What did he want?"

"He came to deliver this." She holds the letter up. "It has your name on it."

I take it from her, glad to see it's unopened, and rip the seal. Inside, there's a letter. It's written in thick black ink, with beautiful penmanship. I glance at the bottom, curious who wrote it, and gasp when I see his name.

Ezekiel.

"What?" Teresa leans forward to peek at it. "What does it say?"

"I haven't read it yet." I pull it to my chest to keep her from reading it before I can. "But it's from Ezekiel."

Without another word, I hurry over to the couch, turn on the lamp beside it, and begin to read.

CHAPTER THIRTY-TWO

My dearest Adriana,

I've been up for hours contemplating how to start this letter. The truth is, I shouldn't be writing it at all. I should let you go on with your life. I should let you find love and happiness, all while striving to stay away from you, to keep you from the dangers that constantly surround me.

But I cannot. I tried—when I resisted calling your name at the end of the ball—but I desire you too much, and I'm far too selfish to let you go so easily.

At the end of our shared dance, when I told you to get used to a life by my side, I meant it. I wanted you, you came to the ball for me, and I planned on having you. Not calling your name hadn't crossed my mind.

Then I lost my temper on that young woman. The darkness overtook my soul, and the next second, she was gone. I will not apologize for what I did, nor will I attempt to explain it. After all, you know what I am. A demon. Just as cursed as everyone else in this city.

You knew it, but you came for me last night anyway.

Immediately after incinerating her, I saw the horror on your beautiful face. In that moment, I realized—if my temper got away from me around you, what might stop me from losing control and lashing out at you the same way I did to her? Reducing you to nothing but a pile of ashes? I couldn't put you in that position, nor could I forgive myself if I allowed that to happen. And so, for the first time in a long time, I put aside my own desires, not calling your name in an effort to keep you safely away from the darkness that haunts my soul.

However, I'm no martyr, and I won't pretend to be what I'm not. So I'm changing my mind. I want you, Adriana, and I'm inviting you to the grand feast in three days' time, at eight in the evening, where you'll be inaugurated as one of my ten chosen concubines and given a suite in the Watchtower for the next year.

If you choose not to accept my invitation, I understand. Hell—I shouldn't want you to accept, because if you don't, you'll be safe. But like I said, I'm selfish, and my desire to have you by my side has consumed me to the point where I can think of nothing else. If you'll still have me, I hope to see you at the feast.

Carlos will return tomorrow morning to retrieve your response. Make this decision carefully, Adriana. Your life may depend on it.

Yours,
Zeke

~

I read the letter once more, my heart pounding with every word. Zeke didn't reject me because he didn't want me.

He rejected me because he wanted to *protect* me.

It's almost as if he's capable of love, and a part of me yearns to have that love all to myself. How must that feel—to be the one person in the world loved by a creature believed incapable of it? To be by his side as his queen?

"Well?" Teresa taps her foot, snapping me out of my thoughts. "What does it say?"

I blink, forcing myself to focus. Whatever I was feeling after reading that letter *must* have been the curse seeping its way into my heart. Those feelings couldn't have been real. I'm being overtaken by greed for a love I can never have.

And so, I push the feelings away, steadying my breathing and getting control over myself. I need to stay focused on my mission. Because Zeke being worried he might lose his temper on me and *incinerate* me is hardly romantic. He's right—if he truly cared about me and believed himself capable of killing me, he would stay far away from me.

But he's not. Because he's a demon… and no matter how tragically romantic his letter might be, demons don't care about anyone but themselves. I can't let myself forget that. I *won't*.

I hand the letter to Teresa, unable to appropriately summarize its contents in words. It's best she read it herself.

Marco hovers over her, and the two of them read it together, silently.

"He's giving you a *choice*?" Teresa says once she finishes reading it. "Since when does Ezekiel give anyone a *choice*?"

"Never," Marco says. "He doesn't give choices. He gives demands." He eyes me suspiciously. "What have you done to bewitch him like this?"

"Nothing." I hold my hands up in innocence. "At least, nothing that I know about. He must have some kind of… primal attraction to Adriana's looks. It could explain why I was commanded specifically to enter her body."

"If that's true, then I suppose Adriana would have become entwined with him whether you were here or not," Teresa says.

"Most likely," I agree. "Although we'll never know, because once I leave her body, Ezekiel will be dead."

"You're accepting his offer, then?" Marco asks.

"Of course I'm accepting his offer." I take the letter back, my heart leaping at the sight of his beautiful handwriting. Stupid, cursed emotions. Fighting them again, I fold the letter so I can't see its contents, hold it to my side, and explain. "Not only will living in the Watchtower be beneficial to my mission, but it also seems as if I'm already on the way to earning Ezekiel's trust. If all goes as planned, it shouldn't be long until I'm able to pry information from him about where he's keeping the Flaming Sword. I'll write my response now and have it ready for Carlos to pick up in the morning."

"Of course," Teresa says, a shadow crossing her eyes. "But when you're in the Watchtower, be careful not to do anything that might set him off. For my sister's sake."

"I will," I promise. "I actually have a plan to help me do that. But I'll need your help."

"What kind of plan?" Marco looks worried.

"Can you get me that meeting with the woman you know who survived a year in the Watchtower?" I ask. "Gloria?"

"I can definitely do that." Teresa nods. "In fact, I'll get in contact with her at once."

CHAPTER THIRTY-THREE

Teresa and I head to Gloria's apartment that afternoon. The building is small, but luxurious. The halls are bright and airy, with papered walls and decorative carpets. Even the air smells sweet and crisp.

Gloria's apartment is on the first floor. Once we arrive at the elegant double doors, Teresa knocks. There's a shuffling from inside, and a few seconds later, the door opens.

Gloria is around my height, and while she's older, slightly hunched over, and her skin is wrinkled, I'm still able to see past that to the beauty she once was. And, of course, gold tattoos circle her wrists.

"Hello, Teresa," she says, and then she turns her gaze to me. Her eyes are green—emerald green—and they shine with love and kindness. "You must be Adriana," she says with a smile. "Please, come in." She opens the door wider, and both of us step inside. "I hope you're hungry, because I've prepared cookies."

I step inside, the smell of chocolate engulfing me. If I

wasn't hungry before, I sure am now. Gloria ushers us to the living room, and Teresa and I take a seat while Gloria grabs the cookies from the kitchen. The apartment isn't large—after all, it's only meant for one person—but everything inside of it screams luxury. Not the flashy luxury of the Watchtower, but traditional luxury reminiscent of a time long past.

"So," I begin once we're all seated and have started enjoying the cookies and drinks. "How do the two of you know each other?"

"As Marco implied at the ball, Gloria is also a witch," Teresa says.

"I can't believe you told her." Gloria shakes her head.

"I wouldn't believe it either," Teresa says. "I never planned on telling my sister. Except... the person we're speaking to right now isn't my sister."

"What do you mean?" Gloria asks. "I thought you were bringing your sister over so I can instruct her how to survive her year in the Watchtower? If this young lady isn't your sister... then who *is* she?"

"Technically, this *is* my sister," Teresa says. "Well, it's her body. Beyond that, it gets a bit complicated..."

And together, Teresa and I catch Gloria up on everything she needs to know.

∾

"Well," Gloria says once we finish the story. "I expected today would be exciting—I rarely get visitors anymore—but I didn't realize it would be *this* exciting."

"You'll help us, then?" I ask.

"I thought I would die before seeing the continent released

from this curse," she says. "Now, I might be able to help break it. So yes—of course I'll help."

"I'm so glad to hear it." I make myself comfortable, ready to begin. "So… I guess we'll just get down to business. What's your advice about surviving life in the Watchtower?"

"The *only* way to survive is to never anger Ezekiel," she says, her eyes serious. "To do that, you must be graceful in your behavior, and always submit to his opinions. Show support of everything he does—even if it's something so horrifying that it makes you feel sick."

"He incinerated a Red for tripping while she was dancing with him." I shudder. "I have to support him even in that?"

"You must," she says. "Criticizing Ezekiel's actions means criticizing who he is, and he doesn't take that lightly. In my year, he killed a woman for simply looking at him wrong after he killed one of our fellow concubines."

"What else does he kill for?" I pick up a cup of tea to have something to do with my hands, but I realize I'm shaking and place it back down.

"The concubines represent Ezekiel himself, and he hates when they look anything but their best," she says. "You must keep up an image of perfection. Every morning when I lived in the Watchtower, I got dressed and ready as if I had a date with Ezekiel—even on days when I never saw him. He'll sometimes call on concubines unannounced, and being unprepared to see him angers him, because it means he must wait around for you to get ready. Ezekiel *hates* waiting. It's important to look fresh and beautiful, even while sleeping. The only time I went without makeup was in the shower. I would freshen it up before going to bed and sleep with my face up to not cause any smudges, just in case he called on me in the night."

"And when he called on you in the night…" I swallow,

dreading the answer to my question. "What did he expect from you?"

"He expected what all men desire when they come to a beautiful woman's bedroom in the middle of the night." Gloria's eyes sharpen, and for the first time since meeting her, I feel like she's challenging me. "And he expects you to be happy to provide that to him. Surely you were aware of this when you decided to audition?"

"I was," I say, although for some reason, that part of being a concubine hadn't felt real until this moment. "I'm simply... inexperienced in such matters, is all."

"A virgin." Gloria smirks. "He'll love that."

My cheeks heat, and I glance down at my lap, saying nothing.

"Let's pray that Rebekah completes her task before it gets that far." Teresa snaps us both to attention, sitting stiffly in her seat. "She's in the body of a Gold. Surely Ezekiel will show her the respect a Gold deserves."

"Perhaps," Gloria says, although from her distant tone, I have a feeling she doesn't believe it.

"What else should she know before going into this?" Teresa asks, looking desperate to change the subject.

"She should know not to eat too many cookies." Gloria glances at my hand, which is midway toward reaching for a cookie.

I pull it back, placing it in my lap.

"Ezekiel chose his concubines based on the way they looked during the ball," she continues. "As I'm sure you noticed, none of the women who made it past the checkpoint to the waiting room were heavy. You must make sure to keep your figure as close to the same size as possible. This is toughest for the Reds and Greens—most of them haven't been exposed to the variety and abundance of food they'll be given as a concubine. They overindulge and gain weight. Ezekiel doesn't like that."

"He *kills* them for that?" I ask, unable to believe it's possible.

"He does," she confirms. "I was born Green myself, but I've never had a large appetite. I can't say the same of the other girls. He killed a friend of mine at breakfast once, simply because she gained weight and wouldn't stop eating pastries."

"He sounds awful." I shudder, even though after witnessing him incinerate that Red girl, I know he's capable of such atrocities.

But the murderous Ezekiel seems like a different person from the Zeke who walked me home and saved my life in that alley. I'm going to have to constantly remind myself that they're *not* different people—they're one and the same.

It's the only way I'll be able to follow through with killing him.

"He mostly *is* awful," Gloria agrees, but then she glances at a framed photograph—of what appears to be a younger version of her with Ezekiel. "But he's also incredibly charming. I have many fond memories of the year I was a concubine. When he's happy, he's capable of making you feel like you're the most wonderful person in the entire world, cherished only by him."

"That's the two of you together?" I motion to the photo.

"Yes." She brushes her fingers against it and smiles. She's glowing with happiness in the photo, and while Zeke's lips are turned up in a closemouthed smile, his eyes tell a different story—one of torment and distress. "It was taken at the bull ring—he brought us there to watch a fight from the royal box," she says. "Right before that photo was taken, he killed the only other remaining concubine from my group. She said something to anger him—something about how sad she got whenever a bull was killed. He said she wouldn't get sad if it was *her* the bull was running toward, and had his guards take her down to the ring to fight. She didn't last a minute before the bull ripped her to pieces in front of the cheering crowd. I cheered the loudest of them all."

"So if something entertains Ezekiel, I must act entertained by it as well," I surmise from the story. "Even if I'm horrified."

"You *must* if you want to survive," Gloria says. "Each time he killed one of my fellow concubines, I pretended to be just as amused as he was. I knew if I didn't, I would be next. Clearly, it worked, as here I am today. *Alive.*"

"Have you heard from him since leaving the Watchtower?" I ask.

"No." She chuckles. "Soon after I moved out, he had ten new girls to keep him entertained. I was used up, old news. He's barely glanced at me since."

"I'm sorry," I say, my heart going out to her.

"Don't be," she says. "I got what I wanted. I'm a Gold. I have more wealth than I could ever dream of. Yes, I still want more, but given the curse, I'm as close to happy as I thought I could ever possibly be."

I frown, because "close" to happy hardly sounds like enough. "Thank you for taking the time to speak with me today," I tell her. "I hope I'm able to please him even half as much as you were."

"Do not hope," she says sternly. "If you only hope, you will fail. You *must* do as I've said. It's the only way to survive."

"You *will* survive." Teresa watches me closely, as if she refuses to accept any other outcome.

"I will," I vow, my gaze unwavering. "I'll do *more* than survive. Because I'm going to break this curse, and free the continent from Ezekiel forever."

CHAPTER THIRTY-FOUR

The feast isn't until tonight, but a chauffeur arrives in a limo to pick me up that morning. I take a small bag of my favorite items—along with my violin, of course—since concubines aren't supposed to bring much. Once we settle into our suites in the Watchtower, we'll have access to anything we desire.

"You'll do great," Teresa says, wrapping me in a hug.

"Thanks." I return her hug, and despite knowing that this is happening—that today's the day—none of it feels real. I don't think it *will* feel real until I'm inside the Watchtower, or until I see Zeke.

"Just remember everything Gloria told you," Teresa says, pulling away. "Stay alive, okay?"

"I will," I promise, although I feel hollow as I say it, since it's technically not a promise I know I can keep.

It doesn't take long to get to the Watchtower. It's a cloudy, depressing day, but the sides of the Watchtower are so shiny that they gleam anyway. It's as if the tower itself is a beacon of light and hope to everyone in the city. But it's a lie. A mirage, placed there to make the citizens believe that this cursed life isn't as terrible as it might sometimes feel.

The driver drops me off at the side door I entered for the ball. I go into the same waiting room, and find that most of the other girls are already there. I spot Elizabeth and hurry to her side.

"I heard a rumor that you would be here, but I didn't believe it until seeing it with my own eyes," she says with a huge smile. "How did it all happen?"

I summarize the story for her as quickly as possible, leaving out the personal contents of Ezekiel's letter. His words were for my eyes only. I didn't even like that Teresa and Marco had read them, although I didn't have much choice there, since they would have read the letter regardless.

"Wow," she says once I finish telling the story. "I *knew* something was strange when he didn't choose you—he almost always chooses the woman he dances with first. But none of that matters now—I'm just so glad you're here with me."

"I'm glad I'm here, too," I say, since it's true—although not for the reasons everyone else might expect.

Another woman enters—Maria—and I'm unsurprised to see that her everyday clothes of a tight skirt and a crop top don't leave much to the imagination. Once she's inside, a Gold guard member locks the door.

I count the girls in the room—there are ten of us, including me.

"Shouldn't there be eleven of us?" I scan the room again and try to remember exactly whom Ezekiel originally chose. I don't remember each of their names, but I *do* know there were three Silvers, four Greens, and three Reds.

Now there are only two Silvers. Elizabeth and another

woman who stands at the other side of the room. Her nose is upturned, and she refuses to look at us—I assume she views us as her fiercest competition.

"There are only ten concubine suites," Elizabeth says. "I suppose Ezekiel revoked Patricia's invitation when he invited you."

"Oh." I frown, hoping he only "revoked" it and didn't do anything too extreme—such as eliminating her existence altogether.

But I don't have much time to worry about it, because the guard comes around and has us each press our thumb against a scanning device so we'll have access to Ezekiel's private elevators. I smile when he comes around to me, happily letting him scan my thumb.

It's a small thing, but being given access to Ezekiel's private elevators makes me feel one step closer to finding the Flaming Sword.

"We'll be assigning each of you a personal servant," he says once he finishes scanning our thumbs. "Whenever you need something, you'll call upon them. Now, I'll introduce you, and they'll escort you to your suites."

My servant's name is Martha—she's small, timid, and appears to be only a few years older than I am. As expected, she's a Red.

She barely speaks to me as she leads me to the elevator. Once inside, she presses the button for floor forty-nine—the top-most one there.

"What floor is Ezekiel's?" I ask.

"The same as yours." She doesn't meet my eyes when she speaks. "Only the concubines are allowed to live on the same floor as His Highness."

"Wonderful." I smile—since I *am* happy to hear it. Better access to Ezekiel is beneficial to my mission.

My ears pop as the elevator ascends, and soon it lets us out on the forty-ninth floor. The hallway is stunningly beautiful, with marbled floors, black shiny walls, and a mirrored ceiling. It's crisp and elegant, like everything in the Watchtower.

Another elevator dings, and I glance behind me to see another girl step out with her servant—the young Red named Yolanda. She wraps her arms around herself, looking scared and out of place. I shoot her a small smile in the hopes of giving her a bit of comfort. Happiness warms my stomach when she smiles in return.

Martha quickens her pace, and I hurry to keep up with her. We pass many double-door entrances, eventually stopping at one near the end. Suite 4901. There's only one suite farther along—suite 4900, at the end of the hall. Unlike the other rooms we passed, it has intricate columns around the entrance.

"Is that Ezekiel's suite?" I ask Martha.

"Yes." Martha nods.

She doesn't elaborate further, instead instructing me to place my thumb on the keypad to suite 4901—the place destined to be my new home until the completion of my mission.

CHAPTER THIRTY-FIVE

The room is huge and stunning. It's decorated in the same flashy style as the rest of the Watchtower, and Martha leads me from room to room for the grand tour. It's a two-bedroom suite, although the second bedroom has a door that leads to the first, and Martha refers to it as my "dressing area." Apparently, the second room is meant to be a massive closet, to hold all the clothes, shoes, and accessories I can dream of owning. Right now, only a few items are inside. It's expected that I'll fill it up during my time living in the Watchtower—if I live long enough to do so.

"There are call buttons in every room, next to the light switches," Martha says, showing me the one closest to where we're standing. "Press it whenever you need assistance."

"Are there certain times when you're not available?" I ask.

"I'm always available," she says. "I live in the servants' quarters of the Watchtower. It will never take me more than five minutes to reach you. You'll also have a Gold guard stationed outside your suite at all times when you're inside of it, so if you have an emergency, you can go to him."

She makes it sound as if the Gold guard is there to protect me, but I can't help but feel like he's also there to keep me in. As if I'm some kind of prisoner.

"I'm allowed to leave my room on my own if I want to, right?" I ask, needing reassurance that I won't be on complete lockdown all the time.

"Of course," Martha says. "Your guard will escort you everywhere you go—for your protection—but you are free to go wherever you please."

I let out a breath, since it's better than being a prisoner. Not *much* better—since the guard will know my whereabouts at all times—but at least I'll have some level of autonomy while I'm here.

～

I don't have much time to settle in before Martha returns to help prepare me for the feast. There are still a few hours to go, but it turns into an entire process—complete with a massage, a facial, manicure, pedicure, hair styling, and makeup. There aren't many items in my closet, but she recommends a beautiful gold gown that matches the tattoos around my wrists—as if to remind everyone watching that I'm a Gold.

I try to ask Martha about her life—since perhaps I can gain information from her about the whereabouts of the Flaming Sword—but she divulges nothing, instead always diverting the subject back to a topic about me. It's the same when I ask her about her life in the Watchtower. Her life is either extraordinarily boring, or she's talented at holding her tongue.

Eventually, it's time for the feast, and Martha gives me one last look over. "Perfect," she says with a satisfied smile. "You look breathtaking."

I glance again at my reflection and stand straighter, unable to refrain from smiling at what I see. Because in my puffy red gown for the ball, I looked like a princess.

In this gold shimmering gown, I look like a queen.

I thank her for her help, and she hands me off to the Gold guard outside my room. I'm thrilled when I see his familiar face—Carlos.

"You're my guard?" I beam, feeling like it's too good to be true.

"Yes." He nods and returns my smile. "All guards remain with the lady they originally escorted at the ball."

"I'm glad of it," I say, meaning it. Because even though I don't know Carlos well, I *do* trust him.

He leads me to the elevator, and we descend to the first floor, taking back hallways to get around once we're there. "Other than Ezekiel and the ten women he selected, the feast is also attended by the top Gold guards, and the women who have survived a year as a concubine," he says as we walk. "All the current concubines arrive and are seated in order of caste."

"So I'm the last to arrive—besides Ezekiel," I realize.

"Yes." He stops in front of a large double-door entrance. "I'll escort you to your spot at the table, and then join my fellow guards at our table nearby. Are you ready?"

"Ready as I'll ever be." I take a deep breath, allowing Carlos to link his arm through mine and walk me into the room.

CHAPTER THIRTY-SIX

Just like everywhere else in the Watchtower, the room for the feast is over-the-top elegant. It's about half the size of the ballroom, but that in no way takes away from its grandness. The ceilings are high, the floors intricate marble, and in the center of the room—right below a gigantic mirrored chandelier—is an elevated table where the other concubines already sit.

As Carlos told me, Gold guard members sit in small circular tables throughout the room. Near the back, I spot a few small tables with older Gold women. I suspect they're the surviving concubines, and my suspicion proves correct when I spot Gloria among them.

There are also men with cameras against the walls, which reminds me of what Ezekiel said at the ball—the event will be televised. A woman stands in front of one of the cameras—a Green—and as I pass, I hear her report on who I am and where I'm from.

"Adriana's being here is already the talk of the continent," the reporter continues. "Not only is she the first Gold to audition in decades *and* chosen for the first dance, but Ezekiel didn't even initially select her to be a concubine! For the first time in history, His Highness had a change of heart and extended an invitation to Adriana at some point *after* the ball. That's all we know at the time, but given how unprecedented all of this is, I say she's certainly one to watch."

Carlos escorts me away from her and toward the only empty seat that's not at the head of the table. I'm thrilled—and relieved—to find I'm next to Elizabeth.

"Your dress is beautiful," she says as I sit down.

"Thank you," I say. I look around at everyone else, glad none of the other women are wearing the same color. They've all been quiet since I approached the table, and I take my cues from Elizabeth's actions when I entered the audition room on the first day—to chat as if I'm not bothered by their silence. "How'd it go with getting settled in?" I ask her.

"Wonderfully!" She brings her hands together and gushes about the luxury of her accommodations. The other girls chime in. Soon enough, we're all talking about the process of preparing for the feast. They were all pampered as much as I was. As we chat, it's like our caste colors are erased, and we're simply ten girls chosen for the experience of a lifetime.

If any of them are fearful about becoming a victim of Ezekiel's wrath, they don't show it.

"Even my *toenails* are painted!" Yolanda gushes from the other end of the table. "I've never known anyone with painted toes."

"Get used to it," the other Silver—Josefina—says. "Remember—no matter where we came from, we'll be treated as Golds from now until the day we die."

Her eyes are hard and full of ambition, and everyone hushes at the reminder of death.

"There's no need to get all serious." Maria smiles smugly and adjusts the top of her dress, making her breasts pop out more than they already were. "After all, I don't know about the rest of you, but *I* plan on surviving. And while I'm here, I'm going to enjoy every second of it."

"I'm sure you will," a smooth, familiar voice says from the head of the table.

I turn to see Ezekiel standing behind his seat, and he smirks as he stares at Maria, like a predator eyeing up his prey.

"Although I assure you that you won't enjoy it nearly as much as I."

CHAPTER THIRTY-SEVEN

Champagne is poured, and I feel Ezekiel's eyes on me as my glass is filled. He raises his glass once everyone has been served.

"To the start of an... entertaining year," he says, and then he downs the entire glass in one gulp. A server is beside him immediately to refill it.

I take a small sip of my champagne, making sure to smile after tasting it. Because like Gloria taught me, if Ezekiel enjoys something, I must show that I enjoy it as well.

Anything else risks angering him and facing possible death.

"You like it?" he asks, and it takes me a second to realize he's speaking to me.

"Yes," I say, taking another sip to show my appreciation. "I love it."

"I'm glad to hear it." His eyes turn intense, and it suddenly feels like we're the only two people in the room. "And I'm pleased you accepted my change of heart. After the letter I sent, I was sure you would say no… but it appears you never cease to surprise me, Adriana."

"I don't see why it's such a surprise," I say playfully. "I haven't stopped thinking about you since we met."

"Neither have I." His eyes darken, and I realize our hands are so close together that if one of us moved an inch forward, we would be touching.

But he leans back, breaking the connection by shifting his attention to the other girls at the table. He asks each of them a question, but I'm so distracted by the connection I just felt between us that I barely hear what they're saying.

Why do I feel such a strong attraction to a demon? It must be the curse.

But that would be easier to accept if my feelings didn't feel so *real*.

I'm glad once the soup is served, since it gives me something to do with my hands. I blow on it and take a small spoonful, pleased to find it's the perfect temperature.

"So, Adriana," he says, and I swallow a mouthful of soup, snapping my attention back to him. "What's your favorite thing about our continent?"

"The stars," I say instantly, since they've been my favorite part of *every* place I've ever seen, regardless of the place and time. Not only do the stars remind me of Heaven, but I've always loved how they're a constant within an ever-changing world. But I can't say that without arousing suspicion, so I add, "The stars are beautiful and mysterious—it's so peaceful to be alone with my thoughts while admiring them at night."

"You've found a good place to see the stars in the city?" he questions.

"They're not as bright as they were back home in my

sector," I say, since I assume that would be true. "But I can still see them."

Someone slurps loudly from the other end of the table, and I glance over to see that the young Red girl, Yolanda, has made quite a dent in her soup.

Ezekiel glares at her, and then returns his attention back to me. "I hope that doesn't mean you prefer your home sector to the city?" he asks.

"Of course not!" My heart races as I try to morph this into a compliment. "I love the city—especially the Watchtower. My suite is beautiful. I was stunned the moment I walked inside. It's so kind of you to give us such wonderful accommodations."

"It's my pleasure," he says. "Although... I do hope your room isn't your favorite thing about living in the Watchtower?"

Heat rises to my cheeks, and I fiddle with the napkin in my lap. "If you're referring to yourself, I assumed my feelings were a given." I raise my eyes shyly, finding myself captured in his gaze once more.

"Nothing is ever a given," he says, his eyes swirling with a never-ending depth of emotion. "Especially feelings—I've always found them to be the most fickle things. They appear without warning and are capable of changing in an instant."

My breath catches at his words—or was it a warning? Why does it seem like there are layers of meaning behind everything he says? I want to talk with him forever and excavate the depths of every crevice in his mind.

But any response I might have made is cut off by another loud slurp of soup.

Ezekiel rips his gaze from mine, shooting another death glare at Yolanda. But she's oblivious—lost in the joy of finishing her food. I notice again how frail she is, and it clicks that she's so thin because she's malnourished. It shows in the way she's eating—like if she doesn't eat quickly enough, the food will be stolen from her hands.

"The same way you appeared without warning the first night we met?" I say to Ezekiel, desperate to pull his attention away from Yolanda. Once this meal is over, I'll have a discussion with her about table manners—for now all I can do is distract Ezekiel from noticing her.

But she slurps again, and it's like he doesn't hear me.

I glance toward the other end of the table in time to see Yolanda tilting her bowl, scooping out more soup and slurping again. Some of the liquid escapes her mouth, and she uses her other hand to wipe it away, licking it from her fingers.

"Disgusting." Ezekiel's eyes blacken, and he doesn't look at his hand as he wraps it around his steak knife—it's as if he's acting on autopilot. "I will *not* dine with animals for a year. Or anyone who eats like one."

He throws the knife, and it flies in an arc across the table, piercing straight through Yolanda's heart.

CHAPTER THIRTY-EIGHT

Yolanda slumps over the table, her face falling into her bowl of soup. Her body twitches a few times and goes still.

Panic races through my mind. She's dead. Ezekiel *killed* her. I shouldn't be shocked—I knew to expect this—but I didn't expect it so *soon*.

I suppose I'd hoped to complete my mission before any of the girls died.

I should have known after the ball that it wouldn't be the case. Now Yolanda is dead. All because she was excited to eat and was enjoying her food.

She didn't deserve to die like that. *No one* deserves to die like that.

But somehow, throughout it all, I keep the horror from my face. I'm here to make sure girls like Yolanda don't have to suffer the same fate in the future. I have a part to play—and no matter how much I hate playing it, I need to do it right if I'm to succeed in my mission.

So I turn away from her body and lift my glass in a toast. "To a more peaceful meal," I say, smiling at Ezekiel in what I hope looks like gratitude.

I catch Gloria's eyes for a second, and she nods in approval.

"Yes," he says, although his voice is robotic and dull. "To a more peaceful meal."

He clinks his glass with mine and tosses back his champagne.

∽

The servants clear away Yolanda's body, and the meal progresses without any more tragedies. But her empty seat haunts me—a reminder of the girl who couldn't even enjoy twenty-four hours as a concubine before being killed by Ezekiel.

How had Ezekiel gone from being charming to murderous in what felt like a split second? I hate myself for being drawn into his spell at the beginning of the meal. Why does he have such sway over me?

The obvious answer is the curse, but I don't fully believe that's it. It feels like something more.

Then again, Ezekiel himself told me that feelings are fickle things.

I'm starting to realize that he might be right.

He makes an effort to speak with each of the girls throughout the meal, asking them about themselves. I listen, hoping to learn more about these girls who I'll be seeing a lot of in the time to come.

I already knew Elizabeth's story, but she gives a much simpler, happier version when Ezekiel asks about her. The other Silver, Josefina, is a manager at a local dress store. I remember the name as one of the stores I visited with Sofia when we were shopping for the ball. She wants us to wear clothes from her store, to give it more publicity, and Ezekiel tells us that we should all go shopping there together.

"You'll find a significant amount of coins in the safes in your closets," he tells us. "Your personal maid will refresh the amount daily."

This results in excited chatter breaking out among the girls. I, too, feel an unfamiliar desire to check out my safe to see how much daily allowance I'm given. I know this desire is the curse taking effect. Are the other women also able to recognize when the curse takes hold of their thoughts? Or are they unaware, having been born after the curse was placed upon the continent?

"And you?" Ezekiel asks Maria once the chatter dies down. "What was your job in the city before coming to live in the Watchtower?"

"I'm a dancer." She pouts her lips in a way I think is supposed to look seductive, and I have to take a bite of my food to stop myself from laughing.

He smirks, his interest apparently piqued. "What kind of dancer?" he asks.

"That's something I'll have to show you in private." She twirls a strand of hair around her finger, her hand so close to her chest that it's clear where she's trying to draw his eyes. Naturally, it works.

My heart pangs with jealously as I watch Ezekiel run his gaze over her breasts.

"I look forward to it," he says, a clear hunger in his eyes.

The Reds, of course, hold service positions. One of them is a waitress, and the other a housekeeper. Both refuse to look at Yolanda's empty chair as they speak with Ezekiel.

When dessert is served, I take only a sliver of cake, remembering Gloria's warning about keeping Adriana's body the same as it was on the night of the ball. Elizabeth, however, isn't as cautious—she cuts the largest slice out of all the girls. But she's a Silver, and she appears well-fed, so I assume she knows what she's doing. She must be blessed with a fast metabolism.

"Adriana," Ezekiel says as the dessert plates are being cleared. "What are your plans on Saturday night?"

"None that I know of," I say automatically, since given everything going on, I've hardly taken time to fill up my social calendar. "Why? Are you throwing another party?"

"No." He chuckles. Then his eyes go serious, and he says, "I'm spending time with you. I'll be at your suite at eight-thirty to pick you up. Don't be late."

I nod, stunned into silence.

Because unless I'm misinterpreting the situation, Ezekiel just asked me out on a date.

CHAPTER THIRTY-NINE

*A*pparently, being asked on the first Saturday-night date is a big deal—the same amount of importance is put on it as the first dance at the ball. It *should* mean that I'm Ezekiel's favorite.

But the morning after the feast, the concubines have breakfast in the penthouse dining room. Maria struts in last, in a short, silky dress that clings to her body. She's walking slowly —deliberately—as if her muscles are sore.

"Sorry I'm late." She smirks and flips her hair over her shoulders, not sounding sorry in the slightest. "Ezekiel simply wouldn't allow me to leave my bed this morning."

"You saw him?" the Red girl who previously worked as a maid—Alicia—asks.

"He came to my room after dinner." She shrugs, as if it's no big deal, but her eyes gleam as she speaks. "So yes, I saw him. Every single bit of him. And let me tell you—he's more delicious than I *ever* imagined."

The other girls ask a million questions at once.

I just stare at Maria, a fire burning in my chest. What does Ezekiel see in her?

She couldn't be more different from me if she tried.

"One at a time," she says as she sits down, raising her arms into the air in an exaggerated yawn. "I'm *so* tired. I don't think I got a wink of sleep last night."

She answers each question. After listening to the play-by-play of her… bedtime adventures with Ezekiel, I'm *glad* he went to her suite and not mine. Because the acts she describes to us—they aren't things people do with someone they care about. They're carnal. Dark. Violent. And as she speaks, I notice the bruises on her body—on her wrists, her collarbones, her neck.

Those bruises weren't there at dinner last night.

If Ezekiel has such desires that need to be satisfied, and if Maria is as happy as she sounds, then I'm glad she's there to fulfill them.

But will he expect such things from me? Last night, he specifically said he would be "picking me up" for our date. That implies we're going out somewhere… or at least, I assumed it did. And he's always been a gentleman toward me in the past. He could have had his way with me in that alley, but he didn't. No—he saved me. He was gentle. Kind.

The person Maria's describing sounds like an entirely different man.

But I know it's not. Ezekiel and that man are one and the same. I can't let myself forget that.

How much longer will it be until he expects from me what he got last night from Maria?

Hopefully I'll be able to kill him before it comes to that.

"Why so quiet?" Maria asks me with a smirk. "You don't

have anything to add to the conversation? Any of your own experiences to share, perhaps?"

My cheeks turn red, and I glance away from her, hoping one of the other girls will change the subject. Because of *course* I don't have my own experiences to add. I'm a messenger angel, bound to love and worship God for my entire existence. Some angels have had relations with humans—and many have even fallen from Heaven for humans they claimed to love—but I've never strayed from my God-given duties.

And while I've always known I might need to be intimate with Ezekiel to complete my mission—although I pray it doesn't come to that—it didn't feel *real* until this moment.

"You're not a *virgin*, are you?" Maria laughs, as if it's the most ridiculous thing she's ever heard. Her smile broadens when I say nothing. "This is great," she says, laughing again. "How do you plan on pleasing Ezekiel as a *virgin?*"

"Don't be mean," Elizabeth snaps, stepping to my defense.

"I'm not being mean," Maria says. "I'm just asking a question."

"No, it's okay." I sit straighter, not about to let Maria get her amusement from me. "There are many ways to please a man," I say calmly, holding my gaze with hers. "In fact, many kings of old were *only* interested in virgins. Virgins were considered pure and untainted—the perfect prize for the worthiest man in the kingdom. I think Ezekiel will be pleased when he learns I've saved my body for him, and him alone. Don't you agree?"

Maria harrumphs and focuses on finishing her food.

And I pray that if Ezekiel ever *does* come to my bedroom in the way he came to hers, I'll have already acquired the sword I need to kill him.

CHAPTER FORTY

On Saturday night, there's a knock on my door at eight-thirty on the dot—just as Ezekiel promised. My stomach's been twisting all day in anticipation. After hearing about what he did to Maria, I haven't stopped worrying if he'll try to do those same things to me.

But I also know that this is a big chance to break through to him and gain his trust.

So I take a deep breath, straighten my dress, and glance one more time at my reflection. I'm wearing a short white dress with swirling rhinestone patterns that I picked out during a group shopping trip to Josefina's store yesterday. I hope the dress makes me appear innocent—bride-like.

Ezekiel won't like it if he's kept waiting, so I push down my anxiety, hurry to the doors, and open them.

He's wearing jeans, a black t-shirt, and the same leather jacket he was in the first two times I met him. Seeing him like this reminds me of the man who walked me home and saved my life—not the man who killed two women in front of me.

He stares at me, transfixed—the same way he did the first time we met. As if he can't believe I'm here.

"Adriana," he says, breaking the silence. "You look beautiful."

"Thank you." I keep my hand on the doorknob, not moving from where I stand.

"You seem nervous," he observes.

"Do I?" I force myself to smile. "I suppose—well, to be honest, I've been looking forward to tonight since you asked. I'm excited."

"And nervous." He tilts his head, as if challenging me to say otherwise.

"Can't excitement and nervousness go hand in hand?"

"Yes," he says. "But I assure you—there's nothing to be nervous about. Because you're going to love what I'm planning to show you."

He holds out his hand and leads me out of my suite. We go to a center elevator, and I'm surprised to see that this one has another floor—a fiftieth floor. He scans his thumbprint and presses the button for floor fifty.

"I didn't know there was a floor above ours," I say as the doors close.

"There's a reason it's called the Watchtower," he says, and the elevator begins its ascent.

The doors open quickly, revealing a lone staircase in front of us. He leads the way up. When we reach the top, we step out into a huge, glass-domed room. It's circular and empty, except for a few bulky, sheet-covered objects scattered throughout.

"Wow," I say, looking every which way to take in my surroundings. From here, I can see out to the entire city—at least until the last lit-up houses. Overhead, the stars shine in the night. The moon is a perfect, glowing crescent—as if it's smiling down at us.

I've looked down at the world from Heaven before, but this is different.

This feels like we're standing on *top* of the world.

"You like it?" he asks from beside me.

"*Like* it?" I say, not having to fake my enthusiasm. "I love it."

"I'm glad," he says. "And that's not all. Come."

His eyes shine with excitement, and he holds his hand out to me. I take it, warmth spreading through my body at his touch. He leads me to one of the covered objects, pulling away the sheet and revealing what's beneath.

"A telescope." I gasp, reaching for it. "Has this always been up here?"

"No," he says, and from the way his eyes dance as he watches me, I can tell he's pleased by my reaction. "I got it for you. I got *all* of them for you." He motions around the room, and I realize that each covered object is another telescope. There must be ten of them in all. "So you can see the stars in the city."

"Wow," I say, truly amazed by the gesture. "Thank you. No one's ever done something like this for me in all the years of my existence."

It slips out of my mouth because it's true. My entire existence has been about devoting myself to God. No one has ever asked me much about myself, let alone given me something because they thought I would enjoy it. No one has ever thought my interests were important.

"I find that hard to believe from a Gold," he says, and I freeze, realizing my slip-up.

I'd spoken as myself—as Rebekah. Not as Adriana.

I frantically search for something to say to cover my mistake, while keeping my face serene.

"I'm given coins, yes," I say quickly. "To buy what I want for myself. And if I told my family I wanted something, they would usually get it for me, no questions asked. But no one has ever cared enough to listen between the lines of a conversation and gift me something I didn't specifically ask for—something they intuitively understood I would love. So... thank you, Ezekiel. This means so much more than I can ever say."

"I thought we were over such formalities," he says, and my heart pounds at the realization that he's standing so close to me that there's barely any space between us. He runs his fingers under my chin, and just like that, I'm trapped under his gaze. "I want you to call me Zeke. Not Ezekiel."

"Right." My cheeks redden at yet another slip-up. "Zeke."

"Much better." He smiles. "Now, do you plan on staring at me all night, or are you going to take a look through the telescope? Not that I would mind the first option, but I *did* position these so you could see the planets at this specific time, so I think you should at least take a peek."

And so, I do.

∽

As promised, each telescope points toward something different —a moon, a planet, or even a cluster of stars that make up another galaxy. He tells me information about each sight we observe, and I'm more impressed by his knowledge with each passing minute.

"I take it you enjoyed this?" he asks after we finish looking through the final telescope.

"Do you even need to ask?" I tease, and I'm surprised when

his eyes flicker with uncertainty. Does he truly not realize how much I appreciate what he did for me? "Of course I enjoyed myself," I tell him. "Tonight has been incredible. Better than incredible. It's been perfect."

"I believe you." He lowers his hand on top of mine, gazing down at me with an intensity that takes my breath away.

The next thing I know, his lips are on mine, his arms around me, and we're kissing with more passion than we had time for in those few stolen moments in the alley. Because here, under this dome, it's like we're in our own private world. And I realize that tonight, he's truly no longer Ezekiel to me.

He's Zeke.

The man who saved my life and gave me the stars.

CHAPTER FORTY-ONE

I toss and turn that night, replaying the date with Zeke in my mind. After kissing in the observatory, he walked me back to my room and said goodnight, like a true gentleman.

But a voice in the back of my mind reminds me that he's *not* a gentleman. He's a *demon*.

I know this. I've *witnessed* this. But it's like there are two sides to him. Ezekiel the demon, and Zeke... the man I fear I'm falling in love with.

The man I'm not sure I could ever bring myself to kill.

These feelings... they're treasonous. I shouldn't be having them. If I don't kill Zeke, then I'm dooming myself to fall from Heaven—to become a demon myself.

I can't let myself become that. I *won't* let myself become that.

But I also don't know if I'll be able to kill Zeke.

Because I want to *love* him. And I want *him* to love *me*.

The thoughts swirl in my mind, tormenting my conscience

and making it impossible to sleep. I need to talk about this with someone. Someone who understands. Someone who knows who—and what—I truly am.

So, first thing in the morning, I have Carlos drive me to Teresa's house.

"I know you're supposed to be with me everywhere I go," I tell him as we walk the path to the house. "But do you think you can wait outside while I'm with my sister?"

"Is there some big secret you don't want me to hear?" he asks.

I still, and my heart feels like it stops beating. Is Carlos onto me? Does he know what I'm up to? Does he know Teresa's involved, too?

"Just kidding," he says with a smile. "Of course, I—along with the entire continent—am curious about how your date with Ezekiel went last night. But I'll give you your privacy."

"Thank you." I let out a long breath, but quickly get ahold of myself and continue the act of being Adriana. "The date was incredible, and I'll tell you more about it later… but there are certain details that should only be shared between sisters, if you know what I mean."

"I do." He chuckles. "I have two sisters of my own, so I know how you girls are. Take as much time as you need. I'll wait for you outside."

∽

Teresa opens the door and eyes Carlos. "Adriana!" she says, smiling brightly and pulling me into a hug. "We have *so* much to catch up on. I can't wait to hear all your stories from the Watchtower."

"And I have so much to tell you." I plaster a similarly bright smile on my face. "Carlos has graciously agreed to wait outside so we can catch up in private."

"How kind of him." Teresa smiles at him and then refocuses on me, ushering me inside. "Spare no details... especially when it comes to your date with Ezekiel!"

She shuts the door, locks it, and mutters a string of Latin under her breath—a spell.

"We can speak freely now," she says, her tone switching from gossipy to business. "I just cast a soundproof spell—no one outside the house will be able to hear a word of our conversation."

"Where's Marco?" I ask.

"He's working today," she says. "The beginning of the month is the busiest for him, since he has to collect all the taxes from those who didn't pay last month."

"Of course." I nod, since it makes sense. Gold men, after they've married, can take on positions as tax collectors. It allows them to spend more time with their families. I was hoping to speak with both, but I'm here now, so I'll have to trust Teresa to relay everything to Marco.

"So?" She sits down on the sofa, and I take the armchair across from her. "Have you found out any more information about the location of the Flaming Sword?"

"No," I say, and my heart hurts at the mention of the sword—the weapon I'm supposed to use to kill Zeke.

"Oh." She frowns. "So why are you here? Shouldn't you be getting as close to Ezekiel as possible, to get him to trust you and tell you where he keeps the sword?"

"That's the problem." I take a deep breath, not knowing how to begin. Teresa will *never* understand. But isn't that why I'm here? To get her to talk some sense into me?

I just have to go ahead and spit it out.

"I feel much closer to him after our date last night," I say. "And I think he does with me, too."

Teresa looks at me blankly. "And that's a problem because..."

"Because there's a whole other side to him—one I didn't expect when I started on this mission," I say, speaking faster as my true feelings spill out. "He's not all evil. Yes, I know a large part of him *is* evil, and I would never say otherwise. But when he's with me—when it's just the two of us—he's a completely different person. A *good* person. A person I don't think I can kill."

"What?" Teresa's eyes widen in disbelief. "You're not falling for his tricks, are you?"

"I don't know." I pick up a pillow from the chair next to me and place it on my lap, running my fingers over the tassels. "It doesn't seem like he's tricking me. But maybe he is? I just... I really don't know."

"Did you sleep with him?" she asks, her tone laced with horror.

"No!" I drop my hands from the pillow. "We kissed, but nothing more."

"Then I think what he's doing is obvious," she says. "He's buttering you up to get you into bed with him."

"I don't think he needs to do that." I balk. "He's a demon—the demon king of the entire continent. If he wanted me in that way, wouldn't he just take it?"

Like he did with Maria, I think, although I don't say it out loud.

"Who knows?" she says. "Like you said, he's a demon. It's probably some sick, twisted game of his to toy with your emotions. He's been known to do things like that with his concubines in the past."

"Things like what?" I ask, dread filling my stomach.

"Make them fall completely and utterly in love with him," she says. "Then he gets bored and kills them. There was one girl a few years ago—a Silver—who fell head over heels in love with him. He appeared to love her, too. Right after the clock struck midnight on New Year's Eve, he kissed her, and she said that her heart was his forever. So he yanked her heart out of her chest, held it up so the entire crowd could see it, and announced that now her heart truly *would* always belong to him, because he would keep it on display forever."

"He wouldn't…" I start, wanting to say that he wouldn't do that to me. But I can't. Because like Teresa said, he's a *demon*. He's capable of anything.

But I truly *can't* imagine him doing such a thing to me.

"Yes, he would," she says, her eyes hard. "He *has*."

"I know," I say. "I do. I just wish… I wish these feelings I'm having for him would go away."

"It's the curse," she says simply. "It must be."

"How so?" I ask. "The curse is *greed*. And I've been fighting it. Otherwise, wouldn't I be traipsing around from store to store with the rest of the girls, spending my coins on everything I could get my hands on?"

"Greed manifests in many ways," Teresa explains. "A greed for material wealth is common. So is greed for power, or for fame. But tell me, Rebekah—have you ever been in love?"

"No," I say quickly. "Well, not *in* love, in the way humans experience. Like all angels, I love God and everything He creates. And He loves me, unconditionally."

"Unless you break one of his rules," she says. "Then he'll toss you out of Heaven, curse you to life as a demon, and damn you to Hell for all eternity."

"Loving God means respecting his rules." I hold her gaze, as if by doing so, I can will her to understand. "Respect and love go hand in hand."

"Right, right." She brushes it away, as if it's unimportant. "So you've never been in love. But… do you *want* to be in love? To experience that unconditional, all-consuming love for one special someone who returns that love for you and you alone? A love like I have for Marco, and he has for me?"

"Angels aren't allowed to love anyone more than God," I repeat. "Especially not a human. Falling in love with a human is forbidden. Angels have been cast from Heaven for far less than that."

"You didn't answer my question," she challenges. "I'm not asking what's allowed. I'm asking what you *want*."

I think back on the date last night—about how special I felt when I realized that Zeke planned the whole date around the stars, because he wanted to make me happy. It worked. Because last night, I *was* happy—not happy for someone else, but happy because of something that someone did for *me*. Because of something *Zeke* did for me.

Last night, I felt cared for… possibly even loved.

"You don't need to answer," Teresa finally says. "Your face says it all. There *is* something you're greedy for—you're greedy for love."

CHAPTER FORTY-TWO

"Greedy for love?" I question, as if testing the words aloud. "From *Zeke*?"

"You have pet names for each other?" Her face twists with disgust. "This is worse than I thought."

"It's what he asked me to call him," I say quietly.

"Then call him that to his face all you like," she says. "But don't *think* of him like that. Because he's not 'Zeke.' He's Ezekiel. A demon who cursed everyone on this continent so he could control them and be their king. You can't forget that. You need to fight the curse. You wouldn't have been sent here to kill him if you couldn't."

"I was sent here to break the curse," I say, an idea forming in my mind. "What if there's a way to break the curse *without* killing him?"

"Do you think the other witches and I haven't been trying to do that for decades?" Teresa asks, exasperated. "*Nothing* we've tried works. This curse is stronger than our magic."

"You can't have tried everything," I say.

"You're right." She looks me dead in the eye. "We haven't been able to kill Ezekiel. We've tried—believe me. But he's impossible to kill. He just killed us instead—it's why the few of us who still survive are forced to live in hiding. But now you're here, and you told me yourself that you were instructed to find the Flaming Sword and kill him. Those *were* your instructions, correct?"

"They were," I say, even though I wish it weren't true.

Teresa doesn't say anymore. She just allows the truth to sit in. Finally, she says, "I know the curse is hard to fight. It embeds itself in the heart and mind, so people don't know the difference between their own desires and what they're being driven to desire by the curse. But you can't forget who Ezekiel truly is. He incinerated a girl because she fell while dancing. He threw a knife into a girl's heart because she was slurping her soup. And it hasn't even been a week! He's going to pick you all off, one by one, until there's no one left. Then he's going to find ten new girls to take the brunt of his wrath. You can't let it get to that point. You have to kill him first. You must end this curse once and for all."

"I know," I say, remembering each murder as she speaks of it. I need to get a grip on myself.

Straightening my shoulders, I sit up, determination filling my soul once more.

"You're right," I say. "These feelings I think I'm having for him—they must be the curse. I need to fight it. Because demons aren't capable of love. Demons aren't capable of caring about anyone but themselves."

"*That's* my girl." Teresa smirks. "I'm glad you're thinking clearly again. Now—do you have *any* leads about where he's keeping the Flaming Sword?"

"No." I sigh and lean back in my chair. "The Watchtower's

huge. And I can't just ask people if they've seen Uriel's Flaming Sword lying around. Not like Ezekiel would just leave it lying around, anyway. I'm sure he keeps it somewhere safe and guarded."

"Okay." Teresa rests her hands on her legs. "I see what you mean, but this isn't hopeless. Because there's something I can work on that will help. A potion."

"What kind of potion?" I balk, but then get ahold of myself. I hate the idea of using anything created by witch magic—especially a brewed *potion*—but I need to get over this prejudice I have toward them. Because like Uriel told me, I need to accept help from witches to succeed in this mission.

And helping Teresa and Marco with the locator spell wasn't as terrible as anticipated. Maybe this won't be so bad, either.

"A truth potion," she says. "But creating it is complicated—*if* I'm able to do it correctly, it'll take at least a month."

"A month," I repeat. "I can manage to keep Ezekiel from killing me for a month."

Hopefully I'll be able to keep him from killing the other remaining girls as well, but after how quickly he murdered the first two, I know that'll be impossible.

"You need to do more than just keep him from killing you," Teresa says. "The potion works best when it's administered by someone the person already trusts. While I'm making this potion, you need to gain as much of Ezekiel's trust as possible. Because the more he trusts you, the stronger the hold of the potion will be."

"And the more likely it'll be that he'll spill the location of the Flaming Sword," I say.

"And the less likely it'll be that he'll suspect anything was amiss once the potion wears off." Teresa smiles, and just like that, we're back on the same team. "I'll get started on the potion immediately," she says. "And you need to get back to the Watchtower. Because you have a demon to seduce."

CHAPTER FORTY-THREE

As suspected, I can't keep the other girls safe from Ezekiel's wrath. Since speaking with Teresa nearly a month ago, three of them have disappeared. Two of them Greens, one of them a Red.

I also haven't seen Ezekiel nearly as much as I would have liked. It's as if whatever connection existed between us that night in the observatory was severed. I'm always seated by his side during major meals, but he pays me no more attention than he does the other girls. There were a few moments when I felt that spark between us again, but each time it happened, he snapped out of it, asked someone else a question, and ignored me for the remainder of the meal.

He visits Maria's bedroom multiple nights a week—I know this because she never fails to brag about it the next morning—but he has yet to ask me on another date. In fact, from what the other girls have said, I'm the only one who *hasn't* spent the night with him.

Luckily, their experiences with him haven't been nearly as

rough as what Maria describes. I'm not sure if she's exaggerating, or if he just likes to take out his aggression on her. Judging from the bruises that constantly pop up on every imaginable place on her body—the ones she tries to cover with thicker and thicker layers of concealer—I suspect the latter.

Perhaps he senses my inexperience in such matters, which is why he's avoiding me. Or maybe he simply lost interest.

But if he doesn't want me anymore, wouldn't he just kill me like he did the other girls?

I don't see what would hold him back.

Despite his reasons, I'm certainly no closer to gaining his trust—or to finding the Flaming Sword.

∽

"Are you eating that?" Elizabeth asks during breakfast, pointing to the untouched strips of bacon on my plate.

"No." I push the plate in her direction. "You can have it."

She picks up a piece, nibbling thoughtfully. "Are you nervous for today?" she asks.

"What's there to be nervous about?" Maria butts in. "It's the Day of the Dead—my favorite holiday of the year! It's Ezekiel's favorite holiday, too. He told me last night."

It takes all my strength to resist rolling my eyes at her obvious attempt to brag. "Of course I'm not nervous," I say instead.

"Then why did you barely touch your breakfast?" Elizabeth asks.

"Maybe she wants to fit into her dress." Josefina eyes the bacon in Elizabeth's hand. "Perhaps you should consider doing the same."

Elizabeth narrows her eyes at Josefina and takes a defiant

mouthful of bacon. I bite the inside of my cheek to stop myself from laughing.

A second later, I worry that Josefina might have a point. Elizabeth has taken to wearing loose tops recently, and she *has* been eating more than the rest of us. I think back to the way she looked on audition night—her cheekbones more prominent, her collarbones more defined—and I remember what Gloria said about how Zeke doesn't like his concubines to gain weight.

"What's with that look?" Elizabeth asks. "Don't tell me you agree with them?"

"Of course not," I tell her. "I think you look beautiful. But… we do have to be careful. We know how particular Ezekiel is about such matters."

"Yes, we do," Maria says, and she studies Elizabeth with a glint of malice in her eyes. "So by all means, eat the bacon. Have a muffin, too! The more weight you put on, the less competition you'll be for the rest of us."

"You don't mean that," the only remaining Red girl—Alicia—says.

Maria raises an eyebrow in challenge. "Wanna bet?"

Alicia bows her head and picks at the remains of her eggs.

"Didn't think so." Maria scoffs.

I glare at Maria and clench my hands under the table, anger rushing through my veins. I've never physically fought anyone in my life, but it would be immensely gratifying to punch that smug smile right off her face.

Instead, I take a drink of water, trying to calm myself. Her malice must be out of greed—because of the curse.

She can't truly want Elizabeth dead.

At least, I pray that's the case.

CHAPTER FORTY-FOUR

We spend the rest of the morning in our suites, getting dressed and ready for the parade. Now, our Gold guards lead us out of the Watchtower and onto the street, where a giant float awaits among the eager crowd.

They cheer and clap as we walk out, screaming our names. Some of them even hold posters to get our attention. I spot one that says, "We love you, Adriana!" and give the group of young girls holding it a small smile. They squeal at the attention.

Judging by the posters and screaming of our names, Maria, Alicia, and I have the most supporters out of the remaining six of us.

We step onto the float in order of caste, which, of course, means I'm last. The float is bright and colorful—like our dresses—and it has a huge, smiling skull statue at the back of it. The symbol of the Day of the Dead.

Unlike most religious holidays, Zeke didn't abolish the Day

of the Dead. He did, however, change its meaning. It used to be a holiday that celebrated the lives of loved ones who passed on. Now, it reminds us that we should be grateful to be in our castes—that we should be grateful not to be Blues.

Because the Blues—trapped in their labor camps, slaving away to keep the city running—are considered as good as dead.

Which is why I assume the smiling skull lady at the back of the float wears a bright blue dress.

I will save you, I think, looking at her as I board the float, thinking of all the slaves toiling away on the outskirts of the continent. *I will save you from your suffering.*

Once all six of us are on board, an announcer steps up onto a platform in front of the Watchtower. "And now, we welcome His Highness, King Ezekiel!" he says, and the crowd goes wild.

Ezekiel steps out onto the second-floor balcony. He's dressed in all black, and he strolls up to the rail, placing his hands upon it. The moment he does, the crowd cheers again. He says nothing as he stares down at them, a knowing smirk on his face as he glances over all the signs.

"I see that your favorite girls align with mine," he says, winking at the group of girls I smiled at earlier. "The citizens of my kingdom have good taste."

This elicits more cheering—and squealing—from the crowd. It takes a while for them to calm down.

"We love Adriana!" the group from before screams in unison.

"So do I," Zeke says, sending them into even more of a frenzy.

I freeze, my heart stopping in my chest. Surely he doesn't mean it? But he's watching me now, his eyes dark and intense as they bore into my soul, as if he wants me to believe him.

Like he wants me to believe that he *loves* me.

But he can't love me. Beyond the obvious fact that we've barely seen each other since our date in the observatory, he's a demon. He's not *capable* of love.

No matter what, I can't let myself forget that.

CHAPTER FORTY-FIVE

I barely have time to think before Zeke disappears into a burst of flames, reappearing instantly in the center of the float. He sends the flames into the sky, and they disappear into the clouds, raining ash onto the crowd. They take a collective breath inward, reaching up to catch it.

But the entire time, I stand still, replaying Zeke's words in my mind.

I want them to be true.

I want him to love me.

But then, a few pieces of ash drift onto my cheeks like snowflakes, reminding me of the girls he murdered. These feelings I'm having—they're the curse taking hold. They're not real.

I push the longing away, down deep into the recesses of my heart, burying it until I can finally think straight again.

Once I do, I realize that Zeke has stepped in front of Elizabeth, his eyes full of disgust. "You were right." He glances at

Maria, and then he reaches forward, pinching Elizabeth's arm. "This blubber wasn't here a month ago."

"I told you so," Maria says smugly. "The rest of us have been trying so hard to remain beautiful for you, while *she* indulges at every meal, stuffing her mouth with as much food as possible. It's disgusting—and completely disrespectful to you. After all, we're here to be beautiful—not to get *fat*."

Ezekiel glares down at Elizabeth and releases her arm, his eyes filling with inky blackness.

I know that look.

It's the way he looks before he kills.

"No!" I throw myself between him and Elizabeth and desperately reach for his hands, as if *that* might be enough to stop him. The crowd is silent, watching me. "Don't hurt her," I beg. "Please."

His eyes bore into mine—fully black now, empty and soulless.

The reality of what I've done crashes down on me. This is exactly what Gloria warned me *not* to do. Concubines have been killed for far less.

I stand frozen in place, my hands still in his, preparing to die.

But he grips my hands tighter—so tightly I fear he's going to shatter my bones. He grunts, his face twisting in agony, as if he's fighting something stronger than himself. As if he's fighting the darkness that's filling his eyes.

"I have to," he finally says, although his voice is tight —strained.

"You don't." I step closer to him, praying to get through to him. "You're the king of this continent. You don't have to do anything you don't want to."

"No," he growls. "You don't understand. It's too late to stop. All of this power—this darkness—it has to go *somewhere*."

"Up to the sky," I beg. "Like you did with the flames."

"It doesn't work like that." He drops my hands, pushing me into Elizabeth. "Someone—one of you—must die."

He turns to Alicia, and she bursts into flames.

∼

I stare at the empty space where Alicia had been standing, speechless.

"Aren't you going to thank me?" Zeke snarls down at me. "For saving your friend?"

I glare at him, saying nothing. My body shakes with hatred. I want to tell him that Alicia didn't deserve to die, either.

But what will that accomplish? She's already dead. I can't save her. If I say that, I'm only risking angering him to the point where he kills me, too. Or someone else.

I glance over his shoulder at the smiling skull lady—a reminder of the people I'm here to save. I *have* to stay alive. They're counting on me.

With difficulty, I swallow and take a deep breath, forcing myself to get ahold of my emotions. "Thank you," I say to him, although the words are hollow. "For saving Elizabeth."

Elizabeth reaches for my hand and gives it a small squeeze. I don't look at her—I'm afraid I'll break down completely if I do—but I return the gesture.

"The parade is cancelled," Ezekiel says, and then he fixes his gaze on Elizabeth. "Get out of here. I don't want you in the Watchtower anymore. I don't want to see you ever again."

"What?" She pulls her hand out of mine and backs away, leaning against the edge of the float. "You're kicking me out?"

"Yes." He smiles, although it's full of threats. "I'm 'kicking you out.' So do yourself a favor and get out."

"Where am I supposed to go?" Her voice is soft, shaking.

"I don't give a shit where you go," he says. "Just get out of my sight forever."

Elizabeth nods and runs off the float, her dress in her hands, her hair flying behind her.

She turns a corner and doesn't look back.

CHAPTER FORTY-SIX

I play the violin as I stare out over my balcony, losing myself in the music as I watch the spectacle of colors as the sun sets over the horizon. Playing music is the only thing that can possibly relax me right now. I've changed into my most comfortable pajamas—yoga pants and a tank top—and washed my face clean of the makeup I wore today. Any other night, I would have taken Gloria's advice and put on a fresh coat of makeup immediately. But now, I don't see the point.

After my display at the parade today, this sunset will surely be my last.

At least Ezekiel let Elizabeth go free. As the song comes to a close, I puzzle over his actions for what feels like the millionth time since I've returned to my suite. He's never sent a girl home—*ever*. He either killed them, or they made it through the year and became a Gold.

What made Elizabeth so different? What made *today* so different?

A knock on the door yanks me out of my thoughts.

I place the violin down on my bed, hurry to the door, and look out the peephole. Carlos is the only person standing there. He's facing the door, waiting for me to answer.

I open it hesitantly. "Yes?" I ask.

"I've just received word that Ezekiel wants to see you in his suite immediately," he says, his expression grim.

My hand rushes to my face, remembering that it's bare. "Give me ten minutes?" I ask. "I can't go to Ezekiel like this."

"My orders are to bring you now," he says. "We both know Ezekiel isn't a patient man."

I glance back into my room, gripping the doorknob. Should I get myself fixed up and risk angering Ezekiel by being late? Or should I go immediately and risk displeasing him with my looks?

"You're the most beautiful girl here—with or without makeup," Carlos assures me, as if he can read my mind.

My thoughts must have been written all over my face.

"So it's better for me to go like this instead of being late?" I ask.

"Yes." He nods. "It most definitely is."

I trust Carlos not to steer me wrong, so I close the door and follow him to Ezekiel's suite. It feels silly to be led there—since the golden double-door entrance is so near my own—but I understand that we must follow protocol.

Once we arrive, Carlos knocks on Ezekiel's door.

"Enter," Ezekiel calls from inside.

"That's strange," Carlos says. "Only Ezekiel's fingerprint accesses his room..." He stares at the door and presses his thumb onto the lock button. Nothing happens. "Perhaps..." He looks at me in question. "You should try yours?"

"Does Ezekiel normally give his concubines access to his suite?" I ask.

"No," Carlos says. "Never. But you, my dear, are far from normal."

I press my thumb to the lock button, and the door clicks open.

CHAPTER FORTY-SEVEN

*E*zekiel is standing in the middle of his foyer, a glass of what appears to be tequila in his hand. "Adriana," he says, no hints of emotion on his face. "I see you've discovered that I've given you access to my suite."

"Yes." I bow my head, my chest surging with hope that he didn't bring me here to kill me. Because if he wanted to kill me, why would he give me access to his suite? "Thank you, Ezekiel," I say, since he prefers me to address him by his full name in front of others.

"No need to thank me," he says. "Carlos—leave us."

Carlos scurries out of the suite, leaving Ezekiel and me alone.

"I would offer you some tequila, but I've noticed during our group meals that the champagne is always your favorite," he says. "Come. I'll open a bottle."

I follow him into the kitchen in a daze. He strolls to one of the paneled doors—if he notices my unease, he doesn't show it. He just opens the door and reveals a room full of wine and champagne. He steps inside, his eyes scanning the rows, eventually stopping on one and pulling out a bottle.

"This will do." He rips off the aluminum, pops the cork, and takes a swig. He swishes it in his mouth—as if he's analyzing all the flavors within it—and swallows. "Delicious," he finally says, holding out the bottle. "Want a taste? Or do you only drink out of a glass?"

He watches me in challenge, and I can't help but feel like this is a test.

Why did he bring me here? Surely not to just share a bottle of champagne?

There must be more to it. And while I'm not sure what kind of game he's playing, as long as he isn't killing me, I'm going to play along. After all, this could be a chance for me to save my mission.

I march over to him, grab the bottle, and take an even longer swig than his. It burns going down my throat—trying to compete with Ezekiel in drinking is stupid, and I know that—but instead of grimacing, I smile and hand the bottle back to him.

"Perfect," I say. "Although I must ask—since I've been curious all my life—can demons get drunk?"

"Yes." He laughs, and I'm surprised by how childlike he seems in that moment. How is it possible that this man is capable of heartless murder? "Our bodies are human in form—it's the magic in our spirit that keeps the body immortal. So yes, we can get drunk, although it takes much more alcohol than it does for an average human."

"Like me," I say, since I assume that must be what he's thinking.

"No." He lowers the bottle to his side, his eyes full of intensity. "You, Adriana, are as far from average as anyone I've ever met."

My heart leaps into my throat, leaving me speechless. How am I supposed to respond to a comment like that? Especially because I shouldn't feel so warm and happy from his compliment—I should feel revolted by this demon in front of me.

It's the curse, I remind myself, trying to get my head back on straight. *These treasonous feelings must be because of the curse.*

He strolls into the kitchen and retrieves a glass, pouring the champagne into it. "For you." He holds it out to me, and after I take it, he picks up both the bottle of champagne and his glass of tequila and heads out of the kitchen. "Let's go somewhere more comfortable," he says over his shoulder, glancing behind himself to make sure I'm following. "Because we have a *lot* to discuss."

He opens another door, and ushers me into his bedroom.

CHAPTER FORTY-EIGHT

I step tentatively inside, taking in the gigantic bed and the floor-to-ceiling windows that overlook the city. I can think of only one reason why he's bringing me in here—he must want to take me to bed. Tonight.

My nerves crackle with anxiety. I knew this was bound to happen, since it *is* the main reason he keeps concubines in the Watchtower. But I'm not ready.

However, if I want to gain his trust, I must go along with it. Reminding myself who I am, I straighten. I'm Rebekah, a messenger angel of Heaven. Angels don't worry about such human concerns. We do what we need to do to get a job done.

So why does being around Zeke make me feel so human?

"Don't look so scared," he teases. "I won't bite."

"I'm not scared," I say, although I tip my glass up and take a long gulp of my champagne, my actions contradicting my words.

He walks toward me and takes the empty glass from my hand, his fingers brushing mine. Electricity rushes over my skin as it connects with his. Then he walks away, the lack of his touch leaving me cold, and refills my glass.

"After today, I'm sure you have many questions for me," he says, bringing the now-full glass back over to me.

"You're willing to answer them?" I ask.

"When have I not been willing to answer to you?" He laughs, although it's dark—hollow. "You got through to me even when the darkness had overtaken my soul."

"You mean when you were about to kill Elizabeth?"

"Yes." He walks toward the window, refusing to look at me.

I join him, walking slowly so as not to startle him. "Were you truly going to kill her?" I ask. "Simply because she gained some weight?"

"I was truly going to kill her," he confirms. "But not for the reason you think."

"Then why?" I ask.

"Because Maria was taunting me in front of the crowd," he says. "She knew what she was doing—she was putting me in a position where I would look weak if I didn't kill Elizabeth. The more she spoke, the more the darkness took over—until it consumed me, making me want to show everyone that I'm a force to be reckoned with. Once the darkness took over, Elizabeth was as good as dead."

"But you stopped yourself," I say. "Why?"

"Because of you." He turns his head sharply, his eyes burning deep into my soul. "You took my hands and spoke to me, and you got past the darkness. In all my years as a demon—since I fell from Heaven—no one has ever been able to do that."

"But I couldn't," I say. "At least not completely. Otherwise, Alicia would still be alive."

"You *were* able to," he insists. "You don't understand. All of that darkness—it needed to go somewhere. And after you opposed me in front of the crowd, the darkness wanted *you*. It wanted me to kill you. But I fought it. Harder than I've ever fought it in my life. Because I could never forgive myself if you died at my hands."

My lips part as I remember how close to death I was this afternoon. But I hadn't realized until now how much it truly meant that Elizabeth and I are still alive. I *still* don't entirely understand what he means.

So I do what he previously invited me to do—I ask.

"What exactly is this 'darkness?'" I start. "You speak of it like it's an entity in itself. Like it's something you can fight."

He walks over to the sofa and takes a seat, motioning to the space next to him. I take it, making sure to leave a few inches between us. The side of my body closest to him buzzes with electricity, and it takes all of my self-control not to move closer and close the gap between us.

He swirls his tequila and takes a slow sip. "What do you know about demons?" he finally asks.

"Not much," I lie, since I doubt Adriana knew a lot about them. "Beyond the fact that you're a demon and rule our continent, of course."

"Of course." He nods. "Did you know that demons aren't created this way? That we all started as fallen angels?"

"No." I shake my head—another lie. "What happened that caused you to fall?"

"That's a story for another day," he says, which only piques my curiosity further. But I don't push him, not wanting to lose this chance of getting information from him. "But after we fall, God abandons us, and darkness fills our soul. Some say this darkness is a piece of the devil himself. The darkness thrives on hate and anger, and it feeds on death. Whenever something angers me—no matter how small that something is—the darkness grows in strength. It builds inside my soul, taking over to do what it needs to survive—to kill."

I sip my champagne, absorbing everything he just told me. Because even though I'm an angel, there are some things that even angels don't know. What he's telling me now is one of those things.

"Are you saying that all of those people you killed... it wasn't actually you who killed them?" I ask. "It was this 'darkness?'"

"It depends on how you look at it," he says. "The darkness lives inside me—it's *part* of me. Most believe that makes us the same."

"But you fought it today," I remind him. "So you're *not* the same."

"I'd like to think so," he says. "But you have to understand—that was the *only* time I've ever successfully fought the darkness. I tried after I first fell—*believe* me, I tried—but it didn't work. Fighting it was impossible, so I gave in. Why fight the inevitable?"

"To keep innocent people alive." I level my gaze with his. "To not be a killer."

"It's not as easy as you think," he says.

"You did it today."

"Because you asked." His eyes stay on mine, the electricity between us buzzing stronger and stronger. "I did it for you."

"What makes me so special?" I ask.

"You remind me of someone I knew," he says simply. "Someone I knew *before* I became what I am today."

"Someone you knew when you were still an angel," I realize. "This someone... did you love her?"

"Like I said, that's another story for another day." He leans back, and disappointment fills my chest. Because I want to know everything about Ezekiel—yet I feel like I'm only grazing the surface of the churning depths within his soul. "But you—ever since I first saw you, you've made me want to be the man I used to be," he says. "A man capable of love."

His words remind me of what he said this morning on the balcony, and I place my champagne flute down on the end table, heat rushing to my cheeks. "Did you mean what you said earlier?" I ask. "When those girls said they loved me, and you said you did, too?"

"Do you want me to mean it?" he asks.

"What I want is irrelevant," I say.

"That's where you're so, so wrong." He leans forward, and I do the same, until our faces are nearly touching. "What you want is *everything*."

Suddenly, his mouth is on mine, and I part my lips for his, heat flooding my body as his tongue brushes my own. I didn't realize how much I'd been wanting this—how much I'd been *needing* this—until right now.

He pulls me closer, and then I'm in his arms, and he's carrying me to the bed, kissing me the entire way there. He lays me down gently and deepens the kiss again, his body on top of mine, igniting a longing deep down inside that I didn't know I could have until this very moment. My body takes on a mind of its own and arches up to him, filling every crevice between us.

"Adriana," he groans, staring down at me with so much intensity that I have to remind myself to breathe. "Do you love me even half as much as I love you?"

"More than that." I pull him back down to me, needing to kiss him again. "So much more."

"How much?" he asks. "Tell me how much."

"Completely," I say, and then we're kissing again, losing ourselves in each other's touch.

His hands explore my body, and then they're on the band of my leggings, coaxing them down. "I want you," he says, and he guides my hand to the space between his legs so I can feel the hardness under his jeans. "All of you."

At the realization of what he means—of what he's ready to do—I can't help but think of Maria.

Of the bruises all over her body.

Is he going to do to me whatever he did to her?

"Wait." I pull away from him, breathing slowly to steady my spinning thoughts.

"What?" he asks. "Don't you want me too?"

"I do," I say. "Of course I do. But…" I pause, searching for a reason he'll understand. I can't risk angering him now—not when we've gotten this far.

He was able to fight the darkness once, but that doesn't mean he'll be able to do it again.

"But what?" he asks.

"I'm a virgin," I rush out, feeling my cheeks redden. "I love you—I truly do, and I hope you never doubt that—but this is all moving so fast. *Too* fast."

He stills at my words, and his eyes go distant. "Just like Julia," he says with a sigh, rolling over so his body no longer hovers on top of mine.

I feel cold at the loss of his touch, but I resist the urge to pull him close again, not wanting to tempt him more than I already have. "You've said that name twice around me now," I say instead. "Who's Julia?"

"It doesn't matter." He blinks, as if trying to get rid of a memory, and sits up in the bed. "But I swear to you, Adriana—I love you, and I want you—*all* of you. But only when you're one hundred percent ready."

"You mean that?" I ask.

"Of course I mean it," he says, and once again, he's proven himself to be completely different than I ever expected.

I can only think of one possible explanation—he loves me. He truly loves me.

I clutch my hands to my chest, terror filling my heart as I realize that I love him as well.

Because if I love him... how can I ever bring myself to kill him?

CHAPTER FORTY-NINE

I stay in my room the next day under the pretense of being sick. It's not a lie—the anxiety I feel truly *is* making me sick to my stomach.

If I don't kill Zeke, I'm condemning everyone on this continent to being cursed—and I'm condemning myself to being cast from Heaven. I'll become the same as Zeke—a demon. The darkness he spoke of will fill my soul and turn me into a murderer.

But if I kill him...

I wrap my hands around my stomach again, sick from the thought. I *can't* kill him.

I can't even pray for guidance. Because if God hears my treasonous thoughts, he'll surely cast me from Heaven on the spot.

I've never felt so lost and afraid in all the centuries of my existence. Now I finally understand why humans go to such extremes for love. Because love—true, all-consuming love—

has the power to make people act in ways they never believed possible.

I toss and turn again that night, unable to sleep. I finally manage to drift off as the first rays of sunlight stream through the blinds, when I'm suddenly awoken by a knock on my door.

I groan and roll over in bed, pulling the pillow around my ears to muffle the sound. But the knocking starts again—harder and more persistent this time.

"Hold on!" I call out, rolling out of bed. "I'll be there in a minute."

I freshen up as quickly as possible, relieved when I glance through the peephole and see that it isn't Zeke who wants to see me—it's Teresa.

I open the door, closing it quickly after she enters. The moment it's shut, she mutters a spell under her breath.

"A sound-barrier spell," she explains. "So no one can listen in on our conversation."

I nod, glad she had the sense to cast it. The Watchtower has eyes and ears everywhere—I suspect even in our suites.

"You look like crap," she observes, giving me a once over. "Didn't Gloria warn you to always look your best?"

"A lot has happened recently." I run a hand through my hair, struggling to get my fingers through the tangles. But fixing it's futile, so I give up and drop my hand down to my side.

"No shit." Teresa crosses her arms and narrows her eyes. "What the hell were you thinking yesterday? Were you trying to get yourself killed? Were you trying to get my *sister* killed?"

I sigh—I should have known that's why Teresa's here.

However, given how insane my actions were yesterday, I can't blame her for being angry.

"He was going to kill Elizabeth," I say. "I had to stop him."

"No." She shakes her head and steps toward me, flinging her

arms down to her sides. "What you *have* to do is find the Flaming Sword and kill him. You can't do that *if you're dead!*" She screams the last part, and I hang my head, knowing she's right. What I did went against everything Gloria taught me to survive here.

But I saved Elizabeth's life. That must count for something.

"Well, I'm *not* dead," I say. "And neither is Elizabeth."

"I don't care about Elizabeth," Teresa snaps. "And I don't care about Alicia, Maria, or any of the other concubines. All I care about is that you keep my sister alive and kill Ezekiel. Got it?"

"About that..." I say, knowing she's going to hate what I have to tell her next. "I don't think I can do it."

"What?" She stares at me, completely still, her voice full of ice. "You mean you don't think you can find the Flaming Sword?"

"No," I say. "Well, I don't know if I can find the Flaming Sword. But that's not what I meant."

"Then what did you mean?" She stares me down, as if she's daring me to say it.

"I don't think I can kill Ezekiel," I say quickly. "No—scratch that. I *know* I can't kill Ezekiel."

"And why do you think that?"

I glance down at my feet, lowering my voice to a whisper. "Because I love him."

"What?" She leans forward and cups a hand around her ear. "Say it again? Because I don't think I heard you correctly."

I lift my head up, holding my gaze with hers. "I can't kill Ezekiel because I'm in love with him." I speak stronger this time, continuing before she has a chance to reply. "You have to understand—*he's* not the one killing all these people. He doesn't want to kill anyone. It's the darkness. But he fought it for the first time yesterday, and I know he can fight it again. He *will* fight it again. Because he loves me, too."

Teresa laughs, although it's dark and hollow. "You've *got* to be kidding me," she says. "The curse is affecting you more than I realized."

"I'm not kidding," I say. "It's the truth."

From there, I explain everything Ezekiel told me about the darkness that takes over his soul and makes him do such terrible things. I feel awful telling his secrets to Teresa—since he told me in confidence—but she *has* to know. It's the only way she might understand.

"None of this changes anything," she says once I'm done. "You were sent here to end the curse, and the only way to end the curse is to kill Ezekiel. You might think he and this 'darkness' are separate from each other, but that's not true. The darkness is a part of him. The only way to get rid of it is to kill him."

"We don't know that," I say. "What if there's another way?"

"There *is* no other way!" She throws her hands up and groans. "Wouldn't Uriel—or God—have told you if there were?"

"Yes," I say, since she's right—God is good, and he wouldn't keep something so important from me. That's something I would never question, no matter what. "But you don't know Ezekiel the way I do. There *is* good in him. He doesn't deserve to die because of what the darkness forces him to do."

Teresa sighs, sits down on the couch, and buries her face in her hands. I don't know what she's thinking, but I don't dare interrupt her.

For all I know, she'll lash out and try to exorcise me again—even if it means possibly damaging Adriana's body by doing so.

"Okay." She lowers her hands and focuses on me again, her

eyes calmer now. "No killing has to be done yet. I'll ask some of the older witches if they know anything about this 'darkness'—maybe there's a way to destroy that part of him while still keeping him alive."

Hope surges through my chest. "You think there might be?" I ask.

"If there is, I'll find out," she says. "But for now, let's focus on the first part of your task—finding the Flaming Sword. Because if there's a way to destroy the darkness without killing Ezekiel, I bet that sword is a part of it."

"Why would you bet that?" I ask.

"Because he used the sword to cast the curse," she explains. "The sword is full of old, powerful magic. It will surely be necessary to break such a strong spell. So, have you gotten any closer to figuring out where it might be?"

"No," I say. "Last night, Ezekiel invited me to his suite for the first time. I thought he might keep it there, but I didn't see it anywhere."

She raises an eyebrow when I say he invited me to his suite, and my cheeks flush, but she doesn't comment any further on the matter. I'm glad—even though Ezekiel and I didn't sleep together, the night we shared felt intimate and sacred. I don't want to share the details of it with anyone.

I want those memories to be his and mine alone.

"All right," she says. "Let's move forward. Because luckily for you, I didn't come here *just* to yell at you."

"Really?" I ask. "Because it sure feels like it."

"Really." She reaches into her bag, bringing out a vial of shimmering silver potion. "I came here to bring you this."

CHAPTER FIFTY

"The truth potion?" I guess. "You were able to successfully make it?"

"Of course I was." She smirks and flips her hair over her shoulder. "I meant it when I told you this potion is one of the hardest to brew. But I'm one of the strongest witches in the city, so I could handle it."

I scrutinize the bottle. "I need to slip that into one of Zeke's drinks?" I ask. Because Zeke's fast, and he notices *everything*. How am I supposed to do this and remain unnoticed?

"Nope." Teresa holds the vial higher, admiring it. "This potion is *much* sleeker than that. That's why it's so much more difficult to make than a run-of-the-mill truth potion."

"How does it work?" I bounce my legs, wishing she would stop complimenting her own skills and get to the point.

"*You* drink the potion," she tells me. "Then for a few hours —nine hours, to be exact—anyone who gets into close contact with you will be compelled to truthfully answer every question you ask them."

"I just drink it, and that's it?" I can hear the skepticism in my voice. Her plan sounds simple—almost *too* simple.

"Yep." Teresa nods. "It'll work on anyone—including those with magic. And the closer bond someone already shares with you emotionally, the stronger the effect of the potion will be on them. Which means—"

"It'll definitely work on Zeke," I say.

"*If* he cares about you as much as you believe he does." She shoots me a knowing smile that gives me the feeling she doesn't believe he could truly care about anyone except for himself. "Then yes—it'll affect him stronger than it would have otherwise."

"And afterward?" I ask. "Will he have any idea he was under a spell?"

"Nope," she says. "He'll believe he told you everything willingly. Sure, he might look back and wish he hadn't said anything at all, but he'll blame his actions on an impulsive decision, and nothing more."

I nod, the possibilities of what I can ask him racing through my mind. Because of course I'll ask about the Flaming Sword. That's a no brainer.

But personally, I'm more interested in finding out if Zeke has been honest with me about his feelings, or if he's been lying to me this entire time.

Now I can finally find out the truth once and for all.

CHAPTER FIFTY-ONE

I wait until after dinner to take the potion, since taking it before dinner could result in drama between the other concubines that I have no interest in dealing with. Plus, I don't think it's fair to force people to tell the truth against their will.

I don't feel good about using the potion on Zeke either—despite my initial thought that it'll be encouraging to know if he's being honest about his feelings for me. But Teresa worked so hard on this potion. And even though I know I won't be able to kill Zeke, the least I can do is retrieve the Flaming Sword for Uriel. It won't make up for being unable to complete my mission, but at least it'll be *something*.

And so, once I return to my room, I freshen up and remove the potion from my bag. I swirl the liquid, and it shimmers under the light—magical and mystical.

I can't believe I'm about to ingest a potion created by a witch. But while I *do* feel queasy at the prospect of drinking the shimmering liquid, I grip it tighter, readying myself.

Now is the perfect chance for me to do this. Zeke didn't join us at dinner tonight, and I'm sure he's worried that I've been avoiding him since the night of the cancelled parade. He gave me access to his suite, so I'm sure he'll be pleased by my coming by. Plus, if I take the potion now, it'll have time to wear off before breakfast.

Staring at the potion is only making me anxious, so I uncap and down it before I can think about it further.

The liquid is cold—ice cold—and I shiver as it slides down my throat. The cold is so strong that it *burns*. I curl over the vanity and hold my head in my hands, as if that can stop the pain.

Did Teresa poison me? It feels like it... but no, she wouldn't do that. Because poisoning me would mean poisoning Adriana.

Teresa would never hurt her sister.

I take a few steady breaths, relieved when the cold dissipates. It takes only a few minutes until I feel normal again. I study my reflection in the mirror, glad to see that besides a watery glaze to my eyes, I look the same as before. I blink a few times and wipe away the water, making sure not to mess up my makeup. Much better.

Now, I'm ready to see Zeke.

～

Carlos walks with me for the short distance to Zeke's suite.

"No doorbell?" I ask.

"Ezekiel would never allow anyone to *ring* for him." He laughs. "If Ezekiel wants to see you, he calls for you."

"Right." I take a deep breath, staring at the door. "I suppose that's why he gave me access to his suite."

"Are you going to use it?" Carlos motions toward the lock.

"In a moment," I say. "First, I'm going to knock."

I knock, but there's no reply. So I knock again, louder this time. Nothing.

"I guess he's not here," I say, disappointed. Frustrated, too. Because I *need* to see Zeke within nine hours. Otherwise, Teresa spent all that time creating the potion for nothing.

I have to find him. But first, I should leave a note so he knows I'm looking for him.

"Wait here," I tell Carlos, pressing my finger against the keypad. "I'll be right back."

The door clicks open, and I reach for the handle, letting myself inside. Nothing has changed since the first time I was here—everything is polished and sleek and in its proper place. I search for a pen and paper, but can't find them in the living room. Perhaps I should try the kitchen?

I take a few steps toward the kitchen, and there's a crash from the other direction.

From his bedroom.

It *must* be Zeke—he's the only one besides me who has access to his suite. Maybe he hadn't been able to hear me knock from his bedroom? His suite is huge, so it would make sense.

I hurry toward his door, relieved I won't have to go on a hunt to find him, after all. And I can't wait to speak with him. Because regardless of my hesitation about using the truth potion for personal needs, it'll be incredible to know with certainty that his feelings for me are as true as he claims.

Eager to see him, I open the door, gasping when I find him mid-thrust on top of a naked—and very bruised—Maria.

CHAPTER FIFTY-TWO

※

The door slams against the wall, and he snaps his head up, his eyes meeting mine. He has Maria pinned facedown on the bed, his pants off as he takes her from behind. A lamp is in pieces on the floor. That must have been the crash I heard.

"Adriana," he growls, although he doesn't move away from Maria.

I stare at him, speechless, watching as Maria backs into him and he shudders in what looks to be pleasure.

His eyes turn black, and he reaches for her neck, snapping it in a second. She goes still—a lifeless heap beneath him.

I don't need to see her face to know that she's dead.

He killed her. In the midst of having sex with her.

It's so twisted that I can barely comprehend it happened.

"I should go," I stutter, unsure why I let myself stay for this long. Why did I let myself in at all? It was so, so stupid.

"No." Zeke pulls himself out of Maria's dead body, grabs his pants, and puts them back on. He doesn't bother with his shirt, and I can't stop myself from running my eyes over his sweaty, defined abs. "I gave you access to my suite. I want you here. I want you to stay."

"But..." I stare at Maria's naked body splayed out on his bed.

He raises an eyebrow. "Did you like what you saw?"

My cheeks heat at the memory of him thrusting into her. "You *killed* her," I say, forcing myself to focus.

I want to ask why he was with her at all, but I know the answer. I'm not oblivious to the purpose of his concubines. He has needs, and the concubines fulfill those. He never said he would stop using them for that purpose, and I didn't expect him to stop doing so—especially since I haven't yet had sex with him.

"Why did you kill her?" I ask instead.

"You've been avoiding me since I told you I loved you," he says swiftly. "I figured you wanted nothing to do with me. I didn't expect you to come here. But you did, and you walked in on me with *her*." He glares at Maria, as though she's a piece of vermin instead of a human being he just killed. "I never wanted you to see that. I was angry—no, I was *infuriated*. So the darkness took over. Maria's been there for me to take out my... less-than-angelic aggressions on—but I never wanted you to see us like that. Besides, she's taunted you and the other girls. Because of that, I didn't try to fight the darkness. It was time for her to go."

I step back, surprised by his brutal honesty. But why should I be surprised? Of *course* he's going to be honest. I took that truth potion.

"It's not right," I say, unable to tear my eyes away from her corpse.

"No," he agrees. "But the darkness had to go somewhere. Better her than you."

"What happens if the darkness takes over and I'm the only one around?" I ask.

"I'll fight it." He holds my gaze. "I'll never kill you."

"Why?" I need to hear him say it now—with the truth potion affecting him.

"You know why."

"I do." I nod. "But after what I just walked in on… I want to hear it again."

"Because I love you, Adriana," he says, as natural as ever. "You've stolen my heart, and I could never live with myself if anything bad happened to you. I'll protect you with my life. I swear it. What do I have to do to get you to believe me?"

His words—his undeniably *truthful* words—make me freeze in place. Demons aren't supposed to be capable of love. But maybe that's not true. Perhaps it's a lie we're told to make us see them as monsters—to make us see them as the enemy.

"I have an idea," I say, forcing myself to remember why I'm here in the first place. I *must* find the Flaming Sword before the truth potion stops working. "But first—can you remove Maria's body? I can't focus with a corpse in the room."

"Fair." He raises a hand and lights her body up in flames. All that remains is a pile of ashes on his bed.

"Thank you." I nod, although the ashes aren't much better.

"You still look distressed," he observes.

"Can you blame me?" I ask. "I may not have liked Maria, but she didn't deserve to *die*."

"She was always going to die," he says simply. "I already explained what happens with the darkness—I will not explain again. I can't change what I am. If you can't accept me for my flaws, then I'm going to have to ask you to leave. Go back to your sector, to your home with your family, where you'll be far out of my reach. I'll never stop thinking about you, but at least you'll be safe."

"What if I don't want to go back?" I raise my chin, more determined now than ever to figure out a way to destroy the darkness and free Zeke from its hold. "What if I want to stay?"

"Then you've chosen to love me despite my flaws, and I'll only love you more for it."

I walk to him slowly. Once I reach him, I lay my hands against his chest, stand on my toes, and press my lips to his. He returns the kiss, slowly at first, and then with more passion. Soon, our bodies are pressed so tightly together that it feels like our souls are intertwined. He's saying he loves me with each kiss, with each touch, and I want to stay here like this with him forever.

But I need to figure out where he's hiding the sword. Reluctantly, I pull away, gazing into his eyes as I figure out how to begin.

"Is that all you needed to believe me?" His voice is low and rough. "A kiss?"

"That's how I showed that I see who you are past the darkness, and that I love you and will fight to be with you," I say. "But I do have a question for you."

"You know you can ask me anything," he says.

"It's a silly question, really." I bite my lip, giving a small shrug. "But I've been wondering about it since the day I arrived at the Watchtower."

"Now you have me curious." His gaze is lighter now—almost playful.

"Okay." I take a deep breath, and begin. "As you know, families pass down the story of how you came to power—how you won the Flaming Sword from Uriel and used it to claim this land as your own, becoming king and building a thriving society out of the ruins of what was left of the world after the realms collided," I say, repeating the twisted history story that Teresa told me all families truly *do* tell their children—or at least tell them in public.

"Yes," he says, his eyes gleaming. "I remember that day well. Why do you bring it up now?"

"Because all my life, I've dreamed of seeing the Flaming Sword with my own eyes." I shrug again, as if admitting a silly childhood fantasy. "I know there's an image of it on our coins, but it's not the same as seeing the *real* sword. Don't you agree?"

"The rendition on the coins is perfect," he says. "But yes, it's hardly the same as seeing the real thing."

"Can you show it to me?" I move closer to him, resting my hands on his hips. "The *real* Flaming Sword?"

"I keep the Flaming Sword in a secret place." His eyes dart around the room. "You must understand—the sword is what I used to claim the city, but it's also very dangerous."

"Even to you?" I laugh, as if the thought of anything being dangerous to him is ridiculous. "I thought you were invincible."

"Nearly invincible." He winks. "There's only one thing in the world that can kill me."

"The Flaming Sword?" I part my lips slightly, as if I'm shocked by this news.

I hate deceiving him like this, but it's for his own good. If Teresa can figure out how to use the sword to destroy the darkness in his soul, he'll be free of it forever. And I wish I could be honest with him about the plan, but witches are persecuted here. I can't risk telling him that Teresa's a witch until she knows for sure that she can do this. I can't risk him having her killed.

"Yes." He nods. "Which is why I keep its location hidden. Only a trusted guard member knows where it is."

"Don't you trust me?" I ask.

"You know I do." He growls and kisses me again, tangling his hands in my hair and pulling me closer. "I gave you access to my *suite*," he says. "What more can I do to prove how much I love and trust you?"

I lean back, my lips nearly brushing against his when I look up at him and say, "I want you to show me the sword."

CHAPTER FIFTY-THREE

"Come with me," he says, holding his hand out for me to take.

I take his hand, and he leads me to the wall on the other side of his bedroom. He pushes against the wooden panel, and it moves back and to the side for him.

"A secret passage," I say.

"Yes," he says. "Only three people in the world know it's here—me, my head guard, and now you."

The passage leads to a small, dark room with a circular iron stairway in the center. From up here, the stairs appear to go on forever.

I rest my hands on the railing and peer down. "How far does it go?" I ask.

"To the basement," he says.

"We're going to walk down seventy floors?"

"No." He laughs. "That's just a failsafe plan. We're going to take the elevator."

He presses a button on the opposite wall—an elevator

panel. The elevator doors blend in with the wall, practically unnoticeable.

They open immediately after he presses it.

"After you," he says, motioning for me to go in first.

The inside of the elevator is industrial and bare. I suppose there's no need to decorate it, since Zeke and the head guard are the only ones who use it. There's a keypad and two unmarked buttons inside. Zeke enters a code into the keypad—0129—and a light above it blinks green. Then he presses the lower unmarked button, and the elevator begins to descend.

What's he thinking right now? I look over at him to try to figure it out, but he stares straight at the doors, his expression blank. Does he wonder why he's showing me this? *Would* he be showing me this if it wasn't for the truth potion?

Eventually, the elevator stops moving and the doors open, revealing an ornate room—with the Flaming Sword floating in an orb in the center.

"Wow." I step out of the elevator and onto a plush Turkish rug, staring up at the sword. It's huge—almost as tall as I am—and made of gold so pure that it shines even in this dim lighting. The orb around it pulses with energy so strong that I can see it waver.

Zeke joins me, and I hear the elevator doors close behind us. "Is it all you imagined it would be?" he asks, placing his hands on my shoulders.

"It's more incredible than I believed possible," I say, since it's true. "But what's the orb thing around it?"

"It's a boundary spell," he explains. "To keep the sword contained, I had a witch cast that spell soon after I came to power. After all, I can't risk anyone getting hold of it."

"Because it's the only thing in the world that can kill you," I say.

"Exactly."

We admire the sword for a few minutes in silence. I can't believe I'm here—staring at the ancient sword forged by Uriel himself. The sword he kept by his side during epic battles throughout history.

The sword Ezekiel stole from him.

"What are you thinking about?" Zeke asks. He's so close that I easily lean back into him, and he wraps his arms around me, holding me steady.

"I'm thinking about how lucky I am that you trust me enough to show me the one object in the world that makes you vulnerable," I say. "Thank you, Zeke. Bringing me here means so much to me."

"The Flaming Sword is no longer the only thing in the world that makes me vulnerable," he murmurs in my ear.

"Really?" My heart races at the intensity of his tone. "What else is there?"

"You." He spins me around and his lips are on mine again, kissing me with more passion than ever before. "Marry me, Adriana," he says, looking at me with so much intensity that it's like he's staring into my soul. "Marry me and become my queen."

CHAPTER FIFTY-FOUR

"What?" I pull back, startled at his proposal.

"You heard me." He drops to one knee and takes my hand. "For centuries, I thought I would never find love again. I gave into the darkness that consumes my soul, convinced I was doomed to an existence of being alone. Then you burst into my world and changed everything. You reminded me of a light that I thought I'd lost—you reminded me of what it feels like to love. I've been around for a long time—long enough to know that a love like the one I feel for you is rare. And I don't intend to lose it. You would be doing me the greatest honor, Adriana Medina, if you agreed to be my wife—and my queen."

I'm so shocked I can barely breathe. I feel like a traitor. Because he thinks he's proposing to Adriana Medina—a Gold who auditioned to be his concubine.

He has no idea that he's proposing to me—Rebekah, a messenger angel of Heaven sent to kill him.

He would never love me if he knew who I really am.

"I don't have a ring yet," he continues. "I'm as shocked at this proposal as you are. But it feels right. And I promise to get you the most beautiful ring you can ever imagine. So… do you accept my proposal? Will you do me the honor of becoming my wife?"

"I don't know what to say." My eyes well up with tears—but not with happiness, as one might expect in a moment like this. They're tears of frustration and guilt.

Because I do love him, and I know he loves me.

But the two of us were doomed from the start. Even if I say yes, there's no way this will end well.

"Say yes." His eyes burn with desire. "What's holding you back?"

"It's just…" I search for an explanation—something that will explain my hesitation without giving away the truth. "You're immortal. I'm not. I'm going to grow old and eventually die, while you remain the same. You love me now, but will you still love me thirty years from now, when I look old enough to be your mother? Or your grandmother?"

"Ah," he says, understanding crossing his face. "I see. But this doesn't need to be a problem. We'll find a solution to your mortality, Adriana. I'll search far and wide for a way for you to become immortal. Together, we'll rule this continent as its king and queen. Just say yes. Say yes, and we'll be together forever."

"Yes." The word slips from my mouth without my realizing it. The moment it does, he stands up and pulls me into his arms, spinning me around and kissing me again.

"Say it again," he says, and my heart's fuller than it's ever been.

At the same time, I feel like I'm falling down a roller coaster, and I don't know if I'll ever find my way back up.

What am I doing? I'm going back on everything I was created to be—I'm turning my back on God and Heaven.

But in all my time as an angel, I've never experienced a love like this. If I get cast out of Heaven—if I get turned into a demon like he is—at least Zeke and I will always have each other.

Maybe I wasn't sent here to kill him.

Maybe I was sent here to *love* him.

At the same time, a voice nags at the back of my mind. A voice reminding me that the people here—they're not just his *subjects*. They're his *slaves*. I've been sheltered in the city, and even more so in the Watchtower. I haven't seen the worst of it—the Blues who spend their lives slaving away in labor camps. I hear Teresa's voice as well—telling me that my love for Zeke isn't real. That it's a mirage—a lie—caused by the curse.

I can't risk my entire existence on something that might be a lie. If my feelings are because of the curse, I have to try to pull myself out of it.

Seeing the Blues—seeing the misery inflicted on them by Zeke himself—might be what I need to do that.

"Yes, Zeke," I say, and as much as I know they shouldn't, the words feel *right*. "I love you, and would love nothing more than to become your wife. But first… I do have one condition."

"Condition?" He stills and places me back onto the ground. "What kind of condition?"

"I want you to come with me to my sector," I say. "I want you to meet my parents."

CHAPTER FIFTY-FIVE

The next night, I board a train headed to Sector Six with Zeke, Teresa, and Marco. The train is wildly extravagant, with plush seating, carved wooden tables, and even a crystal chandelier hanging from the ceiling.

I haven't had time to explain to Teresa why this visit is happening, and she keeps looking at me, clearly curious. But there's no opportunity for me to speak with her alone, so I'm just glad she and Marco agreed to come at all.

"How come you're taking the train?" Teresa asks Zeke over dinner—perfectly cooked steak served to us by personal attendants. "Can't you just teleport yourself instantly?"

"I can," he says. "But it makes no sense to teleport when I can enjoy the journey with Adriana."

He watches me closely as he speaks, and I blush under his gaze.

Luckily, the rest of dinner goes smoothly. It isn't long until we've finished dessert.

"It's time to retire to our cabins." Zeke places his napkin on the table and looks at Teresa and Marco. "My personal guard will show the two of you to your room."

Teresa says nothing as she and Marco follow the guard out of the dining car, although she does raise an eyebrow at me in question.

I'm going to have a *lot* to catch her up on the next time we speak alone.

"Finally, it's just the two of us," Zeke says once the others are gone.

"Yes." I smile and take a small sip of what's left of my wine. "Thank you again for agreeing to come to my sector. It means a lot to me."

"No need to thank me," he says. "If it makes you happy, then it makes me happy."

Suddenly, he's out of his seat and kneeling in front of me. He pulls something out of his pocket—a box.

He opens it and reveals the most beautiful diamond ring I've ever seen.

"Do you like it?" he asks, his eyes sparkling as much as the ring.

"Like it?" I gasp. "I *love* it. It's beautiful. It's perfect."

"I'm glad," he says. "I spent all morning looking for it. It seemed rather inappropriate to announce our engagement to your parents without a ring to show for it." He lifts the ring out of the box, takes my hand in his, and slips it slowly onto my finger.

"It fits perfectly," I say, admiring it under the light. "But won't it ruin the surprise if I show up wearing this tomorrow morning?"

"I had a chain made up for you as well," he says, pulling it out of his pocket. "So that you can wear the ring around your neck until we make the announcement to your parents." He slips the ring off my finger, threads it through the chain, and then steps behind me, fastening it around my neck.

I place it under my shirt—hiding it from public eyes and moving it closer to my heart. The diamond pulses against my skin, full of a life of its own.

"I had a separate sleeping car prepared for you." He moves around me and pulls me to my feet, his tone shifting from loving to more serious. "But if you prefer to stay with me… my door is always open."

My heart races with the prospect of spending the night with Zeke. I *want* to be with him—now more than ever.

But do I truly want to be with him, or is it the curse talking?

I fear that if I spend the night with him, the line between the two will blur and it'll be impossible for me to ever find out. I also can't do that to Adriana. This is her body, and using it in that way without her consent would be immoral.

However, that's a problem to worry about another day. I just pray that once the truth is revealed, Zeke will accept me for who I am, just as I've done for him. Somehow, we'll find a way to be together.

"I want our wedding night to be special—I want our first time together to be on *that* night," I say instead. "If we stay together tonight… I'm not sure if I'll be able to wait."

"Would that be such a terrible thing?" He smirks devilishly.

I freeze, unsure what to say. Because no—when I imagine losing my virginity to Zeke, "bad" is not a word that springs to mind. He loves me, and I love him—being with him will be one of the most incredible experiences of my life.

So incredible that I'll forget about fighting the curse, and will happily allow myself to be cast out of Heaven so I can be with him forever—two immortal demons, ruling this continent side by side.

But I *must* fight the curse.

I need a reminder of the purpose of my mission—I need to see the Blue slave workers. I need to remind myself of the devastation Zeke causes to most people on this continent every day.

I need to remind myself who I am, and why I was sent to kill him.

"I'm sorry," he says, and he sucks in a deep breath as he pulls away from me. "I shouldn't pressure you. You've agreed to become my wife—my queen—but you have to understand that I want you so badly that it's driving me crazy."

"As I do you," I say, the energy between us so strong that the air crackles with it.

"Then why not give in?" His lips are so close to mine that I can practically taste him, and he runs a finger down my arm, sending fiery electric shocks through my body. "Why resist?"

"Because the first time we're together, I want it to be as your wife," I say, using every ounce of control to not give in and kiss him. "As your *queen*."

"Very well." He backs away, teasing me with every step. "If that's what you want, then that's what will be. I'll have my guard escort you to your chamber. But remember—my door is always open."

As if I could ever forget.

CHAPTER FIFTY-SIX

We arrive at Sector Six early the next morning. Three people I recognize from the photos in Teresa's house—Adriana's father, mother, and younger brother—wait for us at the quiet train station. I would have known who they were even without the photos, since they resemble Adriana and Teresa, and they're the only Golds here.

They're polite, but distant at the same time. I wonder if they're always like this, or if they're acting this way because Zeke is here. Either way, it's easy to keep up with the simple chitchat. They continuously glance at Zeke as they lead us to the car—a stretch limo that easily fits all of us—but he barely says a word to them, instead allowing them to catch us up on everything going on in town.

If they're scared for Adriana—if they don't approve of her becoming a concubine—they don't let their feelings show.

Adriana's mom—Silvia—is a chatterbox, and the conversation flows between the members of the Medina family. If they notice anything amiss about me—anything that would make them think I'm *me* and not their daughter—they say nothing. They likely think that any changes in Adriana's personality are because of the time she's spent in the city and the Watchtower —not because she's possessed by a messenger angel who was sent to save the continent from the curse placed upon it.

The drive is pleasant—we don't pass anything that resembles a labor camp. Or perhaps the labor camps are far from the road, so the Golds don't have to see any evidence of the Blues slaving away so they can live in luxury.

"I would like to request a private dinner at your home with the seven of us tonight," Zeke says as we near the village. "I have something important to discuss with the two of you." He looks at Adriana's parents when he says that last part.

"Of course." Silvia sits straighter—if she's surprised by his request, she doesn't let on. "The moment we're back, I'll tell the servants to start preparing a feast at once."

"Perfect." Zeke shoots his perfect smile at her. "I'm looking forward to it."

"Not nearly as much as we are," Adriana's father, Manuel, says. "We're honored to have you at our home. If there's anything you need, please let us know."

Zeke gives a single nod, and returns to staring out the window. His hand hovers close to mine—not quite touching it, but close enough that I can feel the heat of it on my skin. He keeps it there for the entire ride.

Finally, we pass through the wrought-iron gates of the Golden Village and enter the walled town built specifically for the Golds who oversee the sector. The stoic brick buildings remind me of prairie towns in the old west—except that these buildings all have solar panels on the roof, shining as they reflect the sun.

People mill around the town square, going into shops,

restaurants, bars, and more—mostly Golds, with a few other colors mixed in. But our limo doesn't stop at any of those places. We continue down the road, and the shops are replaced with houses. The farther we go, the larger the houses, until we reach the one on the end—the biggest one on the street. It has a circular drive, and we pull up into it until we're right in front of the door.

This must be Adriana's house.

Sure enough, the driver gets out of the car and walks around to our door, opening it and motioning for us to exit.

"Teresa and Adriana, your rooms are ready for your arrival," Silvia says, ushering us into the house. "Ezekiel, will you be staying overnight, or teleporting back and forth from the Watchtower?"

"I'll stay overnight," he says, glancing over at me as he says it. I can tell from the challenge in his eyes that he's sleeping near me on purpose—he wants to tempt me into staying the night with him.

I refuse to give in.

"Very well," Silvia says. "I'll have a servant prepare the guest bedroom. Now, if you'll excuse me, I have a feast to arrange. In the meantime, please make yourselves at home."

She hurries inside, leaving the rest of us to follow.

CHAPTER FIFTY-SEVEN

Teresa and I show Zeke around the house—well, *Teresa* shows him around, and I pretend I know where everything is. Luckily, the layout is simple and utilitarian, and I make sure to memorize the location of each room during the tour.

After all, getting lost in the house that I supposedly grew up in would definitely seem suspicious.

After the tour, Marco goes to Teresa's room to take a nap—apparently, he had trouble sleeping on the train—and the rest of us go down to the library to figure out what to do with the rest of the afternoon. Adriana's father went into work to finish up some stuff for the day, her mother was busy deciding on the menu for tonight, and her brother was in a private tutoring session (being taught how to eventually take over the business from her father), so it's only the three of us.

"We could go into town," Teresa suggests, but then she looks at me, worry passing over her eyes. "But you might run into your friends, and I'm sure they'll annoy you with questions about life in the Watchtower."

While she doesn't say it, I understand what she means—I should avoid Adriana's friends, lest they realize there's something "off" about her.

I know what I want to do with the spare few hours before we have to get ready for dinner—I want to visit the labor camps. But I don't know where they are. Surely, they're not walking distance. I suppose I'll have to take a car. And I'll need a driver, since I won't know where to go.

There's only one way for me to do this—I need to figure out a reason why Adriana would want to see the labor camps. A reason that doesn't raise suspicion.

"I know what I want to do," I say, the perfect reason popping into my mind. "Teresa—would you mind letting me speak to Zeke for a few minutes? Alone?"

"Of course." She marches out and slams the door shut.

I turn to Zeke. The moment I do, he pulls me into his arms and kisses me—long and hard. I wrap my arms around his neck, kissing him back with just as much passion. It's so easy to get lost in his touch.

But I have to focus, so I force myself to pull away.

"What?" He smirks. "Isn't that why you wanted to speak with me alone? Because I don't know about you, but going so long in front of your parents without touching you... it was driving me crazy."

"It was driving me crazy, too." I reach for the chain of my necklace and fiddle with it, the diamond ring hidden beneath my shirt tapping against my chest. "But... there *is* another reason I want to speak with you."

"You're nervous," he observes. "What's going on?"

"Nothing bad," I assure him. "It's just that this request might seem strange to you, but it's important to me, so I hope you hear me out and consider it."

"When have I ever not considered one of your requests?" he says. "You have more power over me than you know. Go ahead, Adriana. If there's something you want, I'll make sure you get it."

"Okay." I take a deep breath and swallow. "Since I'm going to become queen of the continent, I think it's important that I see how *all* the citizens here live. As we were driving to my home, I realized something that distresses me—most of the citizens of the continent are Blues, but I've never once seen where they live. In fact, I don't think I've ever actually *seen* a Blue at all!"

"There's a good reason for that," Zeke says, his eyes darkening. "Someone as pure and wonderful as you shouldn't be around creatures as tainted as them."

"I plan on taking my duty as queen seriously." I hold my gaze with his, making it clear that I won't budge on this issue. "They're more than 'creatures.' They're *people*. They're my future subjects. If I'm to become queen, I must see them. I insist."

"Fine." He runs a hand through his hair and sighs. "Would you like one of them brought here for you to meet?"

"No." I take his hands in mine and squeeze them, bracing him for what I'm going to say next. "I want to see what their living conditions are like. I want to go to a labor camp."

CHAPTER FIFTY-EIGHT

❦

*T*eresa is reading outside, and we pass by her on the way to the car. Not the limo—Adriana's father rented that specifically to pick us up from the train station—but to their family car. One of Zeke's hands holds mine, and the other holds the keys, since he insisted upon driving us to the labor camp himself.

"Where are you going?" Teresa gazes at us suspiciously as we pass, closing her book.

"You wouldn't believe it if we told you," Zeke says, swinging the keys around his fingers.

"Try me," she says. "I've forgotten how boring it gets out here in the country. If you're going to town, I'll definitely hitch a ride." She looks at Zeke again, as if reminding herself who she's speaking to, and adds, "If that's okay with you, of course."

"If you must know, we're visiting a labor camp," I say, since knowing Teresa, she'll force it out of me eventually. "It's hard right now to explain why, but you'll understand tomorrow."

After Zeke and I announce our engagement.

"A labor camp?" Her eyes bulge. "Why?"

"It'll all make sense tomorrow," I repeat. "For now, the best way to explain is that I worry that life in the city has gotten to my head. I've gotten so wrapped up in the excitement and the luxury of life in the Watchtower that I fear I'm losing touch with the person I once was. And on our drive here, I realized I've never seen a labor camp—or a Blue at all. It doesn't feel right."

She scrunches her forehead. "You *have* changed a lot in the past few weeks," she finally says. "You think that visiting a labor camp will remind you more about where you came from?"

I can tell she chose her words carefully—even though we can't speak freely in front of Zeke, she *must* understand that I believe this might be the key to reminding myself about my mission, and possibly breaking through the curse to discover if my love for Zeke is true, or if it's caused by greed like she believes.

"Yes," I confirm. "But we don't have much time, so we should get going."

"Without me?" She drops her book on the step next to her and stands up. "No way. Now that you mention it, I've never seen a Blue either. So if you're doing something crazy like visiting a labor camp, then you can bet I'm coming with you."

She struts to the car and lets herself into the backseat, not allowing us to protest.

CHAPTER FIFTY-NINE

The drive to the nearest labor camp is about a half hour away, and it takes us up into the mountains—which makes sense, since Sector Six specializes in precious metal mining. We pass many people hauling carts along the street on the way there—all of them Reds, since Blues aren't allowed to leave the camps. Zeke informs us that they're taking the mined metals to the train station.

Soon, we arrive at a tall, chain-link fence that expands from one mountain to another. There are a few boxy brick buildings along the perimeter. They have solar panels, so I assume they're for the Golds who guard the camp. In front of the gate are two Gold guards, standing at attention with what looks like automated rifles.

Zeke pulls up to the gate, rolls down his window, and takes off his sunglasses. The guard on his side gapes at the sight of him, but quickly becomes serious again.

"King Ezekiel," he says, his voice shaking slightly. "To what do we owe this honor?"

"Nothing for you to worry about," Zeke says casually. "Just a little sightseeing."

"To a labor camp?" The guard shifts his feet and adjusts his gun.

"Yes," Zeke says. "We don't have all day—let us in."

"Of course." The guard nods, walks over to the gate, and opens it.

Zeke drives through, and I turn around to see the guards closing the gate behind us. We pass the boxy brick buildings, and drive by long log buildings with roofs that are sinking in.

A few people mill about, carrying pails and buckets. They're pale and thin, with hollow cheeks and blue tattoos around their wrists. Their clothes are rags, barely substantial enough to keep them warm in the cool November air. They're covered in dust and dirt, as if they haven't had a shower in weeks.

For the most part, they ignore us, except for one person who turns to look at us—a young boy with circles under his sad, hopeless eyes.

My heart breaks for these poor people. "Are they ever able to leave the camp?" I ask, dreading the answer I know will come.

"No." Zeke doesn't look at me as he speaks. "They're born here, and they die here. They don't know that another type of life exists. They can't miss something they never had."

"I don't believe that," I say. "They see the guards—how they dress and how they live. They *must* know that there's a better life out there somewhere."

"That better life isn't for them." Zeke turns to look at me, his eyes full of passion. "It's for us. We can't live the way we do without people living the way *they* do. That's the way society works."

I say nothing—afraid anything else will raise suspicion. Part of the curse is that the Golds turn their heads from the Blues who slave away their entire lives to provide resources for the continent. They know that acknowledging the *wrongness* of this system and trying to fix it will take away their status in society.

They don't want to overturn the caste system because then they would lose their place as Golds.

But I know better—I know that society doesn't have to function like this. Before the dimensions collided and destroyed the world, many countries had abolished slavery and created governments that provided opportunities for every citizen. Sure, those countries weren't perfect, but they were far better than this.

However, I can't say any of this, since Adriana wouldn't know about the history of the world before the collision.

Teresa's been quiet this whole time, so I glance back at her to make sure she hasn't fallen asleep. She's awake and alert, and she raises her eyebrow, giving me the feeling that I'm going to have a *lot* of questions to answer the next time the two of us are alone.

"Are you ready to leave?" Zeke asks, interrupting my thoughts.

I turn to look at him—he's wearing the same leather jacket that he wore the first night we met, and he watches me closely, his eyes full of love.

If it comes to it, can I kill this man to save this continent?

No, I can't. I want to help the Blues—and everyone else trapped in a low caste—but I love Zeke. Perhaps I can use my position as queen to help these people and make positive changes throughout the continent.

But maybe I simply haven't seen enough to break through the curse yet.

"I hear talking," I say instead, perking up at the warm scent of what smells like a cookout. "Let's keep going to see what they're doing."

"As you wish," Zeke says, and he heads down the road toward the chatter.

We continue around a corner, and I see a campfire being tended to in the center of a clearing. Lines of meat hang from sticks above the fire.

I'm relieved to see that at least the Blues are fed.

But the relief doesn't last long, because I see a young girl near the car who's huddled on the ground in tears. She rocks back and forth, alone, with no one to comfort her.

"Stop the car," I say, and Zeke does as I asked. Once we've stopped, I open the door and rush out to the girl, pulling my sleeves down to cover up my tattoos.

"Adriana!" Teresa calls, but I'm already beside the girl, kneeling to help her.

Teresa follows me, her brow furrowed in concern. "Come back to the car," she begs. "Please."

I ignore her and focus on the girl. "Hi," I say cautiously, and she looks up at me, her eyes pained and confused. "Why are you crying?"

"My mom." She reaches forward, pointing toward the fire.

"She's helping with the cooking?" I ask.

"No." She shakes her head, her hands tucked in her jacket as she rocks back and forth. "She broke her leg. The men with the gold tattoos said she was useless. They…" She glances at Teresa's wrists, her eyes hardening at the gold tattoos around them. "They shot her. And now they're *cooking* her."

"That meat…" I look back at the meat roasting over the fire, horror washing over me. "That's not... it isn't your mom —is it?"

"It is." She takes her hands out of her jacket, the flash of the knife a blur as she thrusts it forward and stabs Teresa in the neck.

CHAPTER SIXTY

"No!" I push the girl away from Teresa and wrestle the knife from her hand.

Suddenly Zeke's there, and he pulls the girl off me, throwing her onto the ground.

His eyes darken, and she goes up in flames before she even hits the dirt.

But I can't think about her right now. Because Teresa—the first person I trusted after arriving to this continent, who's helped me and treated me like a sister even though my presence puts her true sister in danger every day—is laying on the ground beside me, blood flowing from the wound and drenching the ground around her.

I reach for her and roll her over, knowing before seeing her glazed eyes that she's dead.

I do the first thing that comes to mind—I try to access my powers to revive her. Angels aren't supposed to bring people back to life unless God instructs us to do so, but I don't care—Teresa doesn't deserve to die. She deserves to finish helping me break this curse—to live in a city where people don't want to kill her simply because she's a witch.

How am I supposed to continue this mission without her?

But I can't heal her, because while in Adriana's body, I have no access to my angelic powers. I try to exit her body—to take my own form so I can use my magic—but it doesn't work.

Of *course* it doesn't work. I'm stuck in her body until I complete my mission.

So I curl over Teresa and cry, feeling more helpless than ever. It's my fault she died. I'm the one who insisted on coming here—she never would have been here today if it wasn't for me.

But Zeke... he's a demon. A *fallen angel*. He can save Teresa. I've never heard of a demon reviving a human without incentive—some sort of deal—but he *has* the ability to do it. I know he does.

"Bring her back," I beg him, tears streaming down my face. "*Please.*"

"I can't do that." He shakes his head sadly. "I'm a killer. Not a healer."

"That's not true," I say. "You're an angel. A *fallen* angel, but still an angel. You have the power to do this. I know you do."

He stares down at me, his eyes twisting with so many emotions—as if he's fighting within himself to figure out what to do.

"Please," I repeat. "If you love me as much as you say you do, please do this for me."

He kneels beside Teresa and places his hands upon her forehead, closing his eyes in concentration. The wound knits itself together in seconds, color returning to her cheeks. Then a beam of sunlight shines down on her from behind the clouds, and suddenly, her eyes snap open.

"Teresa!" I pull her into a hug, making sure she's real. "You're okay."

"Yeah." She sounds woozy, and she pulls away from me, touching the place where the knife had entered her neck. "What happened?"

"It's a long story," I say. "But Zeke... he saved you." I turn to Zeke, looking at him in admiration. "Thank you," I tell him.

"I've never revived someone without a deal being made," he says, and my heart plummets.

Of course he expects a deal. He might love me, but he's still a demon. Demons don't do anything for free.

"Make the deal with me," I insist. "Not Teresa. It's only fair, since I'm the one who asked you to revive her."

"No." He shakes his head. "I brought her back for you, and I don't want there to be any deals between us. It'll tarnish what we have. I love you, Adriana, and I don't want to think that you might be with me because you owe me, and not because you love me."

"She killed me?" Teresa looks for the girl, but can't find her. So she looks back up at Zeke, question in her eyes. "And you saved me?"

"Yes," I say. "He saved you."

"Thank you." Teresa lowers her eyes, touching the place where the wound had been again. "I don't know how I can ever repay you."

"I'm going to tell your parents tonight that I've proposed to Adriana," he says suddenly. "The only repayment I need is for you to support our union—and to make sure your parents support it, too."

Her eyes go wide as she takes in what he said. That we're *engaged*.

"I'm sure they will," she says slowly.

"To my face, yes," he says. "They wouldn't oppose me—the king of the continent. But parents worry about their children, and I wouldn't blame them for being worried about their youngest daughter marrying a demon. I'm sure they're worried about her enough as it is, and are hoping for her to make it through the year unharmed so she can finally be safe. I want you to take my saving you today as a promise—a promise that I love your sister and will never let any harm come to her, no matter what. And I want you to make sure your parents understand that, so they don't spend the rest of their lives worrying about her. Can you do that for me?"

"Yes." Teresa nods, looking back and forth between the two of us. "I can do that. I promise."

CHAPTER SIXTY-ONE

I toss and turn in my bed that night, unable to fall asleep. I keep thinking about everything that happened today—Zeke saving Teresa's life at the labor camp, and then dinner when he told my parents—*Adriana's* parents—that we're engaged.

As anticipated, her parents took it in stride. What choice did they have? They know that if they speak against Zeke they'll risk being killed. And as promised, Teresa gushed about how perfect Zeke and I are together.

I didn't realize before now that she's a fabulous actress.

Or maybe her opinion about Zeke changed after he brought her back to life this afternoon.

That *must* be it. Because if so, she'll be even more determined to figure out a way to break the curse without having to kill him. And she *needs* to be able to do that. Because after today, I know more than ever that my love for Zeke is real. I can't kill him. I *do* want to break the curse—even more so after seeing the horrors at the labor camp today—but I'll be cast out of Heaven before ever harming Zeke.

I still don't know why God chose me of all the messenger angels for this task. But if this is some twisted test to see if I'm capable of casting my feelings aside for the good of the majority, then I suppose I'll fail.

If love is my weakness, then so be it. I would rather fall from Heaven a million times than kill the man I love. If I lose him, especially by my own hand, my soul will surely die as well.

Thinking of Zeke reminds me how close he is—he's in the bedroom next to mine. After he saved Teresa today and asked for nothing in return, I feel closer to him than ever before. And the distance between us right now—the physical distance—is killing me.

So I leave my room and tiptoe down the hall. Like he promised on the train, his door is open. Only a crack, but it's still open.

I peek inside, not wanting to wake him if he's sleeping. But his eyes open, as if he's attuned to my presence.

"Julia," he says, his voice thick from sleep. "You're here."

Hearing that name again—*Julia*—feels like a punch in the gut.

I walk slowly toward him and sit down next to him on the bed. "Not Julia," I say, taking his hand in mine. "It's me. Adriana."

But as I say it, I'm reminded that it's a lie. Because I'm not Adriana. I'm Rebekah.

How will I ever be honest with him about my betrayal? I'll have to tell him eventually, but I'm scared.

Will he love me once he learns the truth?

"Of course it is," he says with a lazy smile, pulling me down to lay with him. "I wouldn't want it to be anyone else."

I snuggle up against him, saying nothing for a few seconds. But I can't keep it inside—I need to know the answer to the question haunting my mind.

"Who's Julia?" I ask him, slowly and cautiously. "You said her name the first time we met—you thought I *was* her. And you just said it again. I love you, and I know you love me—I'll never doubt that. But clearly this Julia is important to you, too. Please tell me—who is she?"

"*Was*," he says after a few seconds, taking my hand in his. "Who *was* she. Because Julia is gone—she's been gone for a long, long time."

"How long?" I ask.

"Longer than you could ever imagine," he says. "Because you're right that she was important to me. She's the reason I fell from Heaven."

CHAPTER SIXTY-TWO

"A human?" I ask. "You fell from Heaven for a human?"

"Not just any human," he replies. "My first love."

"Oh." My heart pangs at the thought of Zeke in love with someone else. The sadness must reflect on my face, because he cocks his head, looking amused.

"I was created in the time before Christ," he says. "In all that time, you didn't think I'd ever loved?"

"You're a demon," I say simply. "Until now... I didn't think demons were capable of love at all."

"We're not supposed to be," he says. "Most are not. You see, once we fall, the darkness takes over our souls, destroying any parts that were ever capable of love."

"But you love me." I say it as a statement, not a question.

"Yes," he says. "You see—you look practically identical to Julia. The first time I saw you, I thought you *were* her. In that moment, the hope that she was alive sliced through the darkness, allowing me to *feel* again. Allowing me to love again."

"But I'm not her." I lower my eyes so he won't see the disappointment surely shining within them.

"I know that now," he says. "But I didn't then." He places his thumb under my chin, forcing me to meet his gaze. "I've never told anyone about Julia. You'll be the first. If you want to hear it, of course."

"I do," I say. "Of course I do."

"Good," he says, and then he begins, "I was sent to Rome in the year 129 AD on a mission to convert the citizens to Christianity. The religion was just beginning to form, and it needed the support of angels to help people see the light. During my mission, I met a woman—Julia. She and her family weren't Christian, but she had a curious mind and was interested in learning. We spent a lot of time together, and it wasn't long before we fell in love. I eventually told her what I was, and she believed I was her guardian angel sent to save her from the future her family had in store for her. You see, she was from a noble Roman family, and was about to be forced into an arranged marriage with an older, abusive man. She was trapped and miserable—she said the only time she felt alive was when she was with me."

"But angels aren't allowed to fall in love with humans," I say quickly, not realizing until afterward that Adriana might not know that.

If Zeke notices my slip-up, he doesn't let on. "They're not," he agrees. "However, it isn't unheard of for angels to have relations with humans during their times on Earth. Angels love God and all of Gods creations. Humans are one of Gods creations, so it's natural for us to love humans as well. I'd seen it done by my angelic brothers and sisters many times before, so I thought nothing would come of it. But marrying a human… that's another story entirely."

"You married Julia?" I ask.

"Yes," he says. "It was the only way to keep her from a life of misery with that awful man. He would never marry her if she'd been married before. He would see her as *tainted*." He says the word with disgust. "We married in secret, and we planned to run away to the countryside to live the rest of our lives together in peace and happiness."

"She didn't mind that she would grow old while you would remain immortal?" I ask.

"I was going to search to the end of the world for a way to make her immortal," he says. "The same way I will for you."

"But you didn't have a chance," I realize from the way he said it. "What happened?"

"Our marriage was conducted in the traditional Roman manner—it wasn't a Christian wedding," he says. "I thought that would be enough to keep it concealed from Heaven. But it wasn't. The next morning, angels pounded down our doors to force me to face my fate—but first, they killed Julia in front of me."

"Why?" I gasp. "She did nothing wrong."

"Angels aren't as perfect as most want to believe," he says. "They killed her to prevent the conception of a Nephilim child—half-human, half-angel. Immediately after seeing her killed, I was cast out of Heaven and locked away in the demon dimension, where Mammon—one of the seven fallen archangels who rules over Hell—took me under his wing."

"And you stayed there for thousands of years," I realize. "Until the dimensions collided half a century ago."

"Yes." He nods. "During my time in Hell, I grew to resent humans. I blamed the entire race for tempting me to fall in love with Julia and cursing me to life as a demon. Her death was my fault. If I hadn't been so blinded by my love for her, she would have gotten to live a long life. But I wanted her love more than I'd ever wanted anything, and I went to Hell for it. I was doomed to always want that which I couldn't have. And so, after the dimensions collided and I won over this continent, I used Uriel's Flaming Sword to curse the continent with greed, so that everyone living here would be consumed with the same insatiable need that tortured me every day. I was filled with rage—with the darkness—and I thought since I was miserable, *everyone* should be miserable."

His eyes flicker with anger—a trace of what he must have felt all those decades ago when he cast the curse upon the continent. "Do you still feel that same way?" I ask.

"No," he says. "Not since you came into my life."

"Then end the curse," I say. "You cast it—can't you end it?"

"It doesn't work like that," he says. "A curse that strong is bound to my soul. It's irreversible."

Unless he's killed, I think, although I don't say it out loud.

Instead, I remember what Teresa told me the other day—that she thinks she can end the curse without killing Zeke. I want to tell him, but I can't. Not without telling him that Teresa's a witch. And I won't break Teresa's trust like that. Her being a witch is her secret to tell—not mine.

"What if there's another way to break the curse?" I ask instead. "There are rumors of witches who practice magic in secret. What if they can help you?"

"What do you know of such witches?" He jerks his head toward me, suspicion in his gaze.

"Nothing." I reach for his hand, hoping he believes me. I *need* to get him to believe me, for Teresa's safety. "But everyone has heard the rumors. And as king, surely if you ask for their help, they'll come forth."

"I'll do no such thing," he says sharply. "Any witches who

still live on the continent don't want to help me—they want to *kill* me. If their numbers are high enough, they have the ability to do so. It's why all known witches must be killed immediately."

I bite my lip, troubled with where this conversation might go. I'll never forgive myself if I put Teresa and Marco in danger.

"You look worried." He takes my hand again, his voice softer. "What's wrong?"

I can't share my actual thoughts, so I settle on something else that's troubling me. "You noticed me because I look like Julia," I say, swallowing down the lump in my throat. "But that's not why you fell in love with me, right? Because I'm not Julia. I never have been, and I never will be."

"I know that." He chuckles. "You have more fire in you than Julia ever did. The way you risked your own life to save your friend on the Day of the Dead—Julia never had that kind of courage. That's the day I realized I was in love with you. You —*Adriana*—not Julia. The hope that you were Julia was the push I needed to break through the darkness, but it was your love—your light—that captured my heart. With you by my side as my queen, we'll lead the continent into a Golden Age of prosperity and happiness. Together forever."

I lean forward and kiss him, because there's nothing I want more than to marry Zeke and be his queen.

I'm still terrified of what it means for me as an angel. But Zeke was brave enough to fall from Heaven for love, so I need to be that brave, too. He was able to fight the darkness and love again. Surely the love we share will pull me through the darkness as well.

It *has* to. Because I can't rule beside him as an angel.

But I can as a demon.

CHAPTER SIXTY-THREE

We announce our engagement on air the day after returning from the sector. The other concubines have been sent home, and there have been non-stop parties in the street since. But most of my focus has been on planning the engagement party. It's going to be the most extravagant party the continent has ever seen—which will only be topped by the wedding itself.

However, I keep thinking about what I'm giving up by committing myself to this marriage. I've been an angel for my entire existence—it's all I've ever known. I want to give it up for love—like Zeke did—but I'm scared.

Scared of the darkness I'll have to fight every day if I fall from Heaven.

My only hope is that Teresa will be able end the curse without killing Zeke. If so, perhaps I can make a plea to God. I can ask him to forgive Zeke—to welcome him back to Heaven. God is loving and forgiving. After all Zeke has struggled with throughout the years, he deserves a second chance.

One week after announcing the engagement, Teresa comes to my suite unannounced. She shuts the door behind her and mutters the sound-barrier spell.

I hurry toward her, hope welling in my soul. "What did you find?" I ask. "Please tell me it's good."

"It's good," she says, her eyes shining with happiness. "It's more than good. It's *great*."

"You figured out how to stop the curse without killing Zeke?"

"I did." She nods. "I've spoken with many witches in the city, and we figured out an alternative solution. You see—from the story you told me, Ezekiel used the Flaming Sword to cast the curse, correct?"

"Yes." I nod. "That's correct."

"That makes the *sword* a key to undoing the curse," she says, speaking faster. "Both Ezekiel and the sword are tied to the curse. Yes, killing Ezekiel will break the curse, but there's also a ritual—albeit, a complicated one—that can be done with the sword to break the curse as well."

"That's perfect." I smile, peace settling over me at the realization that I can truly complete my mission *and* keep Zeke alive.

"It is," she agrees. "Stealing the Flaming Sword isn't going to be easy, but with enough of us helping, we can pull it off. I have faith in us."

"Steal?" I balk. "Why do we have to steal it? If I tell Zeke that we've figured out a way to break the curse, he'll give the sword to us so we can do so."

"No," Teresa says quickly. "You cannot tell Zeke. Whatever happens, say nothing to him. He can't know anything about this."

"Why?" I ask. "He can help us. After what he did for you in

the labor camp—when he saved your life—I thought you trusted him."

"I do," she says, lowering her eyes. "But he can't know about this. The ritual for breaking the curse will take days. And it'll only work if he doesn't suspect it's coming."

"That doesn't make sense," I say. "I would think it would work *better* if he can help."

"The ways of our spells are complicated," Teresa says gently, placing her hand on mine. "But you believe that I want this curse broken as much as you do, right?"

"Yes," I say, since along with wanting to break the curse, Teresa also wants to get her sister back. She has just as much—possibly even more—desire for this to work than I do.

"Good," she says. "Then please trust me on this. If Zeke expects it's coming, he might put his guard up, which will mess up everything since his spirit is connected to the sword through the curse."

"This ritual you need to do with the sword won't hurt him, will it?" I ask.

"Only a bit." She bites her lip, not meeting my eyes. Then she refocuses on me, more determined than ever. "But he'll survive. Which is better than the alternative way of breaking the curse, don't you agree?"

"Of course."

"So," she says. "Will you help us steal the Flaming Sword?"

"I will," I tell her, and I touch the diamond ring around my finger, smiling. I'm the luckiest person alive for being given this chance to end the curse without killing Zeke. I hate not being able to be honest with him, but once he learns what I did for him—for our love—I know he'll understand. "Just tell me what you need me to do."

From there, she tells me her plan.

CHAPTER SIXTY-FOUR

The engagement party is more incredible than I imagined it could be. Everyone brings out their fanciest, most colorful ball gowns and tuxes, and the ballroom is alive with music and laughter. There's an orchestra, dancing, a nine-course meal, and of course, lots of drinking. No glass becomes less than half full before getting filled back up again.

But my stomach is swirling in anxiety, because tonight is the night I'll be helping the witches steal the Flaming Sword. To do that, I must keep a clear head, so I have to drink the least amount as possible.

"Do you not enjoy your drink?" Zeke asks during the second course, glancing at my untouched glass. "Or the champagne earlier? You barely had more than a sip."

We have an elevated table to ourselves, looking over everyone in attendance. The meal includes a fresh drink with each course—paired to complement the food—so I expected he would notice my not touching my drinks. And I've already come up with a reason why that is.

"The wine is delicious," I say to him with a smile. "But tonight is one of the most incredible nights of my life, and I want to remember every second of it."

He kisses me in response, and the entire ballroom erupts in applause.

By the ninth course, I'm so stuffed that I can barely have a slice of the engagement cake. Looking around at everyone else at the party, and judging from the loud chatter, increased laughter, and red faces, they've all been enjoying their full glasses of wine with each course. The only people who still appear sober are Teresa, Marco, and Gloria—the three witches who will be assisting me in stealing the sword.

Once everyone finishes eating, they stumble to the dance floor to continue the celebration. The dancing is wilder than it was at the beginning of the night, and far less graceful.

"Dance with me?" Zeke asks, holding out a hand to help me up.

"Of course," I say with a smile. "But first, let me run to the restroom. Once I return, we can dance all night."

He nods, and I hurry out of the ballroom, passing the crowded ladies' room nearby and continuing to a lesser-used one farther down the hall. As always, Carlos escorts me and waits outside the door. There's only one other person inside— an older Gold lady who congratulates me on my engagement.

It isn't long before Teresa and Gloria join me inside. We wait for the Gold lady to leave, and then I lock the door as Teresa speaks the soundproof spell.

"Do you have it?" I ask her.

"Of course." Teresa holds up a vial of foggy green liquid. "I just need the final ingredient." She reaches into her purse, pulls out a sewing needle, and hands it to me.

"Can you prick me?" I ask. "I'm not good with blood."

"It has to be you," Gloria insists. "The blood must be given from your own free will. You need to be the one to prick your finger."

"Fine." I huff and take the needle. It gleams silver between my fingers, and I stare at it, as if preparing for battle.

"It'll be easiest it you do it quickly to get it over with," Teresa says.

"Okay." Without allowing myself a second thought, I prick the needle into the pad of my index finger, and a drop of blood pops out.

Teresa uncaps the vial and holds it out to me. "Squeeze the blood into the vial," she instructs.

I do as she says, and the moment the blood falls inside, the liquid transforms into a royal purple.

"Perfect." Teresa stares at the vial, her eyes gleaming in excitement, and holds it out to Gloria. "Your turn," she says, and Gloria takes the vial, swallowing it down in a single gulp.

CHAPTER SIXTY-FIVE

Seconds later, I'm staring at a spitting image of myself. Not my actual self—what I look like when I'm in my angel form—but Adriana. Everything is exact, down to the white dress I'm wearing to the engagement ring around my finger.

But it's not real. It's an illusion.

The person I'm looking at is actually Gloria.

"Are you sure you can do this?" I ask her. "Zeke's extremely perceptive. What if he realizes you're not actually me?"

"I was Zeke's favorite for the year that I was one of his concubines," she reminds me, her voice light and musical. Is that how I sound when I speak as Adriana? "I can handle keeping him happy until you return. And I look exactly like you—he has no reason to doubt that I'm not you. I have this under control. I promise."

"Okay," I say, trying to fight down the worry in my stomach. "But let's do this as quickly as possible. The less time you have to pretend you're me, the less chance we have of getting caught."

"It'll be no longer than three hours," Teresa says, turning to Gloria. "That's how long you have until the spell runs out and you transform back into yourself."

"I know." Gloria rolls her eyes. "I may look eighteen right now, but don't forget that I'm the oldest one in this room."

I clear my throat, and they both look at me. "I think I have a few centuries on you," I say, smiling so she knows I'm not truly offended.

"Flittering around in Heaven is hardly the same as truly living," she says, and I realize that she's right. The time I've spent on Earth in Adriana's body feels more *real* to me than all the centuries I spent in my angel form above. In Heaven, everything is pleasant and perfect, day in and day out. Here, there's uncertainty, there's joy, there's fear, and there's *love*.

I would trade all my centuries as an angel for the chance to live one lifetime as a human on Earth.

"We have no time to waste," Teresa says, forcing me to focus on the present—where we're about to start our mission to reclaim Uriel's Flaming Sword. I like thinking of it that way—*reclaiming*—instead of stealing.

That way, I don't feel like we're doing something wrong.

Teresa mutters a spell, and I glance into the mirror, surprised when I can still see my reflection.

"Was that the invisibility spell?" I ask her.

"No," she says. "It was a spell for luck. Now, I'll cast the invisibility spell."

She does, and our reflections vanish from the mirror. Only Gloria—as Adriana—remains. Teresa says another spell, and she appears again in front of me, but misty, like she's a ghost.

"The spell for true sight," she reminds me. "So we can see each other while we're invisible. Now, let's get on with this. We don't have all night."

CHAPTER SIXTY-SIX

Gloria leaves first, and she holds the door open for long enough that Teresa and I have time to leave the ladies room as well. After all, it would look suspicious if the door opened by itself.

Carlos escorts her down the hall and back into the ballroom. I hold my breath as I watch her walk away, but once she turns the corner, I force myself to relax. Gloria knows Zeke better than most women on the continent. If there was ever a person meant for this job, it's her.

Marco joins us in the hall—also invisible—and we head to the elevators. We're trying to avoid suspicion as much as possible, so we wait for someone else to come and press the button rather than pressing it ourselves.

It's ten minutes before someone approaches the elevators and presses the up button—a Gold man in his thirties who's so drunk he can barely walk. He steps into the elevator, and the three of us scurry inside afterward, standing on the opposite side as the man. He slouches against the wall, presses his finger onto the keypad, and pushes the button for the twentieth floor.

Once he stumbles out onto his floor and the doors close behind him, I hold my finger down on the keypad and push the button for the forty-ninth floor. The elevator rises, and I glance up at the camera in the top corner, praying the guards didn't notice anything strange.

I have to hope they're looking out for suspicious people—not for elevators that seem to take on a mind of their own.

We reach the forty-ninth floor and step out of the elevator. I lead them down the hall to the entrance of Zeke's suite.

"This is it," I tell them once we arrive at the doors.

"The spell to cause a disturbance in the camera will only last while we're chanting," Marco says. "Once it's working, I'll nod to you. After I nod, you get us inside of that suite as quickly as possible."

"Will do," I say.

"Are you sure there are no cameras inside?" Teresa eyes the doors suspiciously.

"I'm sure. He wants complete privacy in his rooms. Plus, he's a demon king. He can protect himself."

That must convince them, because they join hands and start to chant, causing what I know is some sort of electrical disturbance that'll make the cameras fuzzy. We didn't want to use the spell earlier because the guards would surely notice multiple issues with the cameras and would send someone to investigate. However, they'll likely overlook a one-time disturbance.

It isn't long until Marco nods at me.

When I press my finger against the keypad, the door opens. I push my way through, and I'm followed by Teresa and

Marco, who still have their hands together while chanting. They only stop chanting once I close the door behind us.

"We're in." Teresa still holds onto Marco's hands, a smile breaking across her face. "We did it."

"The most difficult part is complete," I say. "But we still have to get to the room where Zeke's hiding the sword."

"Then by all means," Marco says, motioning around the suite. "Lead the way."

CHAPTER SIXTY-SEVEN

I lead them into Zeke's room, thinking about the times I spent with him here. It's impossible to push aside that feeling of *wrong* that I have being here without him. But looking at his bed, I remember the moment he murdered Maria, and I'm reminded about why I'm doing this in the first place.

I'm going to save him. I may not have a cure for the darkness, but we *will* remove the curse, and that's a step in the right direction.

I press my hand against the wall, pushing open the hidden door that Zeke showed me before. "This way," I tell them, walking inside toward the secret elevator. I press the down button and the doors open instantly. The three of us step inside, and I press in the number on the keypad—0129. I didn't realize what it meant before, but now that Zeke's told me about his past, I understand what the numbers represent.

129 AD. The year he met Julia and was cast from Heaven.

I never questioned why angels weren't supposed to involve

themselves romantically with humans. I always assumed it was because as angels, we're incapable of any type of love that isn't love for God. But now—after having fallen in love myself—I know that isn't true.

So *why* aren't angels supposed to fall in love? I don't know. But I do know one thing—it isn't fair.

And I'll do everything to fight for my love for Zeke.

The elevator descends, my ears popping as we get lower and lower, until I suspect we're below the ground itself. Finally, the doors open into the elaborate chamber that I remember from the first time Zeke took me here.

I look down at the Turkish rug in front of the elevator and smile, remembering how Zeke took my hands in his while we were standing on that rug and asked me to be his wife.

Teresa walks forward, her mouth open in awe as she approaches the Flaming Sword. "It's here," she says breathlessly. "It's really here."

"Of course it is," I say. "I wouldn't lie to you."

"I need your help." She looks at me, her expression switching from amazement to determination. "I need to break the boundary spell."

"How am I supposed to help?" I step back. "I don't know a thing about breaking spells."

"You don't need to know anything," she says. "But remember when you helped me with the locator spell?" I nod, and she continues. "It'll be like that. But this time, when you take my hands, I want you to close your eyes and think of what the sword looks like when it's alight with flame. All right?"

"I can do that." I walk slowly toward her, since even though I've been warming up to witches, I'm still not thrilled with the idea of helping with spells.

"Marco will remain on guard near the elevator," Teresa

says, glancing over at where he stands on the rug. "Just in case. Now—are you ready?"

"As I'll ever be." I take her hands in mine and close my eyes. She begins.

CHAPTER SIXTY-EIGHT

Teresa chants for what feels like over ten minutes. Her voice is loud, her hands warm and sweaty in mine. Her grip gets tighter and tighter as she continues. I do my best to picture the sword alight with flames, but so much time is passing that I can't help but worry. Did Teresa overestimate her powers? Is she unable to break the boundary spell alone?

I want to suggest that she get Marco to help, but I don't want to interrupt while she's in the middle of the spell.

Finally, she stops chanting. She mutters another spell—I recognize it as the one she did earlier for luck—and her grip loosens around mine.

"You can open your eyes now." She speaks quickly, clearly excited. "We did it."

I open my eyes and take in the sight of the sword. It's clearer than ever without the orb of the boundary spell around it, the gold shimmering even in the low light. "No." I smile, giving her hands a small squeeze. "*You* did it."

"Don't be so modest," she says. "We wouldn't have gotten this far without your help. And the next move is yours as well. Are you ready to take the sword?"

I nod and turn to face the Flaming Sword. Once again, I'm awed by how elegantly simple it is. There are no complicated engravings upon it—the sword was clearly designed in a utilitarian manner perfect for battle. And it's so close—all I have to do is reach forward and wrap my hand around the handle, and it'll be mine.

I rub my hands on my dress, unsure if the sticky sweat is mine or from Teresa when she was doing her spell. I can barely breathe as I stare up at the sword—it's impossible to control my shaking nerves. Because all angels know that only angels—including fallen angels—can light the sword aflame. Mortals can touch it, but they can't ignite the magic within it. Even witches can't ignite the magic, since they too are mortal.

Which is why it's up to me to take the sword—to prove that this sword is the real deal. I believe it is—Zeke wouldn't have gone to so much trouble to protect it otherwise—but as Teresa said when she first explained our plan, it's better to be safe than sorry. Then, once I prove that it's real, Teresa and Marco will cast an invisibility spell around the sword and walk it out of the Watchtower. They'll bring it back to her house and begin the ritual to break the curse.

"Rebekah." Marco clears his throat, and I glance at him over my shoulder. "Are you going to take the sword? Gloria is still up there pretending to be you—the sooner we can get this over with, the better."

"Yes." I face the sword, straighten my shoulders, and grab it.

The handle slips easily into my grip—as if I were born to hold it. I wrap my other hand around it as well, holding it steadily in front of me, and stare at it in awe. This is the same sword that Uriel forged from the fire in his soul—the sword he used in every battle he fought. I never thought that I—a simple messenger angel—would hold such a holy object. But here I am, doing just that.

Still, there's one more thing left for me to do. And so, I hold the sword up higher, and think of it igniting with flames.

The metal heats under my hands, and the sword glows—a golden glow that reminds me of Heaven itself. Fire bursts forth from the tip, so strong it nearly licks the ceiling. Power surges through my body and I stumble backward, but I steady myself, planting my feet firmly upon the ground.

The flames calm, gently surrounding the sword, caressing it with their light and warmth. My body hums with the power, and I feel invincible.

Then the elevator doors open, revealing Zeke. His eyes connect with mine, widening in shock.

My heart plummets, all that invincibility gone in a second.

"Adriana?" His voice is strained when he says my name, and he clenches his fists, his eyes going black as he rushes toward me.

CHAPTER SIXTY-NINE

He stops running in the center of the rug—it looks like he crashes into a wall, except there's no wall to be seen.

I lower the sword, the flames vanishing. I have no idea how to explain this, but I can't let him see me as a threat.

"Adriana!" He pounds his fists forward, and they stop at the barrier. He tries to go around it, and even back, screaming in frustration when he can't get through. It's like he's stuck in a circle of space in the middle of a rug. "A demon trap?" he says, giving an unsuccessful push at the barrier in front of him. "Really?"

"There's no use in trying to escape." Teresa steps forward, leaving little space between her and Zeke. "You can't walk or teleport out of there while the trap remains intact."

I look at Teresa, stunned. "How did a demon trap get there?" I ask her.

"I drew it under the rug while Teresa kept you busy during the spell to undo the boundary," Marco says, holding up a piece of chalk. "She didn't *actually* need you to do that spell. But it was nice of you to cooperate anyway."

"You were in on this?" Zeke growls, banging his fists against the invisible wall. He's looking at me with murder in his eyes, and I take a step back, swallowing down my fear.

"It's not what you think," I say quickly. "I can explain—I promise I can. But I love you, I truly do. You have to believe me. Everything that you're seeing right now... it's all because I love you."

"You ignited the Flaming Sword." He speaks slowly, his voice so low that it sends a shiver down my spine. "You're not human. You lied to me. How long have you been lying to me?"

"Let's skip the pleasantries and get this over with." Teresa heaves a sigh and faces Zeke. "The girl you met—the one you think you love—isn't Adriana. She's never *been* Adriana. Weeks ago—right before you met her—an angel named Rebekah possessed Adriana's body under God's orders so that she can complete a mission assigned to her—a mission to free this continent from the curse you placed upon it."

"Stop," I command her, holding her gaze and pointing the sword toward her. "This is my story. Let me tell it."

"Be my guest." She motions for me to continue. "I'm sure he'll *love* hearing how you lied to him and deceived him."

"She's telling the truth." Zeke looks at me like I'm a stranger. "You were sent here to kill me."

"Yes." I lower my eyes, but raise them again. "I was. But then I got to know you. I fell in love with you. All of that was real. I didn't mean to fall in love with you, but I did, and I meant it when I said I would marry you. I *want* to marry you. I still will, if you'll still have me."

"I don't even *know* you." He snarls, his eyes turning black.

"Once I'm out of this damn demon trap, I swear on Lucifer himself that I'm going to kill you."

"Not if she kills you first." Teresa glares at him, crosses her arms, and looks at me in challenge. "Did you hear that?" she asks. "He's going to *kill* you. But he can't from inside the demon trap. And you have the Flaming Sword. Ignite it again, sink it into his heart, and not only will you save yourself, but my sister will also be free and you'll save this entire *continent*. Do it. Now."

"No." I tighten my grip around the handle of the sword and look back at Zeke. "You won't kill me," I tell him. "You love me, just like I love you. I'm here right now to *save* you! Teresa found another way to break the curse. She just needed the Flaming Sword to do it, since the sword's what you used to cast it. It will take her a few days to break it, and it would have worked better if you didn't know it was happening, but it can still work. Please, forgive me for lying to you, Zeke. I hated every second of it, but I had no choice. By the time I fell in love with you, it was too late. But I love you—I do. I want to marry you. I'll be your wife, and once the curse is broken, we'll rule this continent and bring it into a Golden Age—together. Isn't that what you want, too?"

"The curse can only be broken if I'm killed by the Flaming Sword," Zeke says darkly. "There is no other way."

"That's not true," I tell him, turning to Teresa for confirmation. "Tell him what you can do!"

"I can't do that," Teresa says, a devious smile forming on her face. "Because he's right. Everything I told you—about the alternate way of breaking the curse—was a lie. The only way to break the curse is for you to finish what you came here to do. You have to kill Ezekiel."

CHAPTER SEVENTY

"You lied to me." I drop my arm to the side, the tip of the sword clanging to the ground. "All of this was a trick."

"I had no choice," she says, her voice cold. "The only way to get my sister back is for you to complete your mission. To complete your mission, you need to kill Ezekiel with the Flaming Sword. But you told me yourself—you weren't going to kill him. I tried to get you to change your mind, but you were too far gone with the curse. Your desire to be loved made you lose touch with reality. I knew after talking with you—after seeing how in *love* with him you think you are—that it was hopeless. You weren't going to kill him, let alone steal the sword. So I had to figure out a way to get it myself. Now—are you going to give me the sword, or am I going to have to take it from you?"

I hold the sword up higher, igniting it into flames. I can't let her take it from me. But right now, it's two against one—her and Marco versus me. Two witches against a human. The only person in this room more powerful than the three of us combined is Zeke.

Somehow, I need to get him out of that demon trap. But I glance over at him, and he glares at me, his eyes covered with black. The darkness is consuming him. He doesn't even *look* like he's trying to fight it.

What will he do when he gets out of there? Will he kill Teresa and Marco? I'm sure of it. Will he kill me? I want to say no, but right now, I honestly don't know. I lied to him—I betrayed him.

I wouldn't blame him if he never forgave me for what I did.

I need to figure out *something* to do. But I don't know what, so I do the only thing I can think to—I stall.

"I'm not going to give you the sword," I tell her. "This is *my* mission. I'm going to kill Zeke myself."

"Really?" Teresa raises an eyebrow. "Why the sudden change of heart?"

"You heard him," I say. "Once he gets out of there, he's going to kill me. He can't forgive me for this. And I don't blame him."

"I don't believe you." Marco walks to join Teresa, the two of them forming a wall in front of me. "But if you're going to do it, now's your chance. Kill him. Now."

"I will," I say. "But first, I have one question. How did Zeke know I was down here at all? Was Gloria in on this, too?"

"No." Teresa laughs bitterly. "Gloria's just as in love with Ezekiel as you are. Why do you think she hasn't remarried? She wouldn't have had it in her heart to kill him. So I told her the same lie I told you. She should have known that the spell I made up—destroying the sword to destroy the curse—was impossible. But she was too blinded by love to face it."

"At least not *everyone* I trusted in this city deceived me," I say, holding tighter onto the sword. "But if Gloria didn't tell him where I was, how did he know?"

"Do you want to tell her?" Teresa smirks at Zeke. "Or should I?"

"You filthy, ungrateful witch," he says instead, sneering at her. "I should have left you for dead in your sector. Once I'm out of here, I'm going to *kill* you."

"Then it's a good thing you're not getting out of there, isn't it?" She smiles at him and turns back to me. "The answer to your question is simple—your engagement ring is more than just a pretty piece of jewelry. It has a tracking spell on it. Whoever cast the spell is a strong witch, but not strong enough to deceive me. I sensed the spell the moment I saw the ring. And remember that spell I did for 'luck?'" She continues before I can reply. "It wasn't *actually* for luck. The first time I cast it, I was blocking the tracking spell. The second time—once I made sure we had the sword and the demon trap was in place—I turned it back on. Just like I predicted, he ran here the moment he realized you weren't actually with him. Tell me, Zeke," she says to him, her voice a low purr. "What *did* you do to Gloria when you realized she wasn't Adriana?"

He glares at her with so much hate that he doesn't even need to speak to get his message across.

Gloria is dead. And once he's out of the demon trap, he's going to kill Teresa, too.

"He wasn't supposed to find out that Gloria wasn't me," I say softly, realizing just how dark Teresa's plan truly was. "But you... you knew he would find out. You knew what he would do once he did. And you let her go through with it anyway. *Knowing* she would die."

"This is a war," Teresa says, her eyes hard and cold. "There are always casualties in war. And if this all ends in getting my sister back and breaking this curse, then so be it. At least Gloria died for a worthy cause."

I back away, staring at Teresa in horror. Didn't Teresa say that the curse didn't affect witches as much as humans? Because right now, she seems just as cursed as the rest of them—willing to do anything to get what she wants.

And if it *isn't* the curse, that's even worse. Because it means this is who Teresa truly is.

I should have known to never trust a witch.

"She's not going to kill him," Teresa tells Marco. "She lied. Get that sword from her. One of us is going to have to do this ourselves."

Marco runs for me, his hands outstretched to attack, and I do the first thing that comes to mind—I light the sword ablaze and swing it through his neck.

CHAPTER SEVENTY-ONE

His head falls to the ground next to my feet, and his body crumples beside it.

A scream pierces through the room—Teresa.

She runs to Marco, and I back away from the pieces of him, my stomach churning at the pool of blood forming where his head was once connected to his neck. Teresa lowers herself beside his head and picks it up, gazing into his sightless eyes. She closes them, places his head back down, and turns to me, her face twisted in rage.

"You're going to die for this," she says, and then she starts saying a familiar spell—the exorcism spell.

I scream as pain wracks through my body, so strong that it feels like my flesh is being slowly carved away. I want to fall to the ground in agony, but I don't. Instead, I stand strong, maintaining my grip on the sword.

If she succeeds—if she exorcises me from Adriana—I'll fail my mission. I'll be cast from Heaven.

Once I'm gone, Teresa will surely take the sword and kill Zeke.

I can't let that happen. I can't let her kill him. I *love* him. And she betrayed me.

The pain digs deeper, and I stare into her eyes as she chants the spell—her eyes that are darkened with hate and revenge. I want to beg her to stop, but the pain is so strong that I can't spare the energy to speak. If I do, I'll surely collapse.

I can't let her win. I need to fight this. I hold tighter onto the sword, and then I remember—this sword is powerful. It has a magic and power of its own. This sword was forged by Uriel to help angels in battle.

I may be trapped in this human form until the end of my mission, but my soul is still mine—an angel. The sword recognizes that. If it didn't, it wouldn't ignite under my command.

I stumble back as another wave of pain reverberates through me, but instead of falling, I focus on the magic of the sword, calling upon its power for help. The magic floods my body, filling me with light, and the pain lessens until it's reduced to a slight hum.

Teresa must notice my sudden recovery, because she chants faster and louder. The hum of the pain grows again, and I know the magic I took from the sword won't last forever.

I need to act—now.

Taking a deep breath, I raise the sword high and start toward Teresa—I run faster than a human can possibly move without magical help—and thrust the sword through her chest.

CHAPTER SEVENTY-TWO

We stare at each other—the sword skewered through her body, my fingers wrapped around the handle.

She sucks in a gasping breath, and blood trickles from her mouth. "You're going to go to Hell for this," she says, and then I yank the sword from her body, and she crumples to the floor next to Marco. Blood seeps from her wound, flowing across the floor until it joins with the puddle of his.

I drop my arm to my side, the tip of the sword clanging to the ground.

They're dead. I *killed* them. I trusted them, they betrayed me, and now they're dead.

I hated what they did to me, but I didn't want them *dead*.

I never wanted to kill anyone.

"You did the right thing," Zeke says, still stuck inside the demon trap. "If you didn't kill them, they would have killed you first."

"No, they wouldn't have." I shake my head sadly, unable to

look away from the bloodbath I'd created. "At least, not while I'm still in Adriana's body."

"It's true then." His voice is empty, and I finally look up at him, shocked by the anger in his eyes. They're still covered in black—covered in darkness. "Everything we had was a lie."

"No," I insist, searching for something—*anything*—I can say that will convince him of the truth. "This may not be my true form, but I'm still me. *That* wasn't a lie. I risked *everything* for you—I was willing to fall from Heaven for you! Because I love you. And I can't kill you. I *won't*."

"You should," he says darkly.

"No." I hold his gaze. "I love you, and I won't kill you. You love me, too. I know you do."

"I don't even know who you are!" He slams his hands against the invisible wall with so much force that it shakes the room.

"I'm going to let you out of there," I tell him softly. "I'm going to free you."

"You shouldn't do that," he warns.

"Why not?" I stand stubbornly, daring him to convince me otherwise.

"Because if you do, I'll kill you."

"No," I insist. "You won't. You might think you will, but I know you, Zeke. I understand that you're angry with me—rightfully so—but you can fight this. I've seen you do it before, and I know you can do it again. You won't kill me. You love me too much to ever kill me."

"You have way too much trust in me," he says, chuckling softly. "Have you forgotten what I am? I'm a *demon*. Killing is in my blood! Sure, I fought it for a bit, but come on—you have to know I just wanted to get you in bed with me, right? *Willingly*. If it took fighting the darkness and proposing to do that, then so be it. We could have had the wedding of your dreams for all I cared—a party's a party, and everyone living here is always down for some fun. Then I would have had you on our wedding night, eventually became bored with you, and then gotten rid of you so the next round of girls could have their turns."

"No." I shake my head, sickened by his words. "You wouldn't."

"You know as well as I do that demons can't love," he says. "You were so stupid to think otherwise—even more so now that I know you're an angel! You should have known better. You most definitely deserve to die for it. It's your own fault, really. But you can't say you weren't warned, can you?"

Everything he says is like a knife piercing into my soul. I hadn't thought there was anything more painful than the feeling I had when Teresa tried to exorcise me.

I was wrong.

Because right now, my heart feels like it's shattering into a million tiny pieces, and that it'll never be able to get put back together again.

"Why are you telling me this?" I ask, choking back tears.

"Because I can't control the darkness anymore." He glances at the sword dangling in my hand. "You *should* kill me. You can do it right now. If you don't—if you let me out of this trap—you'll be dead in a second. Kill me first, Rebekah. Like you did to Teresa and Marco. You have it in you. I know you do."

I shiver when he says my name—*Rebekah*—not Adriana. "You don't mean that," I say, my hands shaking. "Why are you saying all of this?"

"You think I'm making this up?" He smirks. "How much will you bet on that?"

"Everything." I stride toward him, past the invisible line of the demon trap, and press my lips to his.

He kisses me back—slowly at first—and then with more intensity. Heat flows through my body at his touch, and I sink into him, my body flush with his.

He loves me. He might not want to say it, but I can tell from the way he's kissing me—as if I'm the most precious person in the world to him and he never wants to stop.

He finally pulls back and looks down at me, his eyes back to their normal blue. "You really shouldn't have done that," he says.

Then he grabs the sword from my hand, steps back, and plunges it straight into his own heart.

CHAPTER SEVENTY-THREE

I barely have time to scream before I'm ripped out of Adriana's body. Suddenly, I'm floating in a room of bright white light. Uriel stands before me, his Flaming Sword ablaze in his hand.

"That didn't go quite how I imagined it," he says, admiring the sword and sliding it into an invisible shaft on his back. "But you *did* get the job done."

"Zeke," I croak, looking around as if I might find him here. But it's hopeless. I'm no longer in Earth's realm—I'm in Heaven. So I refocus on Uriel and ask, "Where is he?"

He tilts his head and smiles. "Did you truly care for him?" he asks. "Or was it an act?"

"I loved him." I glare at Uriel with as much hate as I can manage. "And he loved me."

"That he did." Uriel nods. "He sacrificed himself for you. Quite unheard of for a demon to willingly sacrifice themselves like that, I must say."

"Where is he?" I ask again. His body might be gone, but I know his spirit still exists.

Even if he's been cast to the depths of the fieriest hell dimension in the universe, I will not rest until I venture there and find him.

"Relax, relax." Uriel smirks. His smirk is so condescending, so *different* from the playful smirk Zeke used to give me that it causes a physical pain in my chest. "Ezekiel sacrificed himself and broke the curse he cast upon the continent. He has been rewarded for his actions."

"How?" My heart leaps at the possibilities. "Has he been accepted back into Heaven? Is he an angel again?"

"No." Uriel shakes his head. "Nothing that extreme. But he's no longer a demon, either."

"Then what is he?" I clench my fists, waiting for his answer.

"A human."

"What?" I gasp.

"You heard me," Uriel says. "Ezekiel's now a human."

"Where is he?" I stand straighter, my gaze unwavering. "Take me to him at once."

"Haven't you gotten feisty since your little adventure on Earth?" Uriel chuckles.

"If you won't tell me where he is, then I'll go down to Earth and find him myself."

"Don't be so rash." Uriel holds a hand up, commanding me to stay where I am. "After all, you just succeeded in your mission. Don't you want to hear what your reward will be?"

"Later," I say. "Right now, I need to see Zeke."

"What will you do when you see him?" Uriel asks. "Marry him?"

I say nothing, since yes, that's exactly what I want to do. If he still wants to marry me, of course.

"If you marry him, you'll be cast from Heaven and will become a demon," Uriel says. "You'll be overcome with the darkness Ezekiel described to you—overcome with the desire to kill. Even if you're able to fight through it and love him, you'll remain immortal. He'll age and die. You'll sacrifice yourself for love, but that love will only be a flicker of time in the eternity of hell you'll live on Earth. Is that really what you want for yourself? Is that really what you think *he* would want for you?"

"No." I step back, appalled by that possibility. "I'll find a way to make him immortal. I'll find a witch. Or a vampire. Or *some* creature that will help me."

"Or you'll stop getting ahead of yourself and listen to your reward."

"Fine." I huff. "But no reward in the entire universe will make me give up my love for Zeke."

"No one ever asked you to give up that love," he says with a small smile. "Because your reward is this—one wish, granted, with no catch. You can take as long as you want to claim your wish, but while you're immortal, I must remind you that Ezekiel is human. His time is much more limited than yours."

"Anything?" I ask. "I can wish for *anything*?"

"Within limits," Uriel says. "You cannot wish for anything that will cause harm upon others, or anything that might catastrophically mess up God's master plan. If your wish is unacceptable, you'll be allowed to make another until you find something deemed appropriate. So tell me, young angel. What do you wish for?"

"I wish to be with Zeke," I say, not needing to think twice about my answer. "I wish to become a human."

EPILOGUE

THREE MONTHS LATER

I stand in front of the door of the dressing room, fidgeting with the bouquet in my hands.

"There's no need to be nervous," a familiar voice says behind me.

I turn around and see Elizabeth. She's wearing a blue dress, and like everyone else on the continent, the tattoos around her wrists are gone. The tattoos all disappeared the moment the curse was broken.

"Of course I'm nervous," I say with a smile. "It's my wedding. Aren't all brides nervous on their wedding day?"

"They are," she agrees. "I certainly was on mine."

"And, hopefully, I'll find out soon," Adriana chimes in, staring wistfully at my engagement ring.

Once I returned to the continent in human form, Adriana rushed to take me in. While she had no control over her body while I possessed it, she *was* aware of everything going on around her. She still hasn't forgiven me for killing Teresa—I don't think she ever will—but she understood what I went through more than anyone else, since she was there through all of it. Since my return, she's been like a sister to me.

Which is why she—and Elizabeth, of course—are bridesmaids in my wedding.

"It's time," Carlos says, opening the door a crack and looking at us.

I didn't know it at the time, but Teresa and Marco weren't the only witches I knew—Carlos was a witch as well. He was the son of the witch who cast the initial boundary spell around the Flaming Sword. Ezekiel practically raised him, and because of that, Carlos was the only witch he trusted. *Carlos* was the one who cast the locator spell on my engagement ring. I was upset with him about that at first—but he was a servant to Zeke, so he really had no say in the matter. Also, he's more than made it up to me.

Because once I returned to Earth as a human, Carlos gathered the witches in the continent. He rallied them to support and protect me in my quest to bring the continent to a Golden Age as its new queen.

Which leaves, of course, the king.

I hear music from the ballroom—the procession must have already begun. Soon, Carlos opens the door again and holds out his arm to me.

As my bodyguard, he's the closest thing I have to a father, so it only seemed appropriate that he would be the one to walk me down the aisle.

He leads me to the large double-door entrance of the ballroom. The first notes of a new song begin to play—my entrance music—and the doors swing open.

Standing at the end of the aisle, gazing at me as if I'm the most beautiful woman in the world, is Zeke.

I walk down the aisle, recalling our story with each step.

Once I returned to Earth as a human, I found him in his suite in the Watchtower and told him everything. We'd faced a lot in the past few months, but we loved each other. Because of that, forgiveness came easy. He still had my engagement ring—Adriana returned it to him after regaining control of her body—and that night, he kneeled before me and asked me to be his wife—again.

I join him at the altar. He reaches out to me, lifting the veil off my face and over my head. "You're beautiful," he whispers, the words meant only for me.

I blush, beaming back at him. One of my biggest worries about my return to Earth as a human was that I would be in my form—not Adriana's. Zeke had said he didn't love me because I looked like Julia, but I worried if my true form would be as appealing to him as hers. After all, with my light blonde hair, pale skin, and sea-green eyes, I couldn't look more unlike Adriana if I tried.

It turned out I had nothing to worry about.

"I love you," I mouth to him, not wanting to disrupt the minister as he speaks his part.

Zeke squeezes my hands, and his message is loud and clear—he loves me, too.

"You may kiss the bride," the minister finally says.

Zeke pulls me toward him and presses his lips to mine. The entire room erupts in thunderous applause.

The future that awaits us will not be easy. As the king and queen of this previously cursed continent, we have our work cut out for us.

But as I lose myself in his kiss, I'm confident that somehow, we will bring this kingdom into a Golden Age—together.

Thank you for reading Demon Kissed! I hope you enjoyed the story. While Demon Kissed is a standalone book in the Charmed Legacy universe, my Dark World Saga features supernatural creatures involved in the battle between Heaven and Hell, too. The Dark World Saga begins with The Vampire Wish. CLICK HERE to grab The Vampire Wish on Amazon, or turn the page to see the cover, description, and read a sneak peak from the first book!

MICHELLE MADOW

THE VAMPIRE WISH

USA TODAY BESTSELLING AUTHOR
MICHELLE MADOW

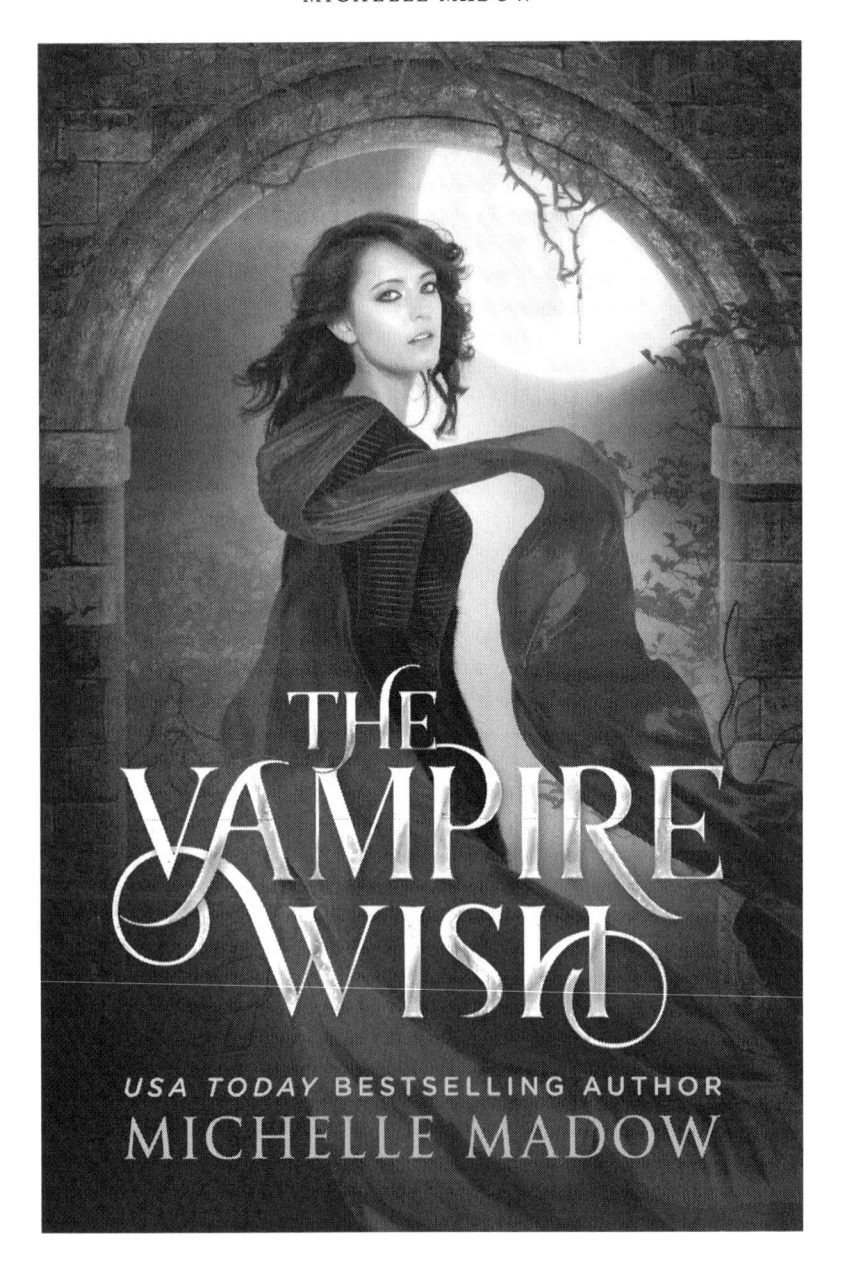

TWILIGHT MEETS ALADDIN in this hot new fantasy series by USA Today bestselling author Michelle Madow!

He's a vampire prince. She's a human blood slave. They should be enemies... but uniting might be their only hope to prevent a supernatural war.

Annika never thought of herself as weak—until the day vampires murdered her parents and kidnapped her from our world to the hidden vampire kingdom of the Vale.

As a brand new blood slave, Annika must learn to survive her dangerous new circumstances... or face imminent death from the monstrous wolves prowling outside the Vale's enchanted walls. But not all in the kingdom is as it appears, and when a handsome vampire disguised as a human steps into her life, Annika discovers that falling for the enemy is sometimes too tempting to resist.

Especially when becoming a vampire might be her only chance to gain the strength she needs to escape the Vale.

Enter the magical world of the Vale in The Vampire Wish, the first book in an addictive new series that fans of The Vampire Diaries and A Shade of Vampire will love!

Turn the page for a sneak peek! Or CLICK HERE to grab The Vampire Wish on Amazon now.

PROLOGUE: ANNIKA

"Race you to the bottom!" my older brother Grant yelled the moment we got off the chair lift.

Mom and Dad skied up ahead, but beyond the four of us, the rest of the mountain was empty. It was the final run of the trip, on our last day of spring break, and we'd decided to challenge ourselves by skiing down the hardest trail on the mountain—one of the double black diamond chutes in the back bowl.

The chutes were the only way down from where we were— the chairlift that took us up here specified that these trails were for experts only. Which was perfect for us. After all, I'd been skiing since I was four years old. My parents grew up skiing, and they couldn't wait to get me and Grant on the trails. We could tackle any trail at this ski resort.

"Did I hear something about a race?" Dad called from up ahead.

"Damn right you did!" Grant lifted one of his poles in the air and hooted, ready to go.

"You're on." I glided past all of them, the thrill of competition already racing through my veins.

Mom pleaded with us to be careful, and then my skis tipped over the top of the mountain, and I was flying down the trail.

I smiled as I took off. I'd always wanted to fly, but obviously that wasn't possible, and skiing was the closest thing I'd found to that. If I lived near a mountain instead of in South Florida, I might have devoted my extracurricular activities to skiing instead of gymnastics.

I blazed down the mountain like I was performing a choreographed dance, taking each jump with grace and digging my poles into the snow with each turn. This trail was full of moguls and even some rocky patches, but I flew down easily, avoiding each obstacle as it approached. I loved the rush of the wind on my cheeks and the breeze through my hair. If I held my poles in the air, it really *did* feel like flying.

I was lost in the moment—so lost that I didn't see the patch of rocks ahead until it was too late. I wasn't prepared for the jump, and instead of landing gracefully, I ploofed to the ground, wiping out so hard that both of my skis popped off of my boots.

"Wipeout!" Grant laughed, holding his poles up in the air and flying past me.

"Are you okay?" Mom asked from nearby.

"Yeah, I'm fine." I rolled over, locating my skis. One was next to me, the other a few feet above.

"Do you need help?" she asked.

"No." I shook my head, brushing the snow off my legs. "I've got this. Go on. I'll meet you all at the bottom."

She nodded and continued down the mountain, knowing me well enough to understand that I didn't need any help—I wanted to get back up on my own. "See you there!" she said, taking the turns slightly more cautiously than Grant and Dad.

I trudged up the mountain to grab the first ski, popped it back on, and glided on one foot to retrieve the other. I huffed as I prepared to put it back on. What an awful final run of the trip. My family was nearing the bottom of the trail—there was no way I would catch up with them now.

Looked like I would be placing last in our little race. Which annoyed me, because last place was *so* not my style.

But I still had to get down, so I took a deep breath, dug my poles into the snow, and set off.

As I was nearing the bottom, three men emerged from the forest near the end of the chute. None of them wore skis, and they were dressed in jeans, t-shirts, and leather jackets. They must have been freezing.

I stopped, about to call out and ask them if they needed help. But before I could speak, one of them moved in a blur, coming up behind my brother and sinking his teeth into his neck.

I screamed as Grant's blood gushed from the wound, staining the snow red.

The other two men moved just as fast, one of them pouncing on my mom, the other on my dad. More blood gushed from both of their necks, their bodies limp like rag dolls in their attackers arms.

"No!" I flew down the mountain—faster than I'd ever skied before—holding my poles out in front of me. I reached my brother first and jammed the pole into the back of his attacker with as much force I could muster.

The pole bounced off the man, not even bothering him in the slightest, and the force of the attack pushed me to the ground. All I could do was look helplessly up as the man dropped my brother into the blood stained snow.

What was going on? Why were they *doing* this?

Then his gaze shifted to me, and he stared me down. His eyes were hard and cold—and he snarled at me, baring his teeth.

They were covered in my brother's blood.

"Grant," I whispered my brother's name, barely able to speak. He was so pale—so still. And there was so much blood. The rivulets streamed from the puddles around him, the glistening redness so bright that it seemed fake against the frosty background.

One of the other men dropped my mom's body on the ground next to my brother. Seconds later, my dad landed next to them.

My mother's murderer grabbed the first man's shoulder—the man who had murdered my brother. "Hold it, Daniel," he said, stopping him from moving toward me.

I just watched them, speechless. My whole family was gone. These creatures ran faster than I could blink, and they were strong enough to handle bodies like they were weightless.

I had no chance at escape.

They were going to do this to me too, weren't they? These moments—right here, right now—would be my last.

I'd never given much thought to what happens after people die. Who does, at eighteen years old? I was supposed to have my whole life ahead of me.

My *family* was supposed to have their whole lives ahead of them, too.

Now their lifeless, bloody bodies at the bottom of this mountain would be the last things I would ever see.

I steadied myself, trying to prepare for what was coming.

Would dying hurt? Would it be over quickly? Would I disappear completely once I was gone? Would my soul continue on, or would my existence be wiped from the universe forever?

It wasn't supposed to be this way. I didn't want to die. I wanted to *live*.

But I'd seen what those men—those *creatures*—had done to my family. And I knew, staring up at them, that it was over.

Terror filled my body, shaking me to the core. I couldn't fight them. I couldn't win. Against them, I was helpless.

And even if I stood a chance, did I really want to continue living while my family was gone?

"We can't kill them all," the man continued. "Laila sent us here to get humans to replace the ones the new prince killed in his bloodlust rampage. We need to keep her alive."

"I suppose she'll do." The other man glared down at me, licking his lips and clenching his fists. "It's hard to tell under all that ski gear, but she looks pretty. She'll make a good addition to the Vale."

He took a syringe out of his jacket, ran at me in a blur, and jabbed the needle into my neck.

The empty, dead eyes of my parents were the last things I saw before my head hit the snow and everything went dark.

JACEN

ONE YEAR LATER

The screams. The hunger. The blood.

I'd never forget the terrified looks on each of my victim's faces as I'd sunk my fangs into their necks and drained the lives from their bodies.

They haunted my dreams since the massacre. I re-lived it every night. The lust for their blood—the scent of it so tantalizingly delicious that my entire body burned for it, my fangs pushing through my gums and craving the silky feeling of the warm, smooth blood flowing down my throat. The way my soul parted with my mind as it gave into the craving—the desire for more and more until I'd consumed so much blood that every inch of my body was bloated and bursting with it.

It had been nearly a year since the massacre, and the nightmares hadn't stopped. I didn't think they ever would.

I would never forgive myself for the pain and heartbreak I'd caused that night when I lost control of my bloodlust and slaughtered those humans in the village. So many of them had died that Queen Laila had to send out troops to replenish their stock.

Stock. As if they were crates of meat, or animals waiting to be slaughtered.

In my dreams, I saw the face of my final victim—the young boy who must have been no older than twelve. Then I woke up with a sharp breath, my fangs out and my gums aching for blood.

As always, a glass of it waited on my nightstand.

I reached for it, downing it in nearly one gulp. It tasted bitter—refrigerated blood always did—but it satisfied the craving enough that after a few deep breaths, I was able to pull my fangs back up into my gums and keep them there.

Still, my body craved more. But I didn't *need* more—I just *wanted* it. The craving was in my mind. It was an addiction—it wasn't real. What I'd just consumed was enough to sustain me for the rest of the day.

The blood I craved was my greatest desire and my greatest enemy.

After first turning, the lust for it controlled my every thought. But as the days had passed—slowly but surely—I'd improved at controlling my cravings. Three glasses in the morning eventually became two, and then became one.

Still, Laila refused to let me leave the palace. Not until I could prove that I could control my bloodlust around humans. After all, she couldn't have me killing any more of them. Not after the *inconvenience* I'd caused a year ago when I'd lost myself to that bloodlust filled haze.

Never mind the *inconvenience* she'd caused me by turning me into a vampire against my will.

And while I was strong, I wasn't strong enough to take

down a group of guards on my own. Trust me, I'd tried. It hadn't ended well.

It was hard to believe it had only been a year ago that I'd been a human, unaware of the existence of supernaturals at all. After being locked in this palace for all that time, that year felt like an eternity.

This extravagant palace hidden in the wilderness of the Canadian Rockies—in an enchanted valley that the vampires called the Vale—had become my prison. Every day, I was suffocating. I needed to get out.

Which was why I'd been working daily on controlling my bloodlust. And slowly but surely, I'd been getting better.

Now, I placed the glass down on my nightstand and looked out my window as the last rays of the sun sunk over the horizon. I took deep, measured breaths, and the craving disappeared, my veins cooling down entirely.

I smiled, knowing this was it. I was ready to prove that I'd gained control of the monstrous creature I'd become.

I was ready to be free.

JACEN

"Your Highness," my vampire guard Daniel said as he stepped inside my room.

I didn't think I would ever get used to being called that. After all, I was no prince. As a human, I'd been an eager swimmer, ready to conquer my first Olympics and get gold medals in as many categories as possible.

That person had died the moment Laila sank her fangs into my neck and damned me to an eternity of hell.

Daniel glanced at the empty glass on my nightstand, no hint of emotion flickering across his eyes. "Would you like another glass of blood?" he asked.

"No." I walked over to the window, observing the nearby village. Lights were starting to flicker on in the small houses the humans lived in. Just as I, they were preparing to start their day. Well, *night*, since we operated on a nocturnal schedule in the Vale.

I turned back to face Daniel. "I would like to speak with Queen Laila," I said.

He pressed his lips together, saying nothing. "Is it an important matter?" he finally asked. "As you know, the queen just returned from visiting the European kingdom, and she has to catch up on everything she missed in her absence."

"It's important." I held his gaze with his, flexing my arms by my sides. "I'm ready."

"For what?" he asked.

"To put myself in the presence of a human."

∽

Laila entered my room thirty minutes later, her trusted witch advisor Camelia following obediently behind her.

Camelia, as always, wore a glass pendant around her neck with a piece of wormwood inside. As a witch, she was the only mortal in the kingdom allowed to use wormwood to protect herself. Laila wore a short, flowing blue dress, and her raven colored hair flowed behind her, making her look more like a teen Hollywood starlet than a centuries year old monster.

She was the worst kind of monster—the kind you never saw coming.

I sure hadn't.

On the night I'd met her in a bar, all I was thinking was that she was a beautiful girl, and that I wanted nothing more than to bring her back to my hotel room and see how far she was willing to go with me.

If someone had told me what she *really* was, I would have laughed in their face.

Because Laila wasn't just an ordinary vampire. She was one of the *original* vampires.

There had been seven of them in all. All part of a cult of witches who were so determined to stay young and beautiful forever that they'd created a spell using dark magic to make them exactly what they'd wanted—immortal.

None of them knew it would turn them into monsters. At least, that's what the six living originals claimed.

But I didn't believe it. Because none of them seemed to hate what they were. In fact, they seemed to *relish* in it.

"Jacen," Laila said my name, the slight lilt in her accent the only evidence that she wasn't from this place and time. "Are you sure you're ready?"

"Especially after what happened last time," Camelia added with a smirk.

As always, the green-eyed witch loved to taunt me. I knew she was referring to four months ago—the last time I tried to drink from a human. They hadn't been able to bring him through the door before I'd caught a whiff of his scent and lost myself to the haze of my bloodlust.

The next thing I'd known, I was staring at his corpse on the ground, the last bits of his blood dripping off my fangs and onto the polished marble floor by my feet.

"I suppose the loss of one human won't be too big of a deal." Camelia waved her hand and turned to Laila. "But of course, the decision is yours, Your Highness."

Laila eyed me up thoughtfully, tilting her head and softly biting her blood red lip. "The loss of one human would be irrelevant," she confirmed. "Daniel—go fetch one from the dungeons. An old one, who wouldn't be much use to us anyway."

Daniel rushed out of the room in a blur, returning ten minutes later dragging a thin, older man with a chain. "Sit," he commanded the man, throwing him onto the nearest armchair.

The man cowered in the chair and curled up into a ball, shaking and not looking up at any of us.

I smelled his blood—the rich, thick liquid pulsing through his veins, and it was so tempting that my fangs itched to protrude. His jugular pulsed and pulsed, calling me closer.

But I swallowed down the urge, forcing my breaths to become shallow. I could control myself. I *had* to control myself.

It was the only way to prove that I was able to leave the palace.

"Very good." Laila nodded after a full minute had passed.

"That's it?" I asked her. "Are we done here?"

"No." She pressed her lips together, mischief dancing in her bright blue eyes. "You've only proven that you can be *around* a human."

"Isn't that what I needed to prove?" I asked. "That I can be around them without losing control?"

"You're a vampire prince." She ran a finger along one of my arms and pulled away, smiling sinfully. "Your stamina needs to be stronger than that."

"How so?" I clenched my fists tighter, ignoring her touch. Instead, I stared at the man's neck again, dreading her next words.

"I want you to drink from him."

JACEN

"You want me to kill him?" I kept my gaze on hers, unwilling to look at the human in question.

"No." The smug smile remained on her deceivingly innocent face. "I want you to drink from him and to control yourself. I want you to pull away *before* killing him. To enjoy your meal and leave him alive."

"I don't think I can do that." I stared her down, since she must know I was right. She was asking me to do this because she wanted me to kill him.

I shouldn't have expected anything less from her.

The vampire queen *looked* young and innocent, but her soul was dark and twisted.

"You can do it," she said simply. "As a great scientist once said—if you put your mind to it, you can accomplish anything."

"That's not a real scientist." I glared at her. "It's a quote from a movie."

"That's irrelevant." She waved my point away. "The point is

that it's the truth. You're a vampire now, Jacen. The strongest of all species."

Camelia gave a small huff, but Laila ignored her.

"When I turned you last year, I gave you a gift," Laila continued.

"A gift I never wanted."

"Nevertheless, I gave it to you," she said. "You're a vampire prince now, Jacen. Show me that you deserve the title."

"And if I don't?" I challenged.

"You do." She laughed, light and melodic. "You may not see it now, but you will. Someday, you will. But for now—feed from him."

I eyed up the human man. How did he get in the prison? How old was he? Did he have a family?

I couldn't ask in front of Laila and Camelia. They viewed the human blood slaves as animals instead of people. Angering them would get me nowhere.

Instead, I created answers to the questions to myself. I imagined that this man had a family—a newborn grandchild he was excited to get to know. That he wanted his family to have more food than their rations allowed, since the rations only afforded bare survival for the humans. So he stole—bread from the vampires. The bread that vampires didn't even *need* to eat to survive, but enjoyed anyway, simply because they could. He got caught, and was unfairly locked in the dungeons, doomed to become a personal blood slave for the vampires in the palace—doomed to have them drink and drink from him until he died of blood loss and his remains were fed to the wolves outside the enchanted boundaries.

I looked into his eyes, trying to convince myself that this story I'd created for him was true.

Humanizing him might be the difference between if I was

able to stop myself from losing myself to the bloodlust or if I killed him.

"Are you ready?" Laila sighed and tapped her foot impatiently. "We don't have all day."

"I'm ready." I stared at the man—examining his wrinkled face and reminding myself of the story I'd created.

I wouldn't kill him.

I would let him live.

I inched toward him and lowered myself down, my fangs sliding out of my gums as the scent of his blood filled my nose. Then my teeth sunk into his flesh and I was gulping down the warm, fresh blood.

How had I thought that the bitter, refrigerated blood could compare? How had I convinced myself that I could live off that garbage for the rest of my immortal existence? Noble vampires in the Vale were afforded the luxury of drinking straight from humans—I should *enjoy* the indulgence, not cower away from it.

It wasn't like I had much else to look forward to anymore. Not after my mortal life—my *soul*—had been taken from me against my will.

If the intoxicating taste of fresh blood was all I could enjoy, then so be it.

Just when I was beginning to enjoy myself, the blood supply stopped. I sucked deeper on his neck, trying to will out the final drops, and I squeezed his arms harder, as if that could push out more blood.

But there was nothing left.

He was drained dry.

CAMELIA

I loved watching Jacen feed.

Ever since he'd been brought to the palace, I'd been fascinated by the vampire prince—the handsome swimmer I'd advised that Laila turn after her previous prince had been driven mad by the bloodlust and had sacrificed himself to the wolves.

As Jacen drained the old man, I reached for the pendant I always wore around my neck—the one filled with wormwood—stroking it and holding my breath. I watched as the man stopped struggling, as his hands went limp, and as his head eventually rolled to the side, his eyes empty and dead.

As predicted, Jacen had lost control again. Consumed by his bloodlust. It wasn't surprising. Because the stronger the vampire, the harder it was for them to control their urge to drain humans dry.

Jacen was shaping up to become one of the most powerful vampires that ever existed.

And I was determined to make him mine.

"Take the body away," Laila told Daniel, barely glancing at the drained corpse.

Jacen didn't tear his eyes away from the old man as Daniel heaved him over his shoulder and walked out of the room.

"You're not ready," Laila told Jacen sharply. "In time you will be, but not yet."

"How do I control it?" he asked her—begged her. "Why don't I know when to stop?"

"You're improving," Laila said. "The fact that you didn't maul him the moment you smelled his blood was significant progress. But you need more time."

"How much more?"

"There's no exact formula," she said. "It will happen when you want it badly enough. In the meantime, I have work to attend to."

She exited the room, leaving Jacen and me alone.

"What are you staring at?" he growled at me. "Don't you have work to do, too? A kingdom to help Laila run?"

"Of course." I nodded. "But I also wanted to let you know that I'm here for you, if you ever want to talk."

"Don't play that game with me." He scowled.

"What game?" I reached for the amulet again, forming my expression into one that I hoped looked like complete innocence.

"The game where you pretend to care about anyone except for yourself."

"There's no pretense here," I told him. "I *do* care about you. I want you to become the strongest vampire prince that ever lived. Perhaps even a king."

"I'll never become a king." He crossed his arms. "I don't *want* to become a king."

"Then what do you want?" I asked, truly curious.

"To be human again."

"Why?" I laughed. "Even if that were possible—which it isn't—why would you refuse the power you've been given? Why would you want to be so weak?"

"I'm not going to bother explaining it to you," he looked away from me and walked over to the window, gazing longingly at the human village below. "You'll never understand."

"I might understand more than you think." I slithered toward him, and when I was close enough, I laid my hand gently on his shoulder. "I understand that you need comfort, Jacen. I can provide that. Let me give it to you."

I leaned forward, looking deep into his eyes, my lips getting closer and closer to his. What would kissing him feel like? I imagined that old man's blood must still coat his tongue—I wished I could know how delicious it tasted to him.

It must have been incredible, to make him lose control like he did.

"Stop." He stepped back, his eyes dilating as he stared into mine. "Leave my quarters. Now."

"Are you trying to compel me?" I laughed again, although disappointment fluttered in my stomach. I wouldn't be turned away that easily. Instead, I leaned forward again, willing him to give into temptation. He'd given in with that human. Why not with me?

He simply backed away and repeated his command.

"You know I'm wearing wormwood," I continued, reaching for my necklace. "Even if you've mastered compulsion, it won't work on me."

He just stared at me, saying nothing.

"Have you?" I tilted my head, bringing my hands together gleefully. "Mastered compulsion?"

Compulsion was an ability that only the originals—and the

vampires they directly turned—possessed. It was the ability to make others do as they willed. It could be used to achieve greatness, but it could also be used to achieve great destruction. Which was why the originals were extremely selective in who they turned into a vampire prince or princess.

They couldn't risk creating a vampire who might use the powers they'd been gifted to destroy their own sire.

"I'm working on it," he said shortly.

"Good." I nodded, at a loss for words. Jacen was like a wall. I couldn't get through to him, no matter how hard I tried.

Which only made me more determined to try.

"We're done here." He took another step away from me, narrowing his eyes. "Unless you have anything more you need to say?"

"No," I said. "At least, not now."

With that, I turned on my heel and headed out the door. Fire ran through my veins as I stomped down the hall—frustration. I hated not getting what I wanted.

Jacen may not want me now. But in time, he would learn to.

Because eventually, I would be his queen.

ANNIKA

I held out my arm, watching as the needle sucked the blood from the crease of my elbow and into the clear vial. I sat there for ten minutes, staring blankly ahead as I did my monthly duty as a citizen of the Vale.

Like all humans who lived in the kingdom, I was required to donate blood once a month.

This was my twelfth time donating blood.

Twelve months. One year. That's how long it had been since my family had been murdered in front of my eyes and I'd been kidnapped to the Vale.

When I'd first been told that I was now a blood slave to vampires, I didn't believe it. Vampires were supposed to be *fiction*. They didn't exist in real life.

But I couldn't deny what I'd seen in front of my eyes. Those pale men, how quickly they'd moved, how they'd ripped their teeth into my parents and brother's throats and drained them dry, leaving their corpses at the bottom of that ski trail.

Why had I been the one chosen to live, and not them?

It was all because I'd fallen on that slope. If I hadn't fallen, I would have been first down the mountain. I would have been killed. My mom would have been last, and *she* would have been the one taken.

But my mom wouldn't have been strong enough to survive in the Vale. So even though I hated that I'd lived while they'd died, it was better that I lived in this hellish prison than any of them. I'd always been strong. Stubborn. Determined.

Those traits kept me going every day. They were the traits that kept me *alive*.

At first, I'd wanted to escape. I thought that if I could just get out of this cursed village, I could run to the nearest town and get help. I could save all the humans who were trapped in the Vale.

I didn't get far before a wolf tried to attack me.

I'd used my gymnastics skills to climb high up on a tree, but if Mike hadn't followed me, fought off the wolf, and dragged me back inside the Vale, I would have been dead meat. The wolves would have eventually gotten to me and feasted upon my body, leaving nothing but bones.

Mike had told me everything about the wolves as we'd walked back to the Tavern. He'd grown up in the Vale, so he knew a lot about its history. He'd told me that they weren't regular wolves—they were shifters. They'd made a pact with the vampires centuries ago, after the vampires had invaded their land and claimed this valley as their own. He'd told me about how the wolves craved human flesh as much as the vampires craved human blood, and how if a human tried to escape—if they crossed the line of the Vale—they became dinner to the wolves.

At least the vampires let us live, so they could have a

continuous supply of blood to feast upon whenever they wanted.

The wolves just killed on the spot.

That was the first and last time I'd tried to escape. And after Mike had saved me, we'd become best friends. He'd offered me my job at the Tavern, where I'd been working—and living—ever since. All of us who worked there lived in the small rooms above the bar, sleeping in the bunks inside.

He and the others had helped me cope with the transition—with realizing I was a slave to the vampires, and that as a mere human amongst supernaturals, there was no way out.

They were my family now.

"You're done," the nurse said, removing the needle from my arm. She placed a Band-Aid on the bleeding dot, and I flexed my elbow, trying to get some feeling back in the area. "See you next month."

"Yeah." I gathered my bag and stood up. "Bye."

On my way out, I passed Martha—the youngest girl who worked at the Tavern. She slept in the bunk above mine, and along with being the youngest, she was also the smallest.

It took her twice as long to recover from the blood loss as it did for me.

"Good luck," I told her on the way out. "I'll see you back at the Tavern." I winked, and she smiled, since she knew what I was about to do.

It was what I always did on blood donation day.

I held my bag tightly to my side and stepped onto the street, taking a deep breath of the cold mountain air. It was dark—us humans were forced to adjust to the vampires' nocturnal schedule—and I could see my breath in front of me. The witch who'd created the shield to keep the Vale hidden from human eyes also regulated the temperature, but she could only do so much. And since it was December in Canada, it was naturally still cold.

I hurried to the busiest street in town—Main Street, as it was so creatively named. Humans manned stalls, and vampires walked around, purchasing luxuries that only they were afforded. Meat, doughnuts, pizza, cheeses—you name it, the vampires bought it.

The vampires didn't even *need* food to survive, but they ate it anyway, because it tasted good.

Us humans, on the other hand, were relegated to porridge, bread, rice, and beans—the bare necessities. The vampires thought of us as nothing but cattle—as blood banks. And blood banks didn't deserve food for enjoyment. Only for nourishment.

Luckily, Mike had taught me a trick or two since the day he'd saved me from the wolves. After seeing me climb that tree, he'd called me "scrappy" and said it was a skill that would get me far in the Vale.

He'd taught me how to steal.

It was ironic, really. Stealing hadn't been something that had ever crossed my mind in my former life. I used to have it good—successful, loving parents, trips to the Caribbean in the spring, skiing out west in the winter, and an occasional voyage to Europe thrown in during the summers. I'd had a credit card, and when I'd needed something, I would buy it without a second thought.

I hadn't appreciated how good I'd had it until all of that was snatched away and I was left with nothing.

Now I walked past the various booths, eyeing up the delicious food I wasn't allowed to have. But more than the food, I was eying up the shopkeepers and the vampires around them. Who seemed most oblivious? Or absorbed in conversation?

It didn't take long to spot a vampire woman flirting with a handsome human shopkeeper. I'd seen enough of vampires as a species to know that if the flirting was going to progress anywhere, it would lead to him becoming one of her personal blood slaves, but he followed her every movement, entranced by her attention.

They were the only two people at the booth. Everyone else was going about their own business, not paying any attention to me—the small, orphaned blood slave with downcast eyes and torn up jeans.

Which gave me the perfect opportunity to snatch the food that us humans were forbidden to purchase.

∼

CLICK HERE to grab The Vampire Wish on Amazon and continue reading now!

ABOUT THE AUTHOR

Michelle Madow is a USA Today bestselling author of fast-paced fantasy novels that will leave you turning the pages wanting more! Click here to view a full list of Michelle's novels.

She grew up in Maryland and now lives in Florida. Some of her favorite things are: reading, traveling, pizza, time travel, Broadway musicals, and spending time with friends and family. Someday, she hopes to travel the world for a year on a cruise ship.

To get free books, exclusive content, and instant updates from Michelle, visit www.michellemadow.com/subscribe and subscribe to her newsletter!

www.michellemadow.com
michelle@madow.com

DEMON KISSED
Cursed Angel Watchtowers (Charmed Legacy)

Published by Dreamscape Publishing

Copyright © 2017 Michelle Madow

ISBN: 1976514649
ISBN-13: 978-1976514647

This book is a work of fiction. Though some actual towns, cities, and locations may be mentioned, they are used in a fictitious manner and the events and occurrences were invented in the mind and imagination of the author. Any similarities of characters or names used within to any person past, present, or future is coincidental.

All rights reserved. No part of this book may be used or reproduced in any manner whatsoever without written permission from the author. Brief quotations may be embodied in critical articles or reviews.

❦ Created with Vellum

34014886R00185

Printed in Great Britain
by Amazon